CENTRAL PARK

The Reunion

The Girl on Paper

Where Would I Be Without You?

Will You Be There?

CENTRAL PARK

GUILLAUME MUSSO

TRANSLATED FROM THE FRENCH BY SAM TAYLOR

BACK BAY BOOKS

Little, Brown and Company

New York   Boston   London

Copyright © 2021 by Guillaume Musso
Translation copyright © 2021 by Sam Taylor

Back Bay Books / Little, Brown and Company
Hachette Book Group
1290 Avenue of the Americas, New York, NY 10104
littlebrown.com

First North American edition: March 2021
Originally published in France as *Central Park* by Guillaume Musso
© XO Editions, 2014

Back Bay Books is an imprint of Little, Brown and Company, a division of Hachette Book Group, Inc. The Back Bay Books name and logo are trademarks of Hachette Book Group, Inc.

ISBN 978-0-316-59096-9
LCCN 2020950107

Printing 1, 2021

LSC-C

Printed in the United States of America

Things that escape you are more important than the things you own.

—W. Somerset Maugham

Part One

HANDCUFFED

1

ALICE

FIRST, A GUST of wind stings her face.

The light rustling of leaves. The distant murmur of a stream. The quiet trill of birdsong. The first rays of sunlight illuminating the tiny blood vessels in her still-closed eyelids.

Then the creak of swaying branches. The smell of moist earth, rotting leaves. The strong, woody odor of gray lichen.

And farther off, an indistinct buzzing, dreamlike and discordant.

Alice Schafer opened her eyes with difficulty. She was blinded by the early-morning sun, her clothes sticky with dew. The frozen sweat on her skin made her shiver. Her throat was dry and her mouth filled with the harsh taste of ashes. Her joints were bruised, her limbs stiff, her mind numb.

When she tried to sit up, she became aware that she was lying on a rough wooden bench. Suddenly, she realized that a large, sturdy man was curled up next to her, his body leaning heavily on hers.

Alice stifled a cry and her pulse raced. Trying to free herself, she toppled over onto the ground and stood up in the same movement. That was when she realized that her right wrist was handcuffed to the left wrist of this stranger. She took a step back, but the man remained motionless.

Shit!

Her heart was pounding in her chest. A glance at her watch—the face of her old Patek was scratched, but the mechanism still worked. According to the watch, it was eight a.m. on Tuesday, October 8.

Jesus Christ! Where the hell am I? she wondered, using a sleeve to wipe the sweat from her face.

She looked around in an attempt to assess the situation. She was in the middle of a forest, the leaves on the trees autumn gold, the undergrowth fresh and dense. A wild, silent clearing surrounded by oaks, thick bushes, and jutting rocks. There was no one else here, which was probably a good thing, considering the circumstances.

Alice looked up. The light was soft, beautiful, almost

unreal. Shards of brightness sparkled through the foliage of a huge flame-colored elm tree. Its roots disappeared into a carpet of damp leaves.

Where was she? She hazarded a few guesses: *The forest of Rambouillet? Fontainebleau? The bois de Vincennes?*

It was like an Impressionist painting on a postcard, the serenity of the image clashing with the surreal weirdness of waking up next to a total stranger.

Cautiously, she leaned forward to get a better view of his face. He was in his late thirties, she thought. Disheveled chestnut hair and the beginnings of a beard.

A corpse?

She knelt down and placed two fingers on his neck, to the right of his Adam's apple. When she pressed down on the carotid artery, she felt a pulse. Relief. The guy was sleeping but alive. She took a moment to look at him more closely. Did she know him? Some thug she was taking to jail? A childhood friend whose face she'd forgotten? No, his features were completely unfamiliar to her.

Alice pushed back a few stray blond locks that had fallen over her eyes, then examined the pair of metal handcuffs that connected her to the man. It was a standard double-locking model, a type used by police departments and private security firms all over the world. Most likely, this was her *own* pair. Alice rummaged in her jeans pocket, hoping to find the key.

It wasn't there. She did, however, find a gun in the inside pocket of her leather jacket. Thinking it must be her service pistol, she sighed with relief as she gripped the butt. But this was not the SIG Sauer used by cops in the Paris Criminal Division. It was a polymer Glock .22, and she had no idea where it had come from. She wanted to check the magazine, but it was difficult with one hand shackled. She did eventually manage it, after a few contortions, taking care not to wake the stranger. One bullet missing. As she handled the pistol, she became aware that the butt was stained with dried blood. Unzipping her jacket all the way, she discovered that there were traces of blood all over her blouse.

My God, what have I done?

Alice rubbed her eyes with her free hand. A migraine was throbbing in her temples now. She felt as if her skull were being crushed in an invisible vise. She took deep breaths, trying to push back her fear, gather her memories.

The night before, she had gone out on the Champs-Élysées with three girlfriends. She'd had plenty to drink, downing glass after glass in a series of bars: the Moonlight, the Thirteenth Floor, the Londonderry... around midnight, the four friends had gone their separate ways. She had been alone when she'd headed to the underground parking garage on Avenue Franklin-Roosevelt, where she'd left her car. And then...

A blank. As if someone had dropped a black veil over her brain. Her mind floundered in the void. Her memory was paralyzed, frozen, jammed on that final image.

Come on, think, for God's sake! What happened next?

She had a distinct memory of paying at the ticket machine, then walking downstairs to the third underground level. She had been drunk, without a doubt. After staggering over to her little Audi, she had unlocked the door, sat behind the wheel, and ...

Nothing.

No matter how hard she tried to concentrate, a white brick wall barred the way to her memories. A vast, unclimbable wall.

She swallowed. Her panic level went up a notch. These woods, the bloodstains on her blouse, this gun that wasn't hers ... whatever was going on, it was a hell of a lot worse than an ordinary hangover. If she couldn't remember how she had ended up here, she must have been drugged. Maybe some creep had spiked her drink. It was far from impossible— as a cop, she'd dealt with several cases involving date-rape drugs in recent years. She filed this idea away in a corner of her mind and began emptying her pockets.

Her wallet and her police badge had disappeared. No ID, no money, no cell phone.

Her fear was compounded by worry.

The crack of a branch sent a flock of warblers flying. A few red leaves fluttered down, brushing Alice's face. With her left hand, she zipped up her jacket, holding the top of it down with her chin. That was how she came to notice the writing, in faded ballpoint, on the palm of her hand— a series of numbers, scrawled on the fly, as if she were some schoolkid trying to cheat on a test:

2125550100

What did they mean? Had she written them? *Maybe, but I can't be sure,* she thought, examining the handwriting.

She closed her eyes for a second, feeling lost and frightened.

But she refused to give in to her fears. Obviously, something serious had occurred last night. She remembered nothing, but the man she was handcuffed to would soon refresh her memory. She hoped so, anyway.

Friend or foe?

There was no way of knowing, so she slid the magazine back into the Glock. With her free hand, she pointed the gun at her companion's head before unceremoniously shaking him.

"Hey! You! Time to wake up!" she said in French.

The man was struggling to open his eyes.

"Come on!" she yelled. "Wake up, asshole!"

He blinked a few times and stifled a yawn before painfully sitting up. His face registered shock as he saw the barrel of the gun a few inches from his forehead.

He stared at Alice, wide-eyed, then turned his head from side to side, apparently flabbergasted by the sight of the surrounding woods.

After a few seconds of shocked silence, he gulped. Then he opened his mouth and asked in English: "Who the hell are you? And what are we doing here?"

2

GABRIEL

T HE STRANGER HAD spoken with a strong American accent.

"Where the hell are we?" he demanded, frowning.

Alice tightened her fingers around the butt of the gun. "That's what I'm asking you!" she replied in English, bringing the barrel of the Glock closer to his temple.

"Whoa, calm down, okay?" he said, raising his hands. "And put the gun down. Those things are dangerous, you know."

Still sleepy-eyed, he pointed with his chin at the steel bracelet around his wrist. "Why did you cuff me? What'd I do this time? Did I get in a fight? Was I drunk?"

"*I* didn't cuff you," she replied.

Alice looked him over. He was wearing dark jeans, a pair of Converse sneakers, a crumpled blue shirt, and a fitted suit jacket. His eyes were clear and engaging but had dark rings of fatigue under them.

"Kinda cold out here," he complained, hunching his shoulders. He looked down at his wrist to check his watch, but it wasn't there. "Shit . . . what time is it?"

"Eight in the morning."

As best he could, he went through his pockets before exclaiming angrily: "What the hell! You've taken everything! My cash, my wallet, my phone . . ."

"I haven't stolen anything from you," Alice assured him. "They got me too."

"And there's a pretty big bump on the back of my head," he noted, rubbing his skull with his free hand. "Let me guess—that wasn't you either?"

He watched her from the corner of his eye. Dressed in tight jeans and a leather jacket, beneath which he could see a bloodstained blouse, Alice was a slender blonde, her hair in a ponytail that was on the point of coming undone. Her face was hard but harmonious—high cheekbones, thin nose, pale skin—and her eyes, spangled with the copper reflections of the autumn leaves, shone intensely.

His thoughts were interrupted by a sudden pain, a burning sensation running up the inside of his forearm.

"What now?" She sighed.

"It hurts." He grimaced. "Like I'm wounded or something."

Because of the handcuffs, Gabriel couldn't take off his jacket or roll up the sleeves of his shirt, but through a series of contortions he managed to see a sort of bandage encircling his arm. The dressing looked like it was freshly applied, but a thin trickle of blood had escaped and was running down to his wrist.

"All right, I've had enough of this bullshit!" he said angrily. "Tell me where we are. Wicklow?"

The young woman shook her head. "Wicklow? Where's that?"

"A national park in the south," he said.

"South of what?" she asked.

"Are you kidding me? South of Dublin!"

She stared at him, wide-eyed. "You really think we're in Ireland?"

He sighed. "Where else would we be?"

"Well, in France, I'd guess. Near Paris. In the forest of Rambouillet, or—"

"Oh, give me a break!" he interrupted. "And who are you exactly?"

"A girl with a gun. So I'm the one who asks the questions."

He stared at her defiantly but, realizing that he was not in control of this situation, stopped talking.

"My name is Alice Schafer. I'm a police captain in the Paris Criminal Division. I spent the evening with friends on the Champs-Élysées. I don't know where we are or how we got here, handcuffed together. And I don't have the faintest idea who you are. Your turn."

After a few seconds of hesitation, the stranger decided to reciprocate.

"I'm American. My name is Gabriel Keyne and I'm a jazz pianist. I live in Los Angeles, but I spend a lot of time on the road, playing gigs."

"And what's the last thing you remember?" she demanded.

Gabriel frowned and closed his eyes in concentration. "Let me see... last night, I played with my bassist and my saxophone player at Brown Sugar, a jazz club in Temple Bar—it's a part of Dublin."

Dublin? This guy is crazy!

"After the concert, I sat at the bar and maybe had a few too many rum and Cokes," Gabriel went on, opening his eyes.

"And then?"

"And then..." His face tensed and he chewed his lip. Evidently, he was finding it as hard as she had to remember the end of his evening.

"Listen, I don't know. I think I may have gotten into a fight with a guy who didn't like my music, then I talked to a few girls, but I was too wasted to actually pick one up."

"Wow, very classy. What a charming guy you are."

He waved away her sarcasm with a casual hand and stood up, forcing Alice to do the same. With an abrupt movement of her forearm, she forced him to sit down again.

"I left the club around midnight," he said. "I could barely stand up. I looked for a taxi in Aston Quay. After a few minutes, a car pulled up and..."

"And what?"

"I don't know," he admitted. "I must have given the driver the address of my hotel and passed out in the back seat."

"And what do you remember after that?"

"Nothing, I'm telling you!"

Alice lowered her weapon and was silent for a few seconds as she digested this bad news. Clearly, this guy was not going to help her get to the bottom of this situation.

"You do realize that everything you've just told me is a huge pile of crap?" she said with a smile.

"Oh yeah? And why's that?"

"Because we're in France—look!"

Gabriel's gaze swept the woods that stretched all around them: the wild vegetation, the dense bushes, the rock walls covered with ivy, the golden dome formed by the autumn leaves. His eyes scaled the length of a giant elm tree and he glimpsed two squirrels racing, leaping from branch to branch in pursuit of a robin.

"I'll bet you my shirt that we're not in France," he said, scratching his head.

"Well, there's only one way to find out," Alice replied irritably, putting her gun in her jacket pocket and dragging Gabriel up from the bench.

They left the clearing and dove into the jungle of dense thickets and leafy shrubs. Cuffed together, they crossed through rolling undergrowth, followed a climbing path, then walked down the other side of the hill, holding on to rocks as they went. It took them a good ten minutes of stepping over little streams and striding along several winding trails to find a way out of this wooded labyrinth. Finally, they came out on a narrow asphalt path bordered by trees that created a leafy vault over their heads. The farther they walked along this paved track, the closer they drew to the sounds of civilization, to the familiar and ever louder buzz of a city.

Propelled by a strange intuition, Alice led Gabriel toward a sunny gap in the foliage. A path led from this clearing to what looked like the grassy bank of a lake.

That was when they saw it.

A cast-iron footbridge arching gracefully over the lake, long and cream-colored, subtly decorated with arabesques and flower urns.

A familiar sight, glimpsed in hundreds of movies.

Bow Bridge.

They weren't in Paris. And they weren't in Dublin either.

They were in New York.

They were in Central Park.

3

CENTRAL PARK WEST

J ESUS CHRIST!" GABRIEL breathed, while Alice's face was a
picture of astonishment.

It might have been difficult to admit the reality, but there
could no longer be any doubt. They were in the Ramble,
the wildest area of Central Park—a genuine thirty-eight-acre
forest stretching out north of the lake.

Their hearts pounded in unison. They approached the bank
and arrived at a busy path, typical of the park's early-morning
energy. Joggers coexisted harmoniously with cyclists, tai chi
enthusiasts, and people walking dogs. The sounds of a big
city seemed to explode in their ears: rumbling traffic, honk-
ing horns, screaming fire-engine and police-car sirens.

"This is insane," Alice muttered.

Disoriented, she tried to think. While she and Gabriel had both been very drunk the night before, to the point where they could not remember everything they'd done, it was inconceivable that they could have been put on an airplane against their will. She had often come to New York on vacation with Seymour, her colleague and best friend. She knew that a Paris–New York flight lasted just over eight hours, but given the time difference, one seemed to land only two hours after takeoff. Usually, when she and Seymour flew together, Seymour would book the 8:30 a.m. flight from Charles de Gaulle airport that arrived in New York at 10:30 a.m. The last international flight left Paris just before 8:00 p.m. But at that time the previous evening, she had still been in Paris. Which meant that she and Gabriel had been flown over on a private jet. Assuming they had been put on a plane in Paris at 2:00 a.m., they would have arrived in New York at 4:00 a.m. local time—early enough for them to wake up in Central Park at 8:00 a.m. On paper, it wasn't impossible. But in reality? Even for a private jet, the red tape involved in entering the United States was complicated. Something did not add up here.

"Oh, sorry!"

A young man on Rollerblades had just bumped into them. Mid-apology, he shot a surprised and suspicious look at their handcuffs.

An alarm went off in Alice's head.

"We can't just stay here like this, in plain sight," she said. "We'll be arrested in under a minute."

"What do you suggest?"

"Quick, take my hand!"

"Huh?"

"Hold my hand—pretend we're a couple," she said brusquely. "Now, let's cross the bridge."

This was what they did. The air was crisp and dry. The outlines of Central Park West's luxurious buildings stood out against the pure blue sky: the two towers of the San Remo, the legendary façade of the Dakota, the art deco apartments of the Majestic.

"Don't you think we should tell the police anyway?" Gabriel asked, continuing to move forward.

"Oh yeah, great idea! Let's throw ourselves to the lions!"

"You should listen to the voice of reason, babe—"

"Call me that again and I'll strangle you with these handcuffs! I'll crush your throat until your face turns blue. You won't spout so much crap when you're dead."

He ignored the threat. "You should at least check in with the French embassy."

"Not until we've worked out what really happened last night."

"Well, don't count on me to play along with your little game. As soon as we're out of the park, I'm going to the first police station we see and telling them everything."

"Are you really this dumb or are you just pretending? In case you haven't noticed, we are *handcuffed together,* you moron! We're inseparable! So until we find a way to break the chain, *you* will do as *I* do."

Bow Bridge was a gentle transition between the wild vegetation of the Ramble and the neatly arranged gardens south of the lake. At the end of the bridge, they took the path that ran along the lake up to the granite dome of the Cherry Hill Fountain.

"I don't understand—why won't you go to the cops with me?" Gabriel asked.

"Because I know what the police will do."

"But what gives you the right to drag me into your mess?" the musician protested.

"How is it *my* mess? I may be in shit up to my neck, but so are you."

"Not at all. I haven't done anything wrong."

"Oh yeah? How can you be so sure? I thought you couldn't remember what happened last night."

This reply seemed to throw Gabriel off balance. "Are you saying you don't believe me?"

"Why should I? All that bullshit about being in a bar in Dublin? It doesn't make any sense, Keyne."

"It makes about as much sense as your story about going out on the Champs-Élysées! And anyway, you're the one with blood on your hands. And a gun in your pocket. And—"

"Yeah, well, at least we can agree on that point," she interrupted. "I'm the one with the gun, so shut your mouth and do exactly what I tell you, okay?"

He shrugged and let out a long sigh of irritation.

Swallowing, Alice felt a burning sensation in her chest and tasted acid at the back of her throat. Stress. Exhaustion. Fear.

CENTRAL PARK   19

How was she going to get out of this fix?

She tried to think straight. In France now, it was early afternoon. The guys on her team must have been surprised when she didn't show up at work this morning. Seymour would have tried calling her cell phone. She had to get in touch with him as soon as possible; he was the one she wanted to investigate this thing. In her head, she began to formulate a checklist: (1) get a hold of the security-camera footage for the Franklin-Roosevelt parking garage; (2) make a list of all the private airplanes that had left Paris for the United States after midnight; (3) locate the place where her Audi had been abandoned; and (4) do a background check on this Gabriel Keyne and find out if he was telling the truth.

The prospect of this investigative work calmed her down a little. For a long time now, the adrenaline rush she got from her job had been her main fuel. In the past, it had been like a drug, and her addiction to it had wrecked her life, but these days it was the only real reason she had to get out of bed in the mornings.

She took a deep breath of the cool Central Park air.

Relieved that the cop inside her was now taking charge, she began to hone her plans: Seymour, under her orders, would investigate the story in France, and she would find out what she could on this side of the Atlantic.

Still walking hand in hand, Alice and Gabriel reached the triangular garden of Strawberry Fields and exited the park on the west side. The cop kept stealing glances at the musician.

She absolutely had to find out who this man was. Was he the one who had cuffed them together? And if so, why?

He gave her a brazen look. "So what exactly do you have in mind?"

She replied with a question of her own: "Do you know anyone in this city?"

"Yeah, actually, one of my best friends lives here—a saxophone player named Kenny Forrest. Unfortunately he's on tour in Tokyo at the moment."

She rephrased her question: "So you don't know anyone who can help us get out of these handcuffs or give us a place to shower and change our clothes?"

"No," he admitted. "How about you?"

"I live in Paris, I already told you that!"

"I live in Paris, I already told you that!" he mimicked in a snooty French accent. "Listen, lady, I don't see how we can avoid going to the police. We have no money, no change of clothes, no way to prove our identities—"

"Oh, quit whining. Let's start by getting a cell phone, okay?"

"And how are we supposed to do that? We don't have a cent between us!"

"Simple. We just have to steal one."

4

HANDCUFFED

LEAVING THE PARK behind, Alice and Gabriel came out onto the stretch of road known as Central Park West. After only a few yards, they felt like they had been sucked into the whirlwind of urban life—the yellow taxis speeding toward Midtown with their horns squealing, the hollering of hot-dog vendors, the battering of jackhammers.

No time to lose.

Alice scrutinized their surroundings. Rising above them on the other side of the avenue was the imposing sand-colored façade of the Dakota, the apartment building in front of which John Lennon had been murdered more than three decades earlier. The edifice looked out of place; with its turrets, gables, dormer windows, and balconies, it was like a Gothic intruder into the Manhattan skyline, a medieval fortress in the middle of the twenty-first century.

On the sidewalk, a street vendor was selling T-shirts emblazoned with the former Beatle's face.

Alice spotted a group of teenagers a dozen yards ahead of her, noisy Spanish tourists taking pictures of themselves with the building in the background. Thirty years later, the legend was still going strong.

After observing them for a few seconds, she decided on her target and worked out a basic plan of attack. She gestured with her chin at the group. "You see the boy talking on his phone?"

Keyne scratched the back of his neck. "Which one? Half of them are on their phones."

"The little fat one with glasses in the Barcelona shirt."

"Seems kind of mean to attack a kid."

Alice exploded. "You don't seem to realize how serious this is, Keyne! He's at least sixteen and we're not attacking him, we're just borrowing his phone."

"I'm starving," he said. "Couldn't we steal a hot dog instead?"

She gave him a murderous look. "Stop being such a smart-ass and listen. You are going to walk very close to me. When we're right in front of the kid, you push me into him, and as soon as I grab the phone, we get the hell out of here. Understood?"

Gabriel nodded. "Sounds easy enough."

"Easy? You'll see how easy it is to run when you're hand-cuffed to someone."

Everything went according to plan—while the teenager was still off balance, Alice snatched his phone, then yelled at Gabriel, "Run!"

The white Walk signal was flashing. They took advantage of this to cross and disappear down the first side street. Running in handcuffs turned out to be even harder than Alice had feared. Not only did they have to try to match their strides, but there was a considerable height difference to deal with. And with every step they took, the steel bracelets dug painfully into their wrists.

"They're following us!" Gabriel shouted, looking back over his shoulder.

Alice turned and saw the group of Spanish teenagers hot on their heels.

Damn it!

She nodded and they increased their pace. They were running down Seventy-First Street, a typically calm Upper West Side block lined by elegant apartment buildings and brownstones. The sidewalks were wide and free of tourists, enabling them to move quickly. The teenagers were not giving up, though, continuing to sprint after the thieves and yelling at passersby to help them.

Columbus Avenue.

More crowds—shops opening for the day, cafés beginning to fill up, students filing out of the neighboring subway station.

"Go left!" Gabriel shouted, veering suddenly to the side.

The change of direction took Alice by surprise. Knocked off balance, she cried out as the handcuffs cut into her skin.

They ran south down the avenue, pushing past other pedestrians, overturning several display stands, and almost crushing a Yorkshire terrier.

Too many people.

Dizziness. Head spinning. A stitch tearing at her side. To avoid the crowd, they tried running a few yards along the road.

Bad idea.

They were nearly hit by a taxi. Brakes screaming, the driver leaned on his horn and yelled a torrent of insults at them. Attempting to get back on the sidewalk, Alice caught her foot on the curb. Again, the handcuffs sliced into her wrist. Her momentum sent her flying headfirst to the ground, dragging Gabriel down with her. The collision took her breath away and she dropped the cell phone that had been the cause of all this trouble.

Shit!

Moving fast, Gabriel grabbed the phone. "Get up!"

They got to their feet and glanced back again at their pursuers. Most of the group had fallen behind, but two of the teenagers were still racing after them, undoubtedly hoping to come out victorious in a chase through Manhattan that would amaze all their friends back home.

"Those little bastards can run, I'll give them that!" Gabriel hissed. "I'm too old for this shit."

"Keep going!" Alice urged, forcing him to match her stride.

Every yard was torture, but they ran through the pain, hand in hand. Ten yards, fifty yards, a hundred yards. A jerky series of images flashed past them: steam rising from manholes, metal ladders leaning against brick façades, children making faces through a school bus's windows. And always that succession of glass-and-concrete buildings, that profusion of store logos and advertising billboards.

Sixty-Seventh Street. Sixty-Sixth Street.

Their wrists were bleeding, their lungs burning, but still they kept running. Driven by the adrenaline in their bloodstreams and the kids on their heels, they found their second wind. Their movements started to synchronize and become more fluid. They reached the point where Columbus met Broadway. Here, the avenue was transformed into a gigantic intersection of three roads and multiple lanes of traffic. They only had to exchange one look.

"Now!"

Taking their lives into their hands, they ran diagonally across the intersection amid a cacophony of screeching tires and car horns.

Between Sixty-Fifth and Sixty-Second Streets, the entire western part of Broadway was occupied by Lincoln Center, built around the Metropolitan Opera House. Alice looked up to get her bearings. Several stories high, the glass-and-steel prow of a gigantic ship protruded over the avenue.

She recognized the Juilliard School; she had been here

before with Seymour. On the upper floors, behind glass walls, ballerinas practiced and musicians rehearsed.

"The parking garage!" she exclaimed, gesturing at a concrete ramp that sloped down.

Gabriel nodded. Stealthily, they went down the ramp, standing aside whenever a car climbed past them heading for the exit. One level belowground, they used a final burst of energy to run across the entire lot, then took the stairs to an emergency exit that came out three blocks away, in the little enclave of Damrosch Park.

Emerging at last into the open air, they were relieved to discover that their pursuers had disappeared.

Leaning against the low wall that circled the esplanade, Alice and Gabriel felt as if they would never get their breath back. Both were sweating and crippled with pain.

"Hand me the phone," she said, gasping.

"Oh, shit, I...I must have dropped it!" He groaned, hand searching his pocket.

"I can't believe it! You—"

"Just kidding." He grinned and passed her the cell phone.

Alice gave him an icy stare and was about to launch into a tirade, when her mouth was suddenly filled with a metallic taste. Her head spun and she felt nauseated. Bending over a window box, she spat out a thin trickle of bile.

"You need water."

"What I need is food."

"I told you we should have stolen a hot dog!"

They walked carefully to a drinking fountain to quench their thirst. Bordered by the New York City Ballet and the immense glass arches of the Metropolitan Opera, Damrosch Park was busy enough that nobody took any notice of them. Workers were putting up tents and podiums on the main square in preparation for an event.

After drinking a few mouthfuls of water, Alice looked at the phone, checked that it was not protected by a code, and called Seymour's cell.

While she waited for him to answer, she trapped the phone in the hollow of her shoulder and massaged the back of her neck. Her heart was still hammering in her chest.

Pick up, Seymour…

Seymour Lombart was the second in command of the investigative team that Alice led. Alice, Seymour, and five other cops made up the "Schafer squad," which shared four small offices on the third floor of 36 Quai des Orfèvres.

Alice checked her watch, calculating the time difference. It was 2:20 p.m. in Paris now.

The cop picked up after three rings, but the clamor of voices behind him made conversation difficult. If Seymour was not in the office, he must still be eating lunch.

"Seymour?"

"Alice? Where are you? I left you a bunch of messages."

"I'm in Manhattan."

"What? Are you kidding?"

"I need your help, Seymour."

"Sorry, I'm having trouble hearing you."

It was the same for her. Bad connection. Her deputy's voice sounded distorted, almost metallic. "Where are you, Seymour?"

"At the Caveau du Palais, on Place Dauphine. Listen, let me go to the office and I'll call you back in five minutes, okay?"

"Okay. You have the number?"

"Yeah."

"Great. But hurry up. I've got work for you." Frustrated, Alice hung up and held out the cell phone to the musician. "If you want to call someone, do it now. You have five minutes."

Gabriel looked at her strangely. In spite of the urgency and the danger, he couldn't help smiling. "Do you always order people around like this?"

"Don't start," she warned him. "Do you want the phone or not?"

Gabriel took it from her and thought for a few seconds. "I'm going to call my friend Kenny."

"The saxophone player? I thought you said he was in Tokyo."

"If we're lucky, he might have left the keys to his apartment with a neighbor or a super. Do you know what time it is in Japan?" he asked as he typed in the number.

Alice counted on her fingers. "Ten at night, I think."

"Damn, he'll be in the middle of a gig."

The call went straight to voice mail. Gabriel left his friend a message explaining that he was in New York and promising to call again later.

CENTRAL PARK   29

He gave the phone back to Alice. She looked at her watch and sighed.

Get a move on, Seymour! she pleaded silently, tightening her fingers around the phone. She had just decided to call her deputy again when she noticed the series of numbers scrawled in ballpoint on her palm. The sweat had almost erased them.

"Does this mean anything to you?" she asked Gabriel, opening her hand in front of his face.

2125550100

"I found it when I woke up this morning, but I have no memory of writing it."

"Probably a phone number, don't you think? Show me again. Yeah, that's it! Two one two is the area code for Manhattan. Hey, are you sure you're a cop?"

How did I miss that?

Ignoring his sarcasm, she typed the number into the phone. It was answered immediately.

"Greenwich Hotel, Candice speaking, how may I help you?"

A hotel?

Alice thought quickly. Where was the Greenwich? Was it possible she'd been there this morning, however briefly? It made no sense, but she gave it a try anyway.

"Could you put me through to Alice Schafer, please?"

There was a silence on the line, and then: "I don't think we have anyone staying at the hotel under that name, ma'am."

Alice persisted. "You don't think? You mean you're not sure?"

"I am sure, ma'am. I'm sorry."

Even before Alice had hung up, Seymour's number flashed on the screen. She answered her deputy's call without even bothering to thank the hotel receptionist. "Seymour, are you at the office?"

"Nearly," a breathless voice replied. "So . . . this thing about New York . . . please tell me you're joking."

"I'm afraid not. Listen, I don't have much time and I need your help."

In less than three minutes, she told him everything that had happened to her since the previous evening: the night out with friends on the Champs-Élysées; the blank in her memory after she entered the parking garage; waking up in Central Park, handcuffed to a stranger; and finally stealing the cell phone so she could call him.

"Oh, come on, Alice, enough with the joke! We're busy here, we don't have time for this. And the judge wants to see you—he refused our wiretap request in the Sicard case. And as for Taillandier, she—"

"Listen to me, goddamn it!" she yelled. There were tears in her eyes and she was close to losing it. Even on the other side of the Atlantic, her deputy must have noticed the desperation in her voice. "I am not joking, for fuck's sake! I'm in danger and you're the only one who can help me."

"Okay. Calm down. Why don't you just go to the nearest police station?"

"Why? Because I have a gun that doesn't belong to me in my jacket pocket, Seymour. Because there's blood all over my shirt. Because I don't have any ID. That's why! They'd throw me in jail without a second thought!"

"Not if there's no body," the policeman pointed out.

"How do I know there isn't? First of all, I need to find out what happened to me. And find a way to get out of these damn handcuffs!"

"What do you want me to do?"

"Your mother's American. You have family here, you know lots of people."

"My mother lives in Seattle, as you know perfectly well. The only family I have in New York is one of my great-aunts. A little old lady living on the Upper East Side. We visited her the first time we went to Manhattan together, remember? She's ninety-five years old—I kind of doubt she has a hacksaw on hand. You need to find someone else to help you."

"Who, then?"

"Let me think. I have an idea, but I need to make a call first. Otherwise I might give you the wrong address."

"Okay, call me back. But please, do it quickly."

She hung up and balled her fists. Gabriel looked into her eyes. He could feel her body quivering with anger and frustration. "Who is this Seymour guy?"

"My deputy in the Criminal Division. And my best friend."

"Are you sure we can trust him?"

"Absolutely."

"My French isn't great, but I didn't get the impression he was exactly rushing to your aid."

She didn't reply. He went on: "What about the hotel? No luck?"

"No, as I'm sure you know, since you were listening to my conversation."

"It would be difficult not to at this distance. Please, madame, I hope you will forgive my indiscretion in light of the current circumstances," he mocked in a posh French accent. "And anyway, as you've already reminded me, you're not the only one who's up shit creek without a paddle!"

Exasperated, she turned away to avoid his gaze. "Jesus, stop staring at me like that! Don't you have someone else to call? A wife, a girlfriend..."

"No. A girl in every port, that's my motto. I'm a free man. As free as the air I breathe, as free as the music I play."

"Yeah, right. Free and alone. I know the type."

"So what about you? Got a husband or a boyfriend?"

She avoided the question with an indecipherable movement of her head, but he sensed that he had touched a nerve.

"Seriously, Alice, are you married?"

"Go fuck yourself, Keyne."

"Okay, I get it," he said. "You are married." As she didn't deny it, he pressed on. "Why don't you call your husband?"

She balled her fists tighter.

"Relationship on the rocks, huh? Can't say I'm too surprised, given your charming personality."

She stared at him as if he had just plunged a dagger into her belly. Then her shock gave way to anger.

"I can't call him because he's dead, you piece of shit!"

Gabriel's face showed his discomfiture at this clumsy faux pas. But before he could offer an apology, an awful ringtone—some improbable mix of salsa and club music—poured from the stolen cell phone.

"Yes, Seymour?"

"I've figured out how to solve your problem, Alice. You remember Nikki Nikovski?"

"Remind me."

"When we went to New York last Christmas, we visited a contemporary artists' collective..."

"In a big building near the docks, right?"

"Yeah, in Red Hook. We had a long talk with an artist who did silk-screen printing on sheets of steel and aluminum."

"And you ended up buying two of her pieces for your collection," she remembered.

"Yep, that's her—Nikki Nikovski. We stayed in touch and I've just talked to her. Her studio is in an old factory. She has the right tools to get you out of the handcuffs and she's agreed to help."

Alice sighed with relief. Clinging to this good news, she laid out her battle plan to her deputy.

"You have to start an investigation, Seymour. Start by getting hold of the security-camera footage from the underground parking garage on Avenue Franklin-Roosevelt. Find out if my car is still there."

"You told me all your things were stolen, right?" Seymour said. "So I can put a trace on your cell phone and check any movements in your bank account."

"Good. And find out about any private jets that left Paris for the United States last night. Start with Le Bourget, then widen the list to all the business airports in the Paris region. Also, try to dig up what you can on a Gabriel Keyne— he's an American jazz pianist. Check whether he was really playing a concert last night in a Dublin club called Brown Sugar."

"You're investigating me?" Gabriel interjected. "You've got nerve!"

Alice signaled him to shut up and continued instructing her deputy. "Question my friends too—you never know. Karine Payet, Malika Haddad, and Samia Chouaki. We were in college together. You'll find their phone numbers on my office computer."

"Okay."

Suddenly, another idea crossed her mind. "Oh, and just in case, see if you can trace a gun for me. A Glock twenty-two. I'll give you the serial number."

She read out the series of letters and numbers engraved on the side of the pistol.

"Got it. I'll do everything I can to help you, Alice, but I have to tell Taillandier about this."

Alice closed her eyes. The image of Mathilde Taillandier,

the chief of the Criminal Division, flashed in her head. Taillandier did not like Alice much, and the feeling was mutual. Since the Erik Vaughn case, Alice had asked several times to be transferred. Up till now, her bosses had refused the request, essentially for political reasons, and Alice knew her position within the division was still fragile.

"No way," she insisted. "Don't tell anyone. You need to deal with this on your own. I've saved your skin plenty of times, Seymour—you owe me this, at least."

"All right." He sighed. "I'll call you as soon as I have any news."

"No, I'll call you. I won't be able to keep this phone very long, but text me Nikki Nikovski's address."

Alice hung up, and a few seconds later, the address of the painter's studio appeared on the screen. She clicked on the link and a map appeared.

"Red Hook? That's pretty far," Gabriel commented, looking over her shoulder.

Alice touched the screen to widen the map. The studio was located in Brooklyn. There was no way they could walk there. And public transit was out of the question.

"We don't even have cash for bus or subway fare," Gabriel said as if reading her thoughts.

"So what do you suggest, Einstein?"

"Easy," he replied. "We steal a car. But this time, you let me do it, okay?"

Near the intersection of Amsterdam Avenue and Sixty-First Street was a little dead-end alley between two apartment buildings.

Gabriel smashed the window of the old Mini with his elbow. He and Alice had spent nearly twenty minutes looking for a car that was parked in a quiet spot and old enough to be started the old-fashioned way.

It was an antique Austin Cooper S with beige bodywork and a white roof, a late 1960s model apparently restored to its original state by a collector.

"Are you sure you know what you're doing?"

Gabriel shrugged off the question. "Nothing in life is certain except death and taxes."

He put his arm through the smashed window and opened the door. Though Hollywood movies suggested otherwise, hot-wiring a car was no easy feat. And it was even more complicated when you were handcuffed to someone.

Gabriel sat in the driver's seat, then crouched under the aluminum-and-polished-wood steering wheel while Alice pretended to talk to him, leaning into the window.

They worked together instinctively, Alice acting as lookout while he dealt with the mechanics of the theft.

With one hard yank, Gabriel pulled off the plastic panels that slotted together to protect the steering column, exposing the electronics. Three pairs of different-colored wires emerged from a scuffed plastic cylinder.

"Where did you learn to do that?"

"School of hard knocks. Englewood, South Side of Chicago."

He carefully examined the bundle of wires before identifying the ones that activated the battery. Pointing to the brown wires, he explained: "These supply all the car's electricity."

"For God's sake, you're not going to give me a mechanics class right now, are you?"

Annoyed, he unclipped two wires from the cylinder, exposed their ends, and twisted them together to turn on the ignition. Instantly, the dashboard lit up.

"Hurry up, damn it! There's a woman watching us from her balcony."

"It's not exactly a piece of cake when you've got only one hand, you know. I'd like to see you try!"

"Well, don't brag about your school of hard knocks, then."

Under pressure and against every rule of common sense, Gabriel used his teeth to expose the end of the starter wire.

"How about giving me a hand instead of standing there whining? Here, take this wire. Rub it gently against where mine are connected. There you go, that's it..."

A spark was produced and they heard the engine fire up. A brief smile of complicity sealed this little victory.

"Move over, quick," she told him, pushing him toward the passenger seat. "I'm driving."

5

RED HOOK

A FORD TAURUS POLICE Interceptor sporting the colors of the NYPD was parked at the corner of Broadway and Sixty-Sixth Street.

Hurry up, Mike!

Inside the car, Jodie Costello, twenty-four years old, drummed her fingers impatiently against the steering wheel.

The young woman had finished the police academy earlier that year, and her job was proving a lot less exciting than she'd hoped. This morning, she had been at work for only forty-five minutes and she already had pins and needles in her legs from sitting still. Her patrol district, west of Central

Park, was a wealthy area and way too quiet for her taste. Since she'd started this job, all she'd done was give directions to tourists, run after purse-snatchers, ticket speeding motorists, and clear drunks from the street.

To make things worse, her partner was a numbskull named Mike Hernandez who was only six months from retirement and chronically lazy. All he thought about was eating and exerting as little effort as humanly possible. Like some cop caricature, he took regular doughnut, burger, and Coke breaks and would hang around to shoot the shit with store-keepers and tourists at the slightest opportunity—his own version of community policing.

Come on, man, that's enough! Jodie seethed. *How long does it take to buy a bag of doughnuts, for God's sake?*

She got out, slamming the door behind her. She was about to go into the Dunkin' Donuts to chew out her partner, when she saw the group of six teenagers running toward her.

"¡Ladrón, ladrón!"

In a firm voice, she ordered the Spanish tourists to calm down and then listened to the explanations they gave in broken English. At first, she thought it was just a simple phone-snatching, and she was about to send them off to the twentieth precinct to file a complaint, when a strange detail grabbed her attention.

"Wait, you're sure the thieves were *handcuffed?*" she asked the boy in the soccer shirt, who seemed to be at once the ugliest and the least dumb of the group, a chubby-faced kid with thick-lensed glasses and an uneven bowl cut.

"I'm sure! Yes!" the Spaniard replied, noisily backed up by his friends.

Jodie chewed her lower lip. *Fugitives?* It was hard to believe. This morning, as she did every day, she had listened to the descriptions of wanted suspects on the APB, and none of them had sounded remotely like these two muggers.

Following a hunch, she took her iPad from the car's trunk. "What kind of phone do you have, kid?"

She listened to his reply and connected to the manufacturer's website. She then asked the teenager to give her his username and password.

Once she'd done this, the app allowed her to access the user's e-mails and contact list as well as the phone's location. Jodie knew how to do this because she had used the same technique six months earlier for personal reasons. In the space of a few minutes, she had been able to trace her boyfriend's visits to another girl's apartment, giving her proof of his infidelity. Now she touched the screen to start the tracking process. A blue dot flashed on the map. Assuming the site was working properly, the kid's cell phone was currently halfway across the Brooklyn Bridge!

Optimistic thoughts were chasing away her bad mood—finally, she had a chance to work a real investigation.

Theoretically, she ought to broadcast this information on the NYPD radio frequency so a Brooklyn patrol could arrest the suspects. But there was no way she was going to just hand this case over to someone else.

She glanced at the Dunkin' Donuts. Still no sign of Mike Hernandez.

Oh, well...

She got behind the steering wheel. At just that moment, her partner came out the door. "Quick! Get in the car!" Jodie called to him.

"What's going on?" he asked, climbing awkwardly into the passenger seat.

"I'll tell you later. Let's go!" And she set off for Brooklyn, siren screaming.

The former working docks jutted out into the East River.

The Mini reached the end of Van Brunt Street, the main road that crossed Red Hook. Beyond that point, the road gave way to a fenced-off industrial wasteland that opened directly onto the docks.

Alice and Gabriel parked next to a broken sidewalk. Still hobbled by their handcuffs, they exited the car through the same door. The sun was shining brightly, but an icy wind roared at their faces.

"Damn, it's cold here!" the pianist grumbled, lifting his jacket collar.

Gradually, Alice began to recognize her surroundings. The rugged beauty of the industrial landscape, the disused warehouses, the strange choreography of the container cranes, the freighters and barges sharing the same stretch of water. It was like the end of the world here, the ferry foghorns barely even audible.

The last time she'd been here with Seymour, the district was still struggling to recover from the ravages of Hurricane Sandy, when the basements and first floors of buildings located too close to the water had been flooded. Today, thankfully, it looked as if most of the damage had been repaired.

"Nikki Nikovski's studio is in that building over there," Alice said, pointing at an imposing brick construction that, to judge from its silos and chimney, must have been a major factory during Brooklyn's industrial golden age.

They headed toward the building, which faced out to sea. The docks were practically deserted. No tourists or joggers here. There were a few little cafés and stores lined up on Van Brunt Street, but none were open yet.

"So who is this woman?" Gabriel asked, stepping over a sewer pipe.

"She was a famous model back in the nineties."

The pianist's eyes lit up. "Really? Like a fashion model?"

"Doesn't take much to get you excited, does it?" Alice said reprovingly.

"No, it's not that," he said irritably. "I'm just surprised by her career change."

"Anyway, her paintings and sculptures are beginning to get shown in galleries."

"So your friend Seymour is a contemporary-art enthusiast?"

"Yeah. He's a collector, in fact. His father passed the passion on to him, and he got a large inheritance that has allowed him to pursue it."

"How about you?"

She shrugged. "Art? It means nothing to me. But to each his own—I'm a collector too, in a way."

"Oh yeah?" He frowned. "And what do you collect?"

"Criminals. Murderers. Killers."

Having reached the former factory, they stood in silence for a moment before noticing that the iron door that barred access to the first floor was not locked. They went inside, entered the cage of an elevator that looked like it had once been used to transport cargo, and pressed the button for the top floor. The cage opened onto a concrete platform that led to a metal fire door. They had to ring the bell several times before Nikki opened it.

A long leather apron, thick gloves, earmuffs, a face protector, black sunglasses. The ex-model's attractive figure was completely hidden behind this metalworker's outfit.

"Hello, I'm Alice Schafer. I think my friend Seymour—"

"Come in, quickly!" Nikki interjected, taking off her mask and glasses. "I'll warn you now: I couldn't care less what kind of shit you're in, I just don't want to be mixed up in it. I'll get you out of those handcuffs, but after that you have to go. Understood?"

They nodded and closed the door behind them.

The place looked more like a blacksmith's workshop than an artist's studio. Illuminated only by daylight, it was a vast room, the walls covered with the widest range of tools imaginable: hammers in all sizes, soldering irons, blowtorches.

Outlined against the fiery embers glowing red in the hearth of the forge were an anvil and a poker.

Following Nikki, they walked across the untreated floor-boards and wound their way between the various metal shapes that filled the space—purple and ocher silk-screened monotypes shining on steel, rusted iron sculptures with sharp edges that threatened to split open the ceiling.

"Sit there," the artist ordered, pointing at two battered chairs.

Eager to be free, Alice and Gabriel sat on either side of a workbench. While Nikki screwed a saw disk to an angle grinder, she told them to trap the handcuff chain in the jaws of a vise. Then she switched on her machine, which vibrated with an infernal noise, and approached the two fugitives.

The disk went through the chain in less than three seconds, and a few blows from a pointed chisel broke the handcuff ratchets.

At last! Alice sighed, massaging her raw, bloody wrist.

She started to mumble a few words of thanks, but Nikovski interrupted her coldly, pointing to the door. "Just get out. Now."

Relieved to be free again, Alice and Gabriel obeyed.

They were both smiling when they emerged onto the docks. This deliverance had not answered any of their questions, but it was still an important step forward—they were autonomous again. Now to find out the truth.

Feeling as if a huge weight had been lifted from their

shoulders, they walked along the docks. The wind had grown less cold. The sky, still perfectly blue, contrasted with the harshness of the postindustrial landscape: abandoned work sites, endless lines of hangars and warehouses. But the view was intoxicating; from where they stood, they could see all of New York Harbor, from the Statue of Liberty to New Jersey.

"Come on, I'll buy you a cappuccino!" Gabriel said cheerfully, gesturing to a tiny café located in an old graffiti-covered train carriage.

Alice was quick to rain on his parade. "And how are you planning to pay for it? Or are we going to steal that too?"

He grimaced at this intrusion of reality into his happiness. Then he touched his injured arm. The pain he had felt on waking was now more intense.

Gabriel took off his jacket. His shirtsleeve was blood-stained. He rolled it up and saw the bandage wrapped around his forearm—a wide cloth compress soaked with coagulated blood. When he lifted it, he discovered a nasty wound that immediately started to bleed again. The entire length of his forearm had been hacked with something like a box cutter. Thankfully the cuts were not too deep. In fact, now he looked at them, they sort of resembled a . . .

"They're numbers!" Alice exclaimed, helping him wipe away the blood.

Engraved in his skin, 141197 appeared in little red notches.

Gabriel's expression had changed. Within a few seconds, the relief he'd felt at being free again had given way to anxiety. "Another code? Damn it, I'm beginning to get tired of this bullshit!"

"Well, this one's not a phone number, anyway," said Alice.

"Maybe it's a date?" he suggested bitterly, putting his jacket back on.

"The fourteenth of November, 1997 . . . it's possible."

Exasperated, Gabriel looked into the Frenchwoman's eyes. "Listen, we can't just keep wandering around like this, with no cash and no ID."

"What do you suggest? Go to the police? You've just stolen a car!"

"Only because you made me!"

"Oh, how brave of you! You're such a gentleman! It's always the same with you—everything is someone else's fault. I can see the kind of person you are."

Deciding that arguing would only make things worse, he let it drop. "I know a pawnshop in Chinatown," Gabriel offered. "The guy's legit. A lot of musicians who are short of cash pawn their instruments there."

She sensed a trap. "And what do you think we should pawn? Your piano?"

He gave a tense smile and looked pointedly at Alice's wrist. "The only thing we have is your watch."

She took a step back. "No chance. Never."

"Come on, it's a Patek Philippe, isn't it? We could get at least—"

"I said no!" she yelled. "It was my husband's watch."

"But what else do we have? Apart from this cell phone."

Seeing him take the phone from his pocket, she came close to strangling him. "Why the hell did you keep that thing? I told you to toss it."

"I don't think so. After all we went through to steal it? Anyway, it's all we have at the moment. It could still be useful."

"But they can track us in three minutes flat with that! Don't you ever read thrillers? Don't you ever watch movies?"

"Chill out, will you? This isn't a movie."

She opened her mouth to insult him, but she was stopped by the distant sound of sirens carried on the wind. She turned in that direction and froze—there was a red light flashing on the horizon. Siren screaming, the cop car was heading straight toward them.

"Come on!" she shouted, grabbing Gabriel's arm.

They ran to the Mini. Alice got into the driver's side and started the engine. Van Brunt Street was a dead end, and the cops had made it impossible for them to escape the way they came.

Impossible to escape at all . . .

The only way out was through a wire gate that led onto the docks. Unfortunately, it was padlocked.

No choice.

"Fasten your seat belt," she ordered as the tires squealed under them.

Hands gripping the steering wheel, Alice accelerated over thirty yards and plowed the Mini into the gate. The chain yielded with a metallic crunch, and the car sped out onto the tracks of the old streetcar line that wound around the abandoned factory.

Sheepishly, Gabriel rolled down his window and tossed out the phone.

"It's a bit late for that!" Alice raged, shooting him a black look.

Sitting only a few inches up from the ground, the young woman felt as if she were driving a go-kart. With its narrow wheelbase and tiny wheels, the Cooper jolted over the uneven ground.

She glanced in the rearview mirror. Unsurprisingly, the cop car was chasing them along the seafront. Alice drove along the docks for about a hundred yards before spotting a street to the right. She took it. The smooth asphalt and the long straightaway enabled her to step on the accelerator and speed northward. At this time of day, traffic was picking up in this part of Brooklyn. Alice ran two red lights, almost causing an accident, but she still didn't manage to shake the cop's Interceptor.

The Mini was not the most comfortable car in the world, but it could certainly move. After negotiating a bend at top speed, tires shrieking, it turned back onto the neighborhood's main road.

Alice saw the Taurus's menacing radiator grille grow larger in the mirror.

"They're right behind us!" Gabriel warned her, turning to look.

Alice prepared to take an underpass that led to the high-way. She was tempted to try melting into the traffic, but on a highway, the Mini Morris would not have the power to escape the Interceptor's V-8.

Trusting her instinct, Alice braked and veered suddenly onto the pedestrian ramp designed to allow maintenance workers to access the top of the underpass.

"You're going to get us killed!" Gabriel screamed, gripping tight to his seat belt with all his strength.

One hand on the steering wheel, the other on the gearshift, Alice drove over gravel for about twenty yards, and then, just as the car was beginning to sink, she managed to swerve onto the concrete ramp that led toward Cobble Hill.

Whew, that was close!

A sudden turn to the left, then right, changing gear.

The car came out on a shopping street edged with brightly colored stores: a butcher, an Italian grocer, a French patisserie, even a barbershop full of customers.

Too many people . . .

Their pursuer was still right behind them, but Alice took advantage of the Cooper's small size to slalom between the cars ahead of them before abruptly turning off the crowded street and going back into the residential area.

The landscape had changed now. The industrial backdrop of Red Hook had given way to a sleepy suburb: a little church, a little school, little front yards placed neatly in front of a row of identical redbrick town houses.

Despite the narrowness of the streets, Alice had not reduced her speed; she was still driving with her foot to the floor, her face almost touching the windshield, on the lookout for an escape. Behind the glass, the landscape rushed past. The Mini's gearbox was on its last legs. At this speed, each time Alice shifted gears, it made a loud creaking noise, as if it were about to break in half.

Suddenly she slammed on the brakes. They had just passed a little back alley. She reversed the car and then turned into the narrow road at top speed.

"Not here—it's a one-way street!"

To make things worse, a delivery van was blocking the other end.

"Slow down! We're going to crash into the UPS truck!"

Ignoring his pleas, Alice stepped even harder on the gas and propelled the Mini onto the sidewalk. The shock absorbers, already struggling, now gave up the ghost. Alice leaned on the car's horn and forced her way through, glancing at the rearview mirror as she went. Unable to follow through the narrow gap, the police car found itself nose to nose with the van.

At least we've won ourselves a few seconds . . .

Still on the sidewalk, the little car sped right and then went back onto the road.

They headed toward a landscaped garden surrounded by an iron fence—Cobble Hill Park.

"Do you know where we are?" Alice asked, slowing down as she went around the park.

Gabriel studied the road signs. "Go right—it'll take us to Atlantic Avenue."

She followed his directions and they found themselves on a four-lane road: the arterial street that crossed New York from east to west, from the neighborhood around JFK to the banks of the East River. Alice recognized it immediately. She'd been in taxis here on her way to and from the airport.

"We're close to the Manhattan Bridge, aren't we?"

"Just behind us."

She made a U-turn and took the ramp to the highway. Soon, she saw signs for the exit that led to Manhattan. The grayish-blue pylons of the suspension bridge came into view in the distance, two steel towers connected by a tangle of cables and ropes.

"Oh, shit! Check your mirror!"

The cop car was just behind them again.

Too late to change direction.

There were now only two possibilities: head for Long Island or return to Manhattan. They took exit 29A, which led to the bridge. Seven lanes of traffic, four subway lines, and a cycling path—the Manhattan Bridge was an ogre that swallowed up travelers and vehicles in Brooklyn and spat them out on the opposite side of the East River.

Suddenly the pavement narrowed. Before reaching the entrance of the bridge, they had to take a long, curving concrete overpass.

The overpass was congested, with cars moving bumper to bumper. The cops were about a hundred yards behind her.

Here, their sirens made no difference, because the way was too narrow for the other cars to move aside and let them pass. At the same time, though, the fugitives could not escape.

"We're screwed," Gabriel said.

"No, we're not. We can cross the bridge."

"Think about it. They have our description and now they know what car we're driving. Even if we do get across, there'll be other patrol cars waiting for us at the end of the bridge."

"Well, let's not forget it's your fault they found us! I told you to get rid of that damn phone."

"Yeah, I know. My bad."

She closed her eyes for a second. She didn't think the cops knew who they were yet, and it didn't really matter much if they did. And Keyne had a point: the real problem was their car.

"You're right."

Seeing that the traffic was easing up farther ahead, she unbuckled her seat belt and opened the door. "You take the wheel," she told him.

"What? But... what do you mean, I'm right?"

"This car is too easy to spot. I'm going to try something."

Gabriel heaved himself over into the driver's seat. On the overpass that led to the bridge, cars were still moving forward at a crawl. He squinted, trying to keep Alice in sight. This girl was full of surprises. She was weaving between cars now, elusive. Suddenly he panicked—she was taking her gun out of her jacket and pointing it at a beige Honda Accord.

Not the kind of car that anyone would notice, he realized.

The Honda's driver, seeing a gun aimed at her face, did not ask questions; she simply got out of her car, climbed over the barrier, and fled down the long grass embankment.

Gabriel could not hold back a whistle of admiration. He turned around. The cop car was right at the foot of the overpass. From that distance, there was no chance they could have seen anything.

He abandoned the Mini and got into the Honda next to Alice just as traffic began moving again.

Gabriel winked at her and, in order to defuse the tension, pretended to complain: "You could have picked something nicer than this! At least that little Mini had style, not like this old clunker."

Alice's features were hardened by the stress of the day. "Instead of trying to be funny, why don't you take a look in the glove compartment."

He did and discovered the one thing he had been most in need of since waking up that morning: a pack of cigarettes.

A lighter was in there too. "Hallelujah!" he said as he lit one.

He took two long drags and handed it to Alice. Without letting go of the steering wheel, she too took a drag. The bitter taste of the tobacco went straight to her head. She desperately needed to eat something or she was going to faint.

She opened the window to get some fresh air. To her right, the Midtown skyscrapers glittered in the sunlight, while to her left, the low-rise buildings of the Lower East Side made her think of the settings of the old thrillers her husband, Paul, used to read.

Paul...

She pushed away her memories and checked her watch. It was more than an hour since they had woken up, oblivious to the previous night's events, in the park. And so far, their investigation had gotten precisely nowhere. Not only was the original mystery still unsolved, but other questions had arisen that made their situation even murkier—and more dangerous.

Their investigation had to move up a gear, and on that point Gabriel was right: they could not accomplish very much without money.

"Give me the address of your pawnshop," she said as they arrived in Manhattan.

6

CHINATOWN

THE CAR PASSED the Bowery and turned onto Mott Street. Alice found a parking spot in front of a Chinese herbalist's shop. The space was not very big, but she maneuvered the car perfectly to squeeze between a delivery van and a food truck selling dim sum.

"If I remember correctly, the pawnshop is a little farther down that way," said Gabriel, closing the door of the Honda.

Alice locked the car, then followed him.

They walked quickly along the narrow street swarming with people and buzzing with movement. Mott Street, a corridor of dark brick buildings latticed with iron staircases, crossed Chinatown from north to south. A wide variety of stores, their windows decorated with Chinese characters, lined the street: tattoo parlors, acupuncturists, jewelers, boutiques selling knockoffs of luxury products, and groceries and delis displaying turtle shells and glazed ducks hanging from hooks.

They soon arrived at a gray façade ornamented with a gigantic neon dragon. The sign flashed the words PAWNSHOP—BUY—SELL—LOAN in the morning light.

Gabriel pushed open the door, and Alice followed him through a gloomy corridor that opened out into a large, dimly lit, windowless room filled with the lingering odor of stale sweat.

All kinds of different objects were piled up on rows of metal shelves: flat-screen televisions, designer purses, musical instruments, stuffed animals, abstract paintings.

"Give me your watch," Gabriel said, holding out his hand.

Cornered now, Alice hesitated. When her husband died, she had—probably too quickly—gotten rid of everything that reminded her of the man she had loved so much: clothes, books, furniture. All that she had left of him was this watch, a Patek Philippe in rose gold with a perpetual calendar and moon phases. Paul had inherited it from his grandfather.

Over time, the watch had become a sort of talisman, a link that connected her to the memory of Paul. Alice wore it every day, repeating each morning the gestures her husband used to make: fastening the leather strap around her wrist, winding the watch, cleaning its face. The object calmed her and made her feel as if Paul were still with her, somewhere—an artificial feeling, admittedly, but a reassuring one.

"Please," Gabriel insisted.

They walked up to a counter protected by bulletproof glass. Behind this partition stood a young, sleek, androgynous-looking Asian man wearing skinny jeans, geek glasses, and a fitted jacket over a fluorescent T-shirt with a Keith Haring design.

"What can I do for you?" he asked, smoothing a strand of hair behind his ear.

His affected air clashed strangely with the grimy ambience of the store. Alice regretfully took off her watch and placed it on the counter. "How much?"

The pawnbroker picked it up and examined it closely. "Do you have a document proving its authenticity? A certificate of origin, for example?"

"Not on me," Alice murmured, giving the man a black look.

The employee handled the watch rather brusquely, changing the position of the hands, squeezing the push button.

"It's very fragile," she scolded him.

"I'm adjusting the time and date," he replied without looking up.

"It shows the right time! Anyway, that's enough now. How much will you give me for it?"

"I can offer you five hundred dollars."

"What?" Alice exploded, grabbing the watch from him. "This is a collector's item. It's worth a hundred times more than that!"

She was about to leave the store, but Gabriel pulled her back. "Calm down," he told her, taking her aside. "We're not *selling* your husband's watch, all right? We're just leaving it here for a while. We'll come back and pick it up as soon as we've solved this mystery."

She shook her head. "No. Absolutely not. We'll have to find another solution."

"Like what? There is no other solution and you know it!" he shouted. "We have to eat something before we collapse and we won't be able to get anything done without money. Go wait for me outside and let me negotiate with this guy."

Resentfully, Alice handed him the watch and left the store.

As soon as she was outside, the mingled odor of spices, smoked fish, and fermented mushrooms hit her, a smell she had not even noticed a few minutes earlier. It made her suddenly nauseated. A convulsion twisted her guts, forcing her to bend forward and vomit a dribble of yellow bile heaved up by her empty stomach. Her head spinning slightly, she stood up and leaned against the wall.

Gabriel was right. She definitely had to eat something.

She rubbed her eyes and realized that there were tears rolling down her cheeks. She felt like she was losing control. She felt claustrophobic in this neighborhood, and her body was threatening to collapse. She was paying for the strain of the morning. Her wrist was on fire with pain where the handcuff had dug into her skin, and her muscles were throbbing.

Worst of all, she felt horribly alone, filled with sorrow and confusion.

Her mind flashed up memories. The pawning of the watch

had brought back painful fragments of the past. She thought about Paul. About their first meeting. How blown away she had been. She thought about how violently she had been in love; it was a force strong enough to destroy all fears.

Memories rose to the surface, erupting into her mind with the power of a geyser. Memories of happy days that would never return.

I remember...

Three years ago

Paris
November 2010

The heavens have opened. The city is deluged.

"Turn right, Seymour, this is it. Rue Saint-Thomas d'Aquin."

The windshield wipers wave frantically from side to side but cannot keep up with the torrent of rain falling on the French capital. No matter how fast the rubber blades sweep across the glass, the translucent curtain remakes itself almost immediately.

Our unmarked car leaves Boulevard Saint-Germain and takes the narrow road that leads to the Place de l'Église.

The sky is black. The storm has been raging since the night before, drowning everything. The city looks liquefied.

In front of us, the pediment of the church has vanished, its decorations and bas-reliefs blurred by mist. Only the stone angels are still distinguishable.

Seymour drives around the little square and parks in a delivery area across from the gynecologist's office. "You think you'll be long?"

"Twenty minutes max," I promise. The gynecologist confirmed the appointment by e-mail. I warned her I was running late.

Seymour checks his phone messages. "Listen, there's a café just up there. I'm going to buy a sandwich while I wait for you. I'll call the station and find out how Savignon and Cruchy are doing with their interrogation."

"Okay, send me a text if you have any news. See you later. Thanks for coming with me," I say. I get out and close the door behind me.

The rain hits me full force. I lift my jacket above my head to protect myself from the downpour and run the ten yards from the car to the doctor's office. The secretary takes almost a minute to buzz me in. When I finally enter the lobby, I notice that she is on the phone. She gestures an apology and points me toward the waiting room. I open the door and collapse into one of the leather armchairs.

Today has been a nightmare thanks to this sudden urinary tract infection. Seriously, it's been torture; I'm in pain and I need to piss every five minutes, and when I do, it burns like fire. I've even had blood in my urine, which freaked me out a little.

And on top of all that, this is *really* bad timing. For the past twenty-four hours, my team has been fighting on all fronts. We're struggling to get a confession from a murderer whom we have no solid evidence against, and now we've just landed another case: the murder of a woman found dead in her own home in a bourgeois apartment building on Rue de la Faisanderie in the sixteenth arrondissement. A young schoolteacher, savagely strangled with a nylon stocking. It is three p.m. Seymour and I arrived at the crime scene at seven this morning. We've been questioning the neighbors ourselves. I haven't eaten, I'm nauseated, and I feel like I'm pissing razor blades.

I grab the compact from my purse and, using the little mirror, attempt to put my hair back into some sort of order. I look like a zombie, my clothes are soaked, and I have the impression that I smell like a wet dog.

I take a deep breath to calm myself down. This isn't the first time I've had these pains. It's horribly unpleasant, but at least I know it's treatable; I'll take some antibiotics, and in a day all the symptoms will disappear. I tried the pharmacy across the street from my apartment, but the guy who worked there wouldn't give me anything without a prescription.

"Ms. Schafer?"

A man's voice. I look up from my compact and see a white coat. Instead of my usual gynecologist, there stands a handsome, olive-skinned man, his face framed by curly blond hair and lit up by laughing eyes.

"I'm Dr. Paul Malaury," he says, adjusting his tortoiseshell glasses.

"But I have an appointment with Dr. Poncelet..."

"My colleague is on vacation. She should have let you know that I was filling in for her."

I lose my temper. "Well, she didn't. In fact, she confirmed our appointment by e-mail."

I get out my phone and look for the message on my screen so I can prove it to him. Rereading it, however, I realize that the guy is right; I had only skimmed the message, noting the confirmation of the appointment but missing the part about her being on vacation.

Shit.

"Please, come in," he says in a gentle voice.

I hesitate, momentarily disconcerted. I've had too many bad experiences with men to want one for a gynecologist. It has always seemed obvious to me that a woman is in a better position to understand another woman. It's a question of psychology, sensitivity, privacy. Still on my guard, I follow him into the office, determined to keep the encounter as brief as possible.

"All right," I say, "I'll get straight to the point: All I need is an antibiotic for cystitis. Dr. Poncelet usually gives me—"

Frowning, he cuts me off mid-tirade. "Excuse me, but you're not trying to write the prescription yourself, are you? I'm sure you realize that I can't prescribe you an antibiotic without examining you."

I try to suppress my anger, but I can now see that things

are going to be more complicated than I'd hoped. "I'm telling you, I get cystitis all the time. There's no other possible
diagnosis."

"That may be true, mademoiselle, but I am the doctor
here, not you."

"You're right, I'm not a doctor. I'm a cop and I'm swamped
right now. So don't waste my time with an examination
that'll take forever!"

"That is precisely what I'm going to do," he says, handing
me a urinalysis cup. "And I am also going to order a cyto-
bacteriological test to be done at the lab."

"God, stop being so stubborn and just give me the antibiotics! I need to get out of here!"

"Please be reasonable and stop acting like a drug addict!
There is more to life than antibiotics."

I feel suddenly weary and stupid. Another shooting
pain tears through my groin. The fatigue that has built
up since I joined the Criminal Division rises in me like
lava in a volcano. Too many sleepless nights, too much
violence and horror, too many ghosts that won't leave
me alone.

I'm at the end of my rope, exhausted. I need sun, a hot
bath, a haircut, a more feminine wardrobe, and a two-week
vacation a long way from Paris. A long way from me.

I look at this guy—elegant, mannered, serene. His handsome face is relaxed; his smile is gentle and charming. I am
exasperated by his improbably blond and curly hair. Even the
little lines around his eyes are gorgeous. And I feel ugly and

dull. Some ridiculous harpy telling him about my bladder problems.

"Are you drinking enough water?" he asks. "Half of cystitis cases can be treated just by drinking two quarts of water a day."

I am no longer listening. This is my strength: I am never discouraged for very long. Images flash up in my mind. The corpse of that woman at the crime scene this morning, Clara Maturin, strangled with a nylon stocking. Her eyes were rolled back, her face frozen in terror. I can't afford to waste time. Can't afford to let myself get distracted. I have to catch the murderer before he kills again.

"What about phytotherapy?" the handsome doctor asks me. "Plants can be very useful, you know, especially cran-berries."

With a quick, sudden movement, I go behind his desk and pull off a prescription sheet from his pad.

"You're right, I am going to write the prescription myself!"

He is so stunned that he doesn't even try to stop me.

I turn on my heel and leave the room, slamming the door behind me.

Paris, tenth arrondissement
One month later
December 24, 2010
7:00 a.m.

The Audi speeds through the night and comes out onto Place du Colonel Fabien. The lights of the city are reflected in the imposing glass-and-concrete structure of the Communist Party headquarters. It is freezing cold. I turn the heating up full blast and enter the traffic circle before driving onto Rue Louis-Blanc. I switch on the radio as I'm crossing the Saint-Martin canal.

France Info—it is seven o'clock. Today's news is brought to you by Bernard Thomasson.

Good morning, Florence; good morning, everyone. It looks as if we may well be in for a white Christmas, but no one will be celebrating. The bad weather is, once again, set to dominate today's news. Météo France has just announced an orange alert, indicating the strong possibility of a major snowstorm due to reach Paris in the late morning. The snow is likely to cause serious traffic disruptions on Île-de-France...

Stupid goddamn holidays! Stupid goddamn family obligations! Thank God Christmas comes only once a year. For me, though, even that is too much.

Paris has not yet been hit by the storm, but the respite

won't last long. I take advantage of the light traffic to roar past the Gare de l'Est, get on Boulevard Magenta, and cross the tenth arrondissement from north to south with my foot to the floor.

I hate my mother, I hate my sister, I hate my brother. And I hate these annual family reunions that always end up a disaster. Bérénice, my little sister, lives in London, where she runs an art gallery on New Bond Street. Fabrice, the middle child, works in finance in Singapore. Every year, with their spouses and children, they spend two days in my mother's villa near Bordeaux to celebrate Christmas before flying off to exotic, sun-filled destinations: the Maldives, Mauritius, the Caribbean.

The traffic information service strongly recommends that drivers avoid using their cars in Paris and in the regions to the west, a warning that would seem difficult to obey on Christmas Eve. The Paris prefecture is also warning that the snow might give way to black ice by early evening, when temperatures will fall below zero.

Rue Réaumur, then Rue Beaubourg. I drive west through the Marais and emerge in the Place de l'Hôtel-de-Ville; the building seems to sag under the weight of its Christmas lights. From a distance, the outline of the two huge towers and the spire of Notre-Dame are visible against the night sky.

Every year, during these two days at my mother's house, we go through more or less same farce. My mother goes into raptures about my siblings' successful careers, the choices they have made in their lives. She swoons over their kids, praising their schools and their fantastic grades. The conversation that follows is always the same: immigration, financial gloom, the terrible state of the country.

For her, for them, I do not exist. I'm not one of them. I am just an overgrown tomboy, without elegance or distinction. A lowly government employee. I am my father's daughter.

The travel chaos threatens to extend to certain Métro and RER commuter-rail train lines. And the same problems will affect air traffic. The Paris airports have warned of multiple delays and cancellations, with thousands of passengers stranded.

The heavy snowfall should, however, spare the Rhône Valley as well as the Mediterranean region. In Bordeaux, Toulouse, and Marseille, temperatures will be between fifteen and eighteen degrees Celsius, while in Nice and Antibes, lucky residents will be able to eat lunch outside, with temperatures rising into the low twenties.

Sick of being judged by those jerks. Sick of their endless predictable remarks: "Still no boyfriend?" "Doesn't look like you'll be having children anytime soon." "Why do you dress in such baggy, unflattering clothes?" "Why do you still act like a teenager?" Sick of their vegetarian meals designed to keep them slim and healthy, their bird food, their disgusting quinoa, their tofu pancakes, their mashed cauliflower.

I turn onto Rue de la Coutellerie and take the Pont Notre-Dame across the river. This is a magical place—to my left, the historic buildings of the Hôtel-Dieu; to my right, the façade of the Conciergerie and the roof of the Tour de l'Horloge.

Every time I go to the family home, I feel as if I am traveling thirty years back in time, reopening the wounds of childhood, rebreaking the fractures of adolescence, bringing back the bitterness of sibling rivalries, and once again being left in absolute solitude.

Every year, I tell myself this will be the last time, and every year I go through the whole charade again without knowing why. Half of me would like to burn those bridges, but the other half would give anything to see their faces the day I turn up dressed like a princess with a perfect man on my arm.

Left Bank. I drive past the quays, then turn left on Rue des Saints-Pères. I slow down, turn on my hazard lights, and park on the corner of Rue de Lille. I get out of the car, put on my orange armband, and ring the intercom of a beautiful, recently renovated building.

I leave my thumb on the buzzer for a good thirty seconds. The idea took root in my mind early in the week and required quite a bit of research. I know what I'm doing is crazy, but being aware of that is not enough to dissuade me.

"Yes, who's there?" a sleepy voice asks.

"Paul Malaury? Judicial police. Please let me in."

"Uh, but…"

"It's the police, monsieur. Open up!"

One of the heavy entrance doors unlocks with a click. Ignoring the elevator, I run up the stairs to the third floor, where I hammer on the door.

"Okay, okay!"

The man who opens the door is indeed my handsome gynecologist, but this morning he doesn't look his best. He's wearing boxers and an old T-shirt, his blond curls are in disarray, and his face is marked with surprise, fatigue, and worry.

"Hang on, I know you—you're..."

"Captain Schafer, Criminal Division. Monsieur Malaury, I hereby inform you that I am taking you into custody. You have the right to..."

"I'm sorry, but there must be some mistake! What am I supposed to have done?"

"Forgery and the use of forged documents. Please follow me."

"Is this a joke?"

"Don't make me send for my colleagues, Monsieur Malaury."

"Can I at least put on a shirt and a pair of pants?"

"Hurry, then. And you'll need a coat too—the heating is out at the station."

While he dresses, I take a quick look around. The Haussmann apartment has been transformed into a sort of loft with a refined décor. A few dividing walls have been knocked down and the herringbone floorboards painted white, but the two marble fireplaces and the original moldings have been preserved.

Behind a door, I see a young redheaded woman, about twenty years old, wrapped in a sheet and staring at me, wide-eyed. I start to grow tired of waiting.

"Get a move on, Malaury!" I yell, banging on the bathroom door. "It doesn't take ten minutes to put on a pair of pants!"

The doctor emerges from the bathroom, dressed to the nines. He has undeniably regained his former splendor, wearing a tweed sport coat, Prince of Wales check pants, a trench coat, and polished ankle boots. He whispers a few words of reassurance to his red-haired girlfriend, then follows me downstairs.

"Where are your colleagues?" he asks when we reach the street.

"I'm on my own. I was hardly going to organize a SWAT team to get you out of bed."

"But that's not a police car, is it?"

"It's unmarked. Now quit stalling and get in."

He hesitates but finally sits down in the passenger seat.

I start the car and we drive in silence as the sun begins to rise. We cross the sixth arrondissement and Montparnasse before Paul decides to ask: "Okay, seriously, what's going on? You know I could have filed charges against you last month for stealing a medical prescription! You can thank my colleague that I didn't; she persuaded me that you had lots of extenuating circumstances. To be perfectly honest, she even used the word *nutcase*."

"Oh, really? Well, I've been doing my homework on you too, Malaury," I say, taking some photocopied documents from my pocket.

He unfolds the bundle of papers and begins to read, frowning. "What is this exactly?"

"Proof that you provided false affidavits of accommodation for two illegal immigrants from Mali so they could apply for residence permits."

He doesn't try to deny it. "So what? Is humanity a crime? Is compassion against the law?"

"No, but forgery and the use of forged documents is. And it's punishable by up to three years in prison and a forty-five-thousand-euro fine."

"I thought the prisons were overcrowded already. And since when does the Criminal Division deal with this kind of thing?"

We are not far from Montrouge. I cut across the Boulevards des Maréchaux, take the beltway, then the A6 to the Aquitaine—the highway that connects Paris to Bordeaux.

When he sees the Wissous exit, Paul begins to get really worried. "Where the hell are you taking me?"

"Bordeaux. I'm sure you like wine—"

"What? You can't be serious!"

"We're going to my mother's place for Christmas Eve. They'll like you, don't worry."

He turns around, looking to see if anyone is following us, then makes a joke to reassure himself. "I've got it—there's a camera in the car. This is some sort of cops' reality show, right?"

I take a few minutes to explain to him, rather proudly, the deal I have in mind: I will drop the forgery charges against him, and in return he will pretend to be my fiancé over Christmas.

For what seems a long time, he stares at me in silence. At first, he is utterly incredulous. Then he realizes the truth.

"Oh my God, you're not even joking, are you? Did you really mount this entire ambush just because you don't have the guts to admit your life choices to your family? Jesus! You don't need a gynecologist, you need a psychiatrist."

I take this on the chin, and then, after a few minutes of silence, I come back down to earth. He's right, of course. I am a coward. And what was I expecting? Did I think he'd enjoy taking part in my role-playing game? Suddenly I feel like the world's biggest idiot. It is both my strength and my weakness, acting on instinct rather than reason. It was thanks to this personality trait that I solved several difficult cases, enabling me to join the Criminal Division at only thirty-four. But sometimes my intuition fails me and I crash and burn. The idea of introducing this guy to my family now seems inappropriate and absurd.

Red-faced with shame, I surrender. "You're right. I ... I'm sorry. I'll make a U-turn and take you back home."

"You should stop at the next gas station. You're almost empty."

I fill up the tank. My hands are clammy and the gas fumes are making my head spin. When I return to my car, Paul Malaury is no longer in the passenger seat. I look up and see him through the window of the restaurant, beckoning me over.

"I got you a tea," he says when I go inside, gesturing to the seat next to him.

"Ah, bad choice! I only drink coffee."

"That would have been too easy." He smiles, stands up, and heads back to the vending machine.

Something about this guy unsettles me—he's unflappable, almost British in the way he maintains his composure in all circumstances.

He returns two minutes later and places a cup of coffee and a croissant in front of me.

"It's not exactly Pierre Hermé, but it's not as bad as it looks," he says to defuse the tension. As if to back up his words, he bites into his own croissant and discreetly stifles a yawn. "I can't believe you dragged me out of bed at seven a.m.! On the one day when I can sleep in!"

"I told you, I'm going to take you home. There'll still be time for you to go back to bed with your sweetheart."

He sips his tea and says, "I have to admit that I don't really understand you. Why would you want to spend Christmas with people who obviously make you unhappy?"

"Drop it, Malaury. As you said, you're not a shrink."

"And what does your father think of all this?"

I sweep the question away. "My father died a long time ago."

"Will you stop bullshitting me?" he exclaims, handing me his cell phone.

I look at the screen, knowing in advance what I will find. While I was putting gas in the car, Malaury Googled me. Unsurprisingly, his search led him to a news item, a few months old, detailing my father's fall from grace.

EX-SUPERCOP ALAIN SCHAFER SENTENCED TO TWO YEARS IN PRISON

Three years ago, news of his arrest exploded like a bombshell within the Lille police department. On September 2, 2007, Chief of Police Alain Schafer was arrested at his home before dawn by Internal Affairs officers investigating his practices and acquaintances.

After an investigation lasting several months, the IA exposed a large-scale system of corruption and embezzlement set up by this high-ranking judicial police officer.

An old-style cop, respected—even admired—by his peers, Alain Schafer admitted while in custody to having "crossed the line" by staying on friendly terms with several well-known criminals. Thus began a downward spiral that led, in particular, to the misappropriation of cocaine and marijuana to pay informants before the drugs were sealed as evidence.

Yesterday, the criminal court in Lille found the former cop guilty of "passive corruption," "association with criminals," "drug trafficking," and "breaches of professional confidentiality."

My eyes tear up and I look away from the screen. I know my father's crimes by heart. "So you're just a lousy snooper."

"Ha—that's the pot calling the kettle black!"

"My dad's in prison. So what?"

"Maybe you should go and see him at Christmas?"

"Mind your own business!"

He does not give up. "May I ask where he's incarcerated?"

"What the hell is that to you?"

"In Lille?"

"No, in Luynes, near Aix-en-Provence. Where his third wife lives."

"Why don't you visit him?"

I sigh and then raise my voice: "Because I don't speak to him anymore. He was the one who inspired me to choose this job. He was my role model, the only person I trusted, and he betrayed that trust. He lied to everyone. I'll never forgive him."

"He didn't kill anyone."

"You can't understand." Angrily, I jump to my feet, determined to escape from this trap I've caught myself in. He holds me back by my arm.

"Would you like me to go with you?"

"Listen, Paul, you're a nice guy—you're very polite and clearly a disciple of the Dalai Lama—but we don't know each other. I messed up your morning, and I've apologized for that. But if I ever feel like seeing my father again, I think I'll do it without you, okay?"

"Whatever you want. Still, Christmas does seem like the perfect time, don't you think?"

"You're getting on my nerves. This isn't a Disney movie!"

He gives a thin smile.

Against my better judgment, I find myself saying to him: "And even if I did want to, I couldn't. You can't just turn up to visit a prisoner like that. You need authorization, you need—"

He interjects: "You're a cop. You could sort that out over the phone."

I decide to call his bluff.

"Aix-en-Provence is seven hours away. With the snow that's supposed to fall on Paris this evening, we wouldn't be able to come back."

"Let's do it!" he says. "I'll drive."

A fire roars in my chest. Unsettled by this turn of events, I hesitate for a few seconds. I want to yield to this crazy idea, but I am not sure of my real motives. Am I excited by the thought of seeing my father again or by the chance to spend time with this stranger who clearly doesn't judge me no matter what I say or do?

I look into his eyes, and I like what I see.

I throw him my keys. He catches them easily.

Évry, Auxerre, Beaune, Lyon, Valence, Avignon...

Our long, surreal trip down the "Sunshine Highway" takes us past all these towns. For the first time in a long while, I have lowered my guard with a man. I let it happen; I let myself get carried away. We listen to music on the radio while nibbling Petit Beurre and Pépito cookies. There are crumbs and sunlight everywhere. Like a summer vacation— Provence, the Mediterranean...freedom.

Everything I need right now.

It's 2:30 p.m. when Paul drops me off in front of the prison in Luynes. Throughout the whole trip, I have deliberately avoided thinking about this confrontation with my father. Now, as I stand before the austere façade monitored by security cameras, it is too late to change my mind.

I emerge a half hour later, in tears but relieved. Relieved to have seen my father again. To have spoken with him. To have planted the seed of a reconciliation that no longer strikes me as impossible. This first step is undoubtedly the best thing I have done in years. And I owe it to a man I barely know. Someone who saw in me something other than what I wanted to show him.

I don't know what you're hiding, Monsieur Malaury—if you're as twisted as I am or simply a unique person—but thank you.

With that weight off my shoulders at last, I fall asleep in the car.

Paul smiles at me.

"By the way, did I mention that my grandmother has a house on the Amalfi coast? Have you ever been to Italy for Christmas?"

When I opened my eyes, we had just crossed the Italian border. We are now in San Remo and the sun is setting. Far from Paris, far from Bordeaux, far from the rain and the police.

I can feel his eyes on me. It is as if I have always known him. I don't understand how we could have grown so intimate in such a short time.

There are rare moments when a door opens and life offers you an encounter you had stopped even hoping for. An encounter with someone who complements you, who accepts you as you are, as a whole person, who senses and tolerates your contradictions, your fears, your resentment, your anger, the torrent of dark thoughts that flows through your mind. And who calms it all. Someone who hands you a mirror into which you are no longer afraid to look.

All it takes is an instant. A look. A meeting. To overturn your entire existence. The right person, the right moment. Chance or fate, the whim of some invisible god.

We spent Christmas Eve together in a hotel in Rome.

The next day, we drove along the Amalfi coast, then crossed through the Valley of the Dragon to the hilltop gardens of Ravello.

Five months later, we were married.

A week later, I discovered that I was pregnant with our child.

There are rare moments in life when a door opens and your existence is filled with light. Rare instances when something unlocks inside you. You float weightless through the air. You drive along a highway with no speed limit. Choices become clear, answers replace questions, fear gives way to love.

Everyone should experience moments like that.

They rarely last.

7

BITING THE DUST

Chinatown
Today
10:20 a.m.

THE SOUND OF the crowd. The nauseating stink of dried fish. The creak of a metal door.

Gabriel emerged from the pawnshop and took a few steps along Mott Street. Seeing him, Alice was jerked abruptly from her memories.

"Are you okay?" he asked, seeing the expression on her face.

"I'm fine," she assured him. "So, my husband's watch?"

"I got sixteen hundred dollars for it," he said, proudly waving the sheaf of bills. "And I promise we'll get it back soon. In the meantime, I think we've earned a good breakfast."

She nodded and they left Chinatown in search of the more

welcoming sidewalks of the Bowery. They walked back up
the sunny side of the busy street.

Not so long ago, this part of Manhattan had been
a dangerous area, rife with drug dealers, prostitutes, and
homeless people. These days, it was a chic, lively, pleasant
place. The street was light and airy, its architecture varied,
its store windows colorful. The disconcerting shape of the
New Museum stood out from the buildings, little shops, and
restaurants that surrounded it. Its seven stories looked like a
precariously balanced pile of shoeboxes. With its bold lines
and the strange color of its façade—an immaculate white
crisscrossed by silver ropes—it exploded like a pale bomb
amid the bright colors of the Lower East Side.

Alice and Gabriel went into the first café they found, the
Peppermill Coffee Shop. They sat in a booth with cream
banquettes, facing each other. White-tiled walls, moldings,
a large bay window, wide oak floorboards—the place was
both cozy and refined, a warm and welcome respite from
the frenetic energy of Chinatown. Beautiful autumn sunlight
poured through a large skylight, illuminating the room and
making the espresso machines behind the counter shimmer
and sparkle.

Embedded in the middle of each table, a digital tablet
allowed customers to consult the menu, go online, or read a
selection of newspapers and magazines.

Alice looked through the menu. Her stomach was so
twisted by hunger that she could hear it growling. A waiter
dressed in a shirt, vest, and fedora quickly took their orders.

She asked for a cappuccino and a bagel with cream cheese, smoked salmon, shallots, and dill. Gabriel went for a latte and a Monte Cristo sandwich with fries.

They devoured their food and drank their coffees in practically a single gulp. Alice polished off her salmon bagel. Her hunger sated, she closed her eyes and let her mind drift to the sound of the old blues songs playing on the varnished wooden jukebox. It was an attempt to empty her head and "put her brain cells in order," as her grandmother used to say. After a moment, she opened her eyes.

"We must have missed something," Gabriel said, eating the final bite of his sandwich.

He signaled for the waiter to refill their coffee cups. Alice nodded in wholehearted agreement.

"Yes. We have to start again from scratch. Make a list of all the clues and try to find a pattern. The phone number for the Greenwich Hotel, the number scratched into your arm—"

She stopped mid-flow. A shaggy-haired waiter had just flinched after noticing the bloodstains on her blouse. She discreetly zipped up her jacket.

"I suggest we divide up the money," Gabriel said, taking out the sixteen hundred dollars. "There's no point putting all our eggs in one basket."

He handed eight hundred-dollar bills to Alice, who put them in the pocket of her jeans. That was how she found the small cardboard rectangle at the bottom of the pocket. Frowning, she unfolded it on the table.

"Look at this!"

It was a claim ticket, the kind given out by coat checks in chic restaurants and hotel luggage drops. Gabriel leaned forward to read the number on the ticket: 127. A watermark of the intertwined letters *G* and *H* formed a discreet logo.

"The Greenwich Hotel!" they exclaimed simultaneously.

In a single second, their despair was gone.

"Let's go!" Alice said.

"But I haven't finished my fries yet!"

"You can eat later, Keyne!"

Already, Alice was checking the hotel's address on the touchscreen in the center of the table. Gabriel went to the counter to pay their bill.

"Corner of Greenwich and North Moore Streets," she told him when he returned.

She picked up a knife from the table and slipped it into her jacket pocket. He threw his jacket over his shoulder.

They left the café together.

The Honda came to a halt behind two double-parked taxis. In the heart of Tribeca, the Greenwich Hotel was a tall brick-and-glass building not far from the bank of the Hudson.

"There's a parking lot just down there, on Chambers Street," said Gabriel, pointing at a road sign. "I'll park the car and then—"

"Forget it," Alice interrupted. "I'm going in on my own. You wait for me here, with the engine running, in case anything goes wrong."

"And what do I do if you're not back in fifteen minutes? Call the police?"

"I am the police," she replied, getting out of the car.

Seeing her walk toward the entrance, a doorman smiled and opened the door for her. She nodded her thanks and went into the lobby.

It was a discreetly luxurious space that led into an elegant and dimly lit library-salon. A Chesterfield sofa and some armchairs were arranged around a large fireplace where two huge logs burned. Farther on, through glass doors, was a flower-filled interior courtyard reminiscent of Italy.

"Welcome to the Greenwich, ma'am. What can I do for you?" asked a young woman with wispy auburn bangs. Her outfit conformed to the hotel's eclectic, trendy décor: tortoiseshell glasses, a blouse with a geometric design, and a wrap skirt.

"I've come to pick up a bag," Alice announced, handing her the claim ticket.

"Of course. Just one minute, please."

The woman gave the ticket to her male assistant, who disappeared into a small adjoining room and reemerged thirty seconds later with a black leather briefcase, the handle bearing a tag with the number 127.

"Here you go, ma'am."

Too good to be true, Alice thought, taking the briefcase. She decided to push her luck. "Now I'd like you to tell me the name of the person who left this bag here."

The receptionist frowned. "Well, ma'am, I presumed it

was you. Otherwise I wouldn't have given it to you. If the bag does not belong to you, I would kindly ask you to return it—"

"Detective Schafer, New York Police Department," Alice said, unfazed. "I'm investigating a—"

"You have a pretty strong French accent for a New York police detective," the woman interrupted. "I'd like to see some identification."

"Just give me the customer's name!" Alice demanded, raising her voice.

"That's enough. I'm calling the manager."

Realizing she had lost this duel, Alice retreated. Gripping the briefcase, she quickly crossed the lobby and went out the door.

No sooner had she stepped outside than an alarm went off, a piercing siren that made every pedestrian on the street stare instantly at Alice. In a panic, she realized that the sound was coming not from the hotel, as she had first thought, but from the briefcase itself.

She ran a few yards down the sidewalk, looking for Gabriel and the car. She was just about to cross the road, when an electric shock ran through her body.

Dazed and breathless, she dropped the briefcase and collapsed onto the asphalt.

Part Two

MEMORY OF PAIN

8

MEMORY OF PAIN

THE SIREN SCREAMED for a few seconds longer, then went silent as suddenly as it had come to life.

Lying on the ground, Alice struggled to recover full consciousness. Her ears were buzzing and her vision was blurred, as if someone were holding a veil in front of her eyes. Still woozy, she saw a figure loom over her.

"Get up!"

Gabriel helped her to her feet and then guided her to the car. He put her in the passenger seat and went back to retrieve the briefcase, which was a little farther down the street.

"Quick!" Alice said.

He got in and started the car and drove off at full speed. A sudden turn to the right, then another, and they were back on the West Side Highway, which ran along the river.

"Shit, they must have seen us!" Alice yelled, emerging from the mental fog caused by the electric shock. White as a sheet, she felt nauseated, and her heart was pounding. Her legs were weak. Bile burned inside her chest.

"What happened to you?"

"You saw for yourself!" she replied, exasperated. "The briefcase was booby-trapped. Someone must have known we were at the hotel. They must have remotely triggered the alarm and the electric shock."

"You sound kind of paranoid, you know."

"I wish you'd had that shock instead of me, Keyne! Listen, there's no point in us trying to escape if someone is tracking our every move!"

"But who does the briefcase belong to?"

"They wouldn't tell me."

The car sped north. The sun was bright on the horizon. To their left, there were ferries and sailboats floating on the Hudson, the skyscrapers of Jersey City, the metal gantries of old piers.

Gabriel changed lanes to pass a van. When he turned to look at Alice, he noticed that she was gripping the knife she had stolen from the café and slashing at the lining of her leather jacket.

"Stop! What the hell are you doing?"

Trusting her instincts, she didn't even bother responding to this. Carried away by her excitement, she reached down to remove her ankle boots and used the knife to cut off the heel of the first one.

"Alice, my God, what's the matter with you?"

"This is what I was looking for!" she said, triumphantly brandishing a tiny casing that she had just extracted from her outer sole.

"What is it, a microchip?"

"No, a miniaturized GPS system. That's how they were able to track us. And I would bet anything that you have the same thing in one of your shoes or in the lining of your jacket. Someone is following us in real time, Keyne. We need to change our clothes and our shoes. Now!"

"All right," he agreed, looking worried.

Alice opened the window and threw the tiny snitch away, then picked up the briefcase. It was a rigid, smooth leather case with a double combination lock. The handle no longer seemed electrified. She tried to open the case but without success.

"Hardly surprising," Gabriel said.

"We'll find a way to break the lock later. For now, let's just concentrate on finding somewhere discreet where we can buy new clothes."

Eyelids drooping, Alice massaged her temples. Her migraine was coming back, and her eyes were burning. She searched through the glove compartment and fished out an old pair of sunglasses that she had spotted earlier. They had glittery cat's-eye frames. She put them on. The architectural diversity of this part of the city mesmerized her and made her head spin. From afar, she recognized the bluish outline of the Standard Hotel, like an enormous open book perched on stilts, rising above the High Line. There was something chaotic and jarring about this clash of modern buildings—all geometric lines in glass and steel—and the red brick of old New York.

And then, like a pearl-colored iceberg in the distance, an irregularly shaped translucent building broke up the skyline and dazzled the surrounding landscape with an unreal light.

They wandered around for a while between the Meatpacking District and Chelsea before finding a little boutique on Twenty-Seventh Street that was like a cross between a military-surplus store and a thrift shop. It was a long single room filled with a glorious mess of clothes, a mix of combat gear and designer labels.

"Be quick, Keyne," Alice said sternly as they entered. "We're not here for a nice, relaxed shopping trip. Understood?"

They rummaged through the racks of clothes and shoes—combat boots, canvas lace-ups, bomber jackets, fleeces, camouflage jackets, leather belts, kaffiyehs.

Alice quickly found a black turtleneck sweater, a fitted T-shirt, a pair of jeans, a pair of ankle boots, and a putty-colored army jacket.

Gabriel was not as decisive.

"Hurry up! Look, just take this and this," she urged, throwing him a pair of khaki pants and a faded cotton shirt.

"But it's not exactly the right size, and it's not my style either."

"Look, it's not Saturday night and you're not going out to pick up girls, Keyne," she replied, unbuttoning her blouse.

The pianist completed his outfit with a pair of work boots and a three-quarter-length coat with a sheepskin collar. Alice spotted an old holster she could carry her Glock in and a canvas satchel with two leather straps. There were no changing rooms, so they undressed and dressed within a few yards of each other. Gabriel could not resist stealing a sideways glance at Alice.

"Don't ogle me, you pervert!" she scolded him, covering her bare torso with the wool sweater.

She said it more vehemently than she'd intended, and Gabriel looked away sheepishly. What he saw had chilled him, however: a long scar running from Alice's belly button down to her crotch.

"A hundred and seventy for all of it," said the store owner, a huge, stocky bald man with a long, ZZ Top–style beard.

While Gabriel finished taking off his shoes, Alice went out to the street and threw all their old clothes into a trash can. The only thing she kept was a scrap of bloodstained fabric torn from her blouse.

Evidence, she thought, slipping it into her army satchel.

Noticing a little bodega on the other side of the road, she crossed the street and bought some wet wipes to clean herself up, a packet of ibuprofen for her headache, and a small bottle of water. Then she had an idea. She retraced her steps, looked through the aisles, and finally found a small section devoted to cell phones. She chose the most basic model, for $14.99, and also bought a 120-minute prepaid phone card.

Coming out of the store with her purchases, she was surprised by a gust of wind. The sun was still shining brightly, but the air was cold and blustery now, with dead leaves and clouds of dust whipping around in a frenzy. She put her hand to her face to protect her eyes. Leaning against the hood of the car, Gabriel watched her.

"Waiting for someone?" she teased.

Waving one of his old shoes at her, he said, "You were right: there was a bug in my sneaker too." And, like a basketball player, he threw the Converse into the nearest garbage can. It hit the rim and fell inside. "Whoo, a three-pointer!"

Alice rolled her eyes. "Have you finished screwing around now? Can we go?"

A little wounded, he turned up the collar of his jacket and shrugged, like a kid who had just been scolded.

Alice sat in the driver's seat and placed the bag from the convenience store and her canvas satchel on the back seat, next to the briefcase.

"We have to find a way to open that thing."

"Let me take care of that," Gabriel said, buckling his seat belt.

To put as much distance as they could between their bugged shoes and themselves, they drove farther north, crossing

Hell's Kitchen to Forty-Eighth Street. They parked in a dead end that led to a community garden, where a group of children were picking pumpkins, watched over by their schoolteacher.

It was a quiet neighborhood. No tourists, no crowds. So quiet, in fact, that it was hard to believe they were still in New York. They parked under the yellow foliage of a maple tree. Orange rays of sunlight filtered through its branches, intensifying this feeling of tranquility.

"So what do you have in mind for the briefcase?" she asked, pulling the parking brake.

"I'm going to use the knife you stole to open the locks. They don't look very solid to me."

She sighed. "You've got to be kidding."

"Do you have a better idea?"

"No, but yours will never work."

"We'll see!" he said defiantly, turning to the back seat to pick up the briefcase.

She gave him the knife and watched, skeptically, as he attempted to insert the blade between the jaws of the lock with no luck. After a while, losing patience, Gabriel tried to force it, but the knife slipped and grazed his palm. "Ow!"

"Jesus Christ, concentrate on what you're doing!" Alice scolded.

Gabriel gave up. His face was serious now. Something was very obviously bothering him.

"What's up with you?" she demanded.

"You."

"Me?"

"Back in the store, I saw the scar on your stomach...what happened to you?"

Alice's face suddenly darkened. She opened her mouth to retort, but, overcome by a vast weariness, she turned away, sighing as she rubbed her eyes. This guy was just going to keep causing her problems. She'd sensed it from the very beginning.

When she opened her eyes again, her lip was trembling. The pain was returning. The memories resurfacing, large as life.

"Who did that to you, Alice?" he insisted.

Gabriel could feel that he was trespassing on sensitive ground. He said more softly, "How do you expect us to get out of this fix if we can't even trust each other?"

Alice took a drink of water. Her determination not to confront the past was fading.

"It was early November three years ago," she began. That was where the story started—with the murder of the young schoolteacher named Clara Maturin...

I remember...

Two and a half years ago

A year of blood and fury

ANOTHER WOMAN MURDERED
IN THE WEST OF PARIS
(Le Parisien, May 11, 2011)

Nathalie Roussel, a 26-year-old flight attendant, was found this morning strangled in her home on Rue Meissonnier, a quiet street in the 17th arrondissement. The young woman lived alone and was described by her neighbors as "a quiet person who kept to herself and often traveled for work." The man who lived across the hall from her saw her a few hours before she was murdered: "She was in a good mood because she'd just bought tickets to see a concert the next day at the Olympia. She didn't act as if anything was wrong."

According to sources close to the investigation, several witnesses claim to have seen a man rushing from the premises and driving away on a Piaggio three-wheel scooter. The suspect is described as a man of medium height and slim build, wearing a dark-colored motorcycle helmet.

The investigation is being carried out by the judicial police. Initial reports do not suggest that theft was the primary motive for the attack, even though the victim's cell phone appears to have been taken.

This murder has strange similarities to that of Clara Maturin, a young schoolteacher in the 16th arrondissement, who was savagely strangled with a nylon stocking in November of last year. Asked about these similarities, the public prosecutor said that nothing was being ruled out at this stage of the investigation.

MURDERS IN THE WEST OF PARIS: POLICE SUSPECT A SERIAL KILLER
(Le Parisien, May 11, 2011)

Forensic analysis shows that flight attendant Nathalie Roussel was strangled with a pair of tights belonging to

Clara Maturin, the young schoolteacher murdered last November, says a source close to the investigation.

This fact, until now kept secret by the police, establishes a macabre link between the victims, leading investigators to believe they are tracking a fetish killer whose modus operandi is to use the underwear of his previous victim to murder the next one.

For the moment, the police refuse to confirm this conjecture.

NEW MURDER VICTIM
IN THE 16TH ARRONDISSEMENT
(Le Parisien, August 19, 2011)

Maud Morel, a nurse at the American Hospital in Neuilly, was murdered the day before yesterday, in the evening, in her apartment on Avenue de Malakoff. The building's concierge discovered the young woman's body this morning. She had been savagely strangled with a pair of stockings.

Although police refuse to confirm it officially, this last detail would seem to point to an obvious connection between this homicide and those committed last November and this May in the 16th and 17th arrondissements.

While the motive for the murders remains mysterious,

investigators are certain that the three women knew their attacker well enough that they did not suspect him. All three victims were found inside their apartments without any suggestion of breaking and entering. Another disturbing detail: none of the victims' cell phones have yet been found.

MURDERS IN THE WEST OF PARIS: MORE CLUES POINT TOWARD A SERIAL KILLER
(Le Parisien, August 20, 2011)

After the savage murder of Maud Morel, a nurse from the American Hospital in Neuilly who was murdered three days ago, investigators no longer have any doubt that there is a link between this homicide and the two others committed in the same area since November of last year.

Questioned about the possibility of this being the work of a serial killer, the public prosecutor was forced to acknowledge that "the three murders do show similarities in their MOs." The pair of stockings with which Mademoiselle Morel was strangled belonged to Nathalie Roussel, the flight attendant murdered last spring, who was herself strangled with a pair of tights belonging to the schoolteacher Clara Maturin.

This fact has led to a rethinking of the judicial treatment of the three crimes. They are now under the authority of a single investigating judge. Questioned yesterday on the France 2 television news, the minister of the interior assured viewers that "all human and material resources are and will be mobilized to find the person or people responsible for these crimes."

MURDERS IN THE WEST OF PARIS: A SUSPECT IN CUSTODY
(Le Parisien, August 21, 2011)

A taxi driver considered to be a serious suspect in the series of murders committed since November in the west of Paris was questioned and placed in custody on Friday evening. A search of his home led to the discovery of the cell phone belonging to the killer's latest victim, Maud Morel.

TAXI DRIVER RELEASED!
(Le Parisien, August 21, 2011)

... The man has an alibi for all three murders.

Questioned by police, he stated that Maud Morel was

a passenger in his taxi a few days earlier, and that the young woman simply left her phone in his taxi.

ANOTHER WOMAN MURDERED: WESTERN PARIS TRAUMATIZED
(Le Parisien, October 9, 2011)

Virginie André, a divorced bank employee and the mother of a little boy, was found this morning strangled in her apartment on Avenue de Wagram. Her body was discovered by her ex-husband as he was dropping off the three-year-old son, whose custody they shared.

FEAR IN THE CITY: HUNDREDS OF POLICE TRACK THE WEST PARIS KILLER
(Le Parisien, October 10, 2011)

This extraordinary investigation has now mobilized hundreds of police on the trail of a murderer who remains nameless and faceless, but who has been terrorizing single women in the 16th and 17th arrondissements for the better part of a year.

What connects Clara Maturin, schoolteacher, strangled on November 12, 2010; Nathalie Roussel, flight attendant, killed on May 10, 2011; Maud Morel, nurse, found dead on August 19; and Virginie André, bank employee, murdered last Sunday? These young women were all single or divorced, and their pasts and personal relations have been investigated by police, but so far no significant clues have been discovered.

Four homicides conforming to the same modus operandi. Four victims without any apparent connection, but all of whom seem to have been sufficiently intimate with their killer to have invited him into their apartments.

This series of murders has caused disbelief and terror among inhabitants of these two arrondissements. To reassure the populace, the prefecture has vastly increased the number of police on patrol and asked citizens to report any suspicious behavior.

Paris
November 21, 2011
Solferino Métro station

I struggle breathlessly up the station steps. At the top of the stairs, rain blows into my face. I open my umbrella facing the wind to keep it from turning inside out. I am seven and a half months pregnant and I have an appointment with

Rose-May, the midwife who is supposed to be with me when I give birth.

November has been one long, dark, rainy tunnel, and today is no exception. I do not rush. The white façades of Rue de Bellechasse shine in the downpour.

My feet are swollen, my back is killing me, and my joints ache. I am having a hard time adapting to the weight gain caused by my pregnancy. I have grown so fat that I need Paul to help me tie my shoes! Pants tend to cut into my crotch, so I am condemned to wear only dresses. My nights are short, and whenever I want to get out of bed, I have to roll over to the side before I can put my feet on the floor. And just to add to my misery, I've had nausea for the last few days, as well as sudden waves of exhaustion that wipe me out.

Thankfully, the distance between the Métro exit and Rue Las Cases is only about two hundred yards. I reach the clinic in less than five minutes. I walk in, sign in at the reception desk, and—under the disapproving glare of the other patients—grab a coffee from the vending machine in the waiting room.

I am worn out. My belly jumps as if huge bubbles are moving under the skin, as if there is an ocean inside it. Paul finds it very funny when this happens at home.

My own feelings are more complicated. Pregnancy is an amazing, magical state, but I find it hard to surrender to it. My excitement is always tempered by a vague worry, a bad feeling, a series of painful questions without answers: Will I be a good mother? Will my son be healthy? Will I know how to look after him?

I have, theoretically, been on maternity leave for the past week. Paul has done his part by decorating the baby's room and fitting the car seat in my car. I have made plans to do lots of things—buy clothes, a stroller, a baby bathtub, toiletry products—but I keep putting them off.

The truth is that I have never really stopped working on the investigation—*my* investigation—into those four women strangled in the west of Paris. My team was put in charge of solving the first murder, but we failed. After that, the case became too big and we lost it. I was sidelined, but I can't stop seeing those faces frozen in horror. This obsession is polluting my pregnancy, preventing me from thinking about the future. The same images keep appearing in my mind, the same theories circling in my head. I lose myself in conjectures, trying to find the missing thread.

The thread...

I must find the invisible thread that connects Clara Maturin, Nathalie Roussel, Maud Morel, and Virginie André. Even if no one has spotted it yet, there has to be a link. Those four women have something in common that is eluding the investigators.

Even me.

Especially me.

I just know that some crucial piece of evidence is right under my nose, unseen, and this certainty is ruining my life.

If we don't stop him, this man will continue killing women. One woman, two women, ten women...he is careful, invisible, uncatchable. He leaves no trace, no fingerprints or DNA. No one can explain why the four victims opened the door to him quite late in the evening. All we have is a vague eyewitness account of a man in a black helmet fleeing on a three-wheel scooter. And there are thousands of vehicles like that in the Paris area.

Another vending-machine coffee. It's cold and drafty in this room. I grip the plastic cup with both hands in search of some warmth. Staring into space, I go over the case in my head for the thousandth time, reciting the facts to myself like a mantra.

Four victims—four women living alone. Three of them single, one a divorced mother. In the same geographic area. Killed with the same MO.

For a long time, the newspapers nicknamed the murderer "the phone-thief killer." Even the cops thought at first that he was stealing the victims' cell phones in order to erase certain compromising information: calls, videos, photos...but this theory doesn't hold up. In spite of what the press claimed, the phones of the first and fourth victims were eventually found. And while the phone of the second victim, the flight attendant, has never been located, that of the third victim— the nurse—was simply forgotten in a taxi.

I look at my own phone. I have downloaded hundreds of photos of the four victims onto it. Not those morbid crime scene shots but images from their daily lives, taken from their computers.

I scroll through these, always coming back to those of Clara Maturin. The first victim, the schoolteacher. The one I feel closest to. One of her photos particularly moves me. It's a traditional class picture, dated October 2010, taken on the school playground. All the kindergartners from the Joliot-Curie school are gathered around their teacher. The image is full of life. The kids' faces fascinate me. Some children are very serious, while others fool around—silly grins, fingers up nostrils, bunny ears, and so on. At their center, Clara Maturin smiles openly. She is a pretty, reserved-looking woman with blond hair cut in a bob. She is wearing a beige raincoat over a rather elegant pantsuit and a Burberry silk scarf. She must have especially liked this outfit, because she wears it in quite a few other pictures: at a friend's wedding in May 2010 in Brittany; during a vacation in London in August of the same year; and even in the last photo of her, taken a few hours before her death by a security camera on Rue de la Faisanderie. I scroll from one to the next, finding the same favorite outfit in each one: raincoat, *Working Girl* suit, Burberry scarf around her neck like a cowl. When I linger over this last detail, however, something hits me: It's not the same scarf. To make sure, I zoom in, using three fingers on the touchscreen. In spite of the poor resolution of the security-camera image, I am almost certain—the scarf has a different print.

The day she died, Clara was not wearing her favorite scarf.

A faint shiver runs down my back.

An unimportant detail?

Maybe, but my brain goes to work anyway, trying to make sense of this fact. Why did Clara Maturin change her scarf that day? Did she lend it to a friend? Did she take it to be dry-cleaned? Did she lose it?

Maybe she lost it.

Maud Morel, the third victim, also lost something—her cell phone, which was finally discovered in a taxi. And Nathalie Roussel's phone, which we assumed had been stolen—maybe that had been lost too?

Lost.

Two phones, a scarf…

And Virginie André? What did she lose?

Her life.

But what else? I quit the photo app on my phone and call Seymour. "Hey, it's me. Listen, about Virginie André's murder, do you know if anything was ever mentioned about her having lost something just prior to her death?"

"Alice! You're supposed to be on maternity leave! Just concentrate on getting ready for your baby!"

I ignore this. "Do you remember or not?"

"No, I have no idea, Alice. We're not working that case anymore."

"Could you find her ex-husband's number? Text it to me. I'll ask him myself."

"All right." He sighs.

"Thanks, Seymour."

Three minutes after I hang up, I receive his text. I call the ex-husband immediately and leave a message on his voice mail asking him to contact me as soon as possible.

"Madame Schafer! You walked here again!" Rose-May exclaims, wide-eyed.

She is a plump woman from Réunion with a strong creole accent, and every time I see her, she gives me a scolding as if I'm a little girl.

"No, I didn't. Honestly!" I say, following her into one of the third-floor rooms where she gives her birthing classes.

She asks me to lie down, then takes her time examining me. She assures me that the cervix is still closed, that I am not at risk of giving birth prematurely. She is pleased to see that the baby has turned over and is no longer breech.

"The head is pointing down now, and the baby's back is to the left. The perfect position! He's even begun to descend a little."

She straps sensors to my bare belly and connects the monitor that records the baby's heartbeat and my Braxton-Hicks contractions.

I hear my son's heartbeat.

I am deeply moved—tears well in my eyes—but at the same time, my chest tightens with anxiety. Rose-May explains what I have to do when I begin to feel contractions, which should normally happen in about four to five weeks.

"If they're happening every ten minutes, take a Spasfon tablet and wait thirty minutes. If the pain goes away, it was a false alarm. If it persists and—"

I feel my phone vibrate in the pocket of my parka, which is close by. I interrupt the midwife, sit up, and lean down to grab the phone.

"Jean-Marc André," a voice announces. "I was just checking my messages and—"

"Thank you for calling me back, monsieur. I'm Captain Schafer, one of the officers investigating the murder of your ex-wife. I was wondering if you remember whether she lost something in the days prior to her death?"

"Lost what?"

"I don't know, I'm afraid—that's the point. Maybe an item of clothing? Or a piece of jewelry? Her purse?"

"What does this have to do with the murder?"

"Maybe nothing, but we have to pursue every line of investigation. So this doesn't ring any bells for you—something she may have lost?"

He pauses to think for a moment, and then: "Actually, there was—"

He breaks off midsentence; I sense that his voice is tight with emotion. He starts again.

"It was one of the reasons we argued the last time she left our son with me. I was annoyed with her because she'd lost Gaspard's favorite teddy bear; he couldn't sleep without it. Virginie said she'd lost it in Parc Monceau. She was talking about the lost-and-found office there, but..."

Lost-and-found office...

My heart speeds up in my chest. A burst of pure adrenaline.

"Wait a minute, Monsieur André, I want to make sure I've fully understood. Had Virginie gone to the lost-and-found office herself or was she planning to go?"

"She told me she'd already been and that she'd filled out a form so they would let her know if the bear was found."

I can't believe my ears. "All right, thank you. I'll call you back if I have any news."

I remove the electrodes, stand up, and hurriedly get dressed. "I'm sorry, Rose-May, but I have to go."

"No! This is ridiculous, Madame Schafer. In your state, you should—"

But I am already through the door. I am already in the elevator. I get out my phone to call a taxi. I shuffle my feet impatiently in the lobby while I wait for it to arrive.

This is my investigation.

My pride rises again. I think of all those cops in the Criminal Division who have gone through the victims' diaries with a fine-tooth comb and yet may have missed something vital.

Something I *have just found.*

36 Rue des Morillons, fifteenth arrondissement, just behind Parc Georges-Brassens

The taxi drops me off at the door of the lost-and-found office, housed in a handsome 1920s building in pink brick and white stone. Although the department is part of the Paris police prefecture, there are no cops in this office, and I have never set foot here before.

I show my badge at the reception desk and ask to see the manager. While I wait, I glance around me. Behind the counters, a dozen employees apathetically deal with people turning in objects they've found or those who have lost something or come to pick something up.

"Stéphane Dalmasso, pleased to meet you."

I look up. A bushy mustache, hanging jowls, little round glasses with colored plastic frames—the boss of the lost-and-found office has a pleasant face and a strong Marseille accent.

"Alice Schafer, Criminal Division."

"Welcome. Are you due soon?" he asks, looking at my belly.

"Six weeks, maybe less."

"A child, huh? Your life is about to change forever!" he says, inviting me into his office.

I enter a spacious room laid out like a little museum, an exhibition of the oddest objects ever handed in to the department: a Legion of Honor medal, a wooden leg, a human skull, a shard of metal from the World Trade Center, an urn containing the ashes of a cat, a yakuza sword, even a wedding dress.

"A taxi driver brought it here a few years ago," he explains, pointing to the dress. "He was driving a couple who had just gotten married. They had a fight and broke up during the trip."

"It's like Aladdin's cave in here…"

"Yes, but most of what we receive are wallets, glasses, keys, phones, and umbrellas."

"Impressive," I say, glancing at my watch.

"I have an endless store of anecdotes, but I imagine you're in a hurry," he says, gesturing for me to sit down. "So, to what do I owe this visit?"

"I'm working a murder case. I would like to know if a certain Virginie André came here recently."

"In connection with what?"

"To ask if you'd found her son's teddy bear, which he lost in Parc Monceau."

Sitting on a wheeled office chair, Dalmasso rolls toward his desk and touches his computer keyboard. The machine hums in response.

"Virginie André, you said?" he asks, curling his mustache.

I nod. He types the name into his computer.

"No, sorry, there hasn't been any request made under that name in the past few months."

"She might have reported a missing object online or by phone."

"It would have shown up if she had. All requests are automatically registered in our database. The forms our employees fill out are all electronic."

"That's strange—her husband told me she'd reported it missing with your office. Could you check three other names for me, please?"

I write the names on the spiral-bound notebook lying on the desk and turn it around so he can read what I've written.

Dalmasso deciphers my handwriting and enters the three names, one by one: Clara Maturin, Nathalie Roussel, Maud Morel.

"No, nothing for any of those."

I feel so disappointed. It takes me a few seconds to accept my mistake.

"Oh, well, never mind. Thanks for your help."

As I stand up, I feel a tingling sensation in my belly and put my hand to it. The baby is still moving a lot. He pushes so hard sometimes, it's as if he's trying to stretch my skin. At least I'm not having contractions.

"Are you all right?" Dalmasso asks. "Should I call you a taxi?"

"That would be great," I say, sitting down again.

"Claudette!" he shouts to his secretary. "Please call a cab for Mademoiselle Schafer."

Two minutes later, a small woman with a severe, irritable face and badly dyed red hair enters the office, carrying a steaming cup. "The taxi will be here very soon," she assures me. "Would you like some sweet tea?"

I accept the drink and gradually start to feel better. Although I have no idea why, the little woman continues to give me a disapproving look. Out of nowhere, the question suddenly crosses my mind.

"Monsieur Dalmasso, I forgot to ask you: Do any of your employees own a three-wheel scooter?"

"Not that I'm aware of. That's more a guy thing, isn't it? And, as you can see, most of our employees are women."

"Erik drives one of those machines," his secretary interjects.

I look Dalmasso in the eyes. "Who is Erik?"

"Erik Vaughn is a temp. He fills in here during holidays and busy periods or when one of our employees is out sick for a while."

"Is he here today?"

"No, but we'll probably hire him again for the Christmas season."

Through the office's fluted glass wall, I see the taxi waiting for me in the rain. "Do you have his address?"

"We'll find it for you," he says, handing a blank Post-It note to his secretary, who leaves the room.

This new revelation has rekindled the fire inside me. I don't want to waste time. Hastily, I scrawl my phone number and e-mail address in Dalmasso's desk diary. "Check the periods when Vaughn worked for you over the past two years and send them to me by e-mail or text them to my cell phone, please."

Claudette returns and I grab the note that she is holding out for me, walk outside, and dive into the taxi.

The inside of the taxi stinks of sweat. The radio is on full blast and the meter is already showing ten euros. I give the address to the driver—a building on Rue Parent-de-Rosan, in the sixteenth arrondissement—and tell him to lower the volume. His response is contemptuous until he sees my cop's badge.

I feel feverish and start shivering, overcome by hot flashes.

I need to calm down. In my mind, I test out an improbable theory, but one I want to believe. Erik Vaughn, an employee in the lost-and-found office, uses his job to target his victims. Clara Maturin, Nathalie Roussel, Maud Morel, and Virginie André all came to see him, but he never entered their names in the office computer. That is why Dalmasso couldn't find any trace of them. Vaughn managed to win their trust, got them to talk, squeezed as much information as he could out of them. He knew their addresses; he knew they lived alone. After that first meeting, he let a few days go by and then went to his target's home, claiming to have brought her the missing object. Unfortunately for them, all four women invited him inside. Who ever suspects a bearer of good news? Each was so relieved at having found her favorite scarf, her cell phone, or her son's teddy bear that she opened the door, even if it was past nine p.m.

No, I'm just raving. What are the chances of this theory being correct? One in a thousand? And yet . . .

The trip passes quickly. After driving back up Boulevard Victor-Hugo, the car passes the Georges-Pompidou hospital and crosses over the Seine, not far from the Porte de Saint-Cloud.

Don't do this on your own . . .

I know as well as anyone that solving a crime is not a solo job but the culmination of a long-term team effort. There are well-defined procedures and clear rules, which is why I would really like to call Seymour and let him know what I've discovered. I hesitate, then decide to wait until I've learned the dates that Erik Vaughn worked in the lost-and-found office.

My phone vibrates. I check my e-mail. Dalmasso has sent me an Excel file showing Vaughn's work schedule. I click on my screen, but the file refuses to open. Incompatible format.

Fuck.

"This is it." Unsmiling, the driver lets me out halfway along a small, one-way street between Rue Boileau and Avenue Mozart. The rain is falling even harder now. It streams down the back of my neck. I can feel the baby's weight, very low and very dense, making it increasingly painful to walk.

Turn around.

Among the town houses and small residences, I spot a grayish façade that bears the number the secretary wrote on the Post-It note. A typical 1970s apartment building—a long concrete construction with a sinister, ugly look.

I see the name VAUGHN on the intercom and press the button.

No response.

Out on the street, in the parking spaces reserved for two-wheel vehicles, there is a motorcycle, an old Yamaha Chappy, and a three-wheel scooter.

I keep pressing the buzzer and eventually try all the buttons until someone in the building lets me in.

I note the floor where Vaughn lives, then walk slowly upstairs. I can feel the baby kicking inside my belly again. As if he's trying to warn me.

I know this is a dumb idea, but something urges me onward. *My investigation.* I don't turn on the light. I climb the stairs one by one in darkness.

Sixth floor.

Vaughn's door is half open.

I take my gun from my purse, congratulating myself on the intuition that made me bring it along. I hold it in two hands.

Sweat and rainwater trickle down my back.

I yell: "Erik Vaughn? Police. I'm coming in."

I push open the door, both hands still gripping the butt of the gun. I move along the corridor. I press the light switch, but the power has been cut. Outside, rain hammers on the roof.

The apartment is half empty. No light, almost no furniture, a few cardboard boxes on the living-room floor. Clearly, this bird has flown.

My anxiety goes down a notch. I remove my right hand from the gun to reach for my phone. As I'm typing in Seymour's number, I sense a presence behind me. I drop my phone and spin around. A man in a motorcycle helmet.

I open my mouth to scream, but before any sound comes out, I feel the blade of a knife sink into my flesh.

The blade that is killing my son.

Vaughn stabs my stomach again and again.

My legs give way and I collapse to the ground.

In a blur, I feel him pulling off my tights. Then I feel myself swept away on a river of hatred and blood. My last thought is of my father. More precisely, I think of the words he had tattooed on his forearm:

The devil's finest trick is to persuade you that he doesn't exist.

9

RIVERSIDE

Hell's Kitchen, New York
Today
11:15 a.m.

ALICE HAD FINISHED telling him her story a minute ago. Still frozen in shock, Gabriel said nothing. He tried to think of something comforting to say, but, fearful of making things worse, he decided it was better to stay silent.

Alice squinted at the yellow leaves as they flew around in the wind. The buzz of the city was very distant. They could almost hear the sound of birdsong and the murmur of the fountain that stood in the center of the little garden. It had been painful but cathartic to relive the past in front of this stranger. Like talking to a shrink. Suddenly, out of the blue, a thought startled her.

"I know how to open the briefcase!" she exclaimed to Gabriel's surprise. She grabbed it and placed it flat on her knees. "Two locks controlled by a double code of three figures," she muttered.

"Sure," he agreed, raising his eyebrows. "So?"

She leaned forward and lifted up the sleeve of his shirt, revealing the series of numbers carved into his skin: 141197.

"Let's see..."

She tested the combination by playing with the different thumb wheels, then pulled at the two locks at the same time. There was a click and the briefcase popped open.

Empty.

Or at least so it appeared. Alice spotted a detachable compartment separated by a zipper. She opened it, revealing a false bottom. Inside was a little tan alligator-skin travel bag.

Yes!

Hands trembling, she pulled it open. Inside, secured against the lining by an elastic, lay a large syringe, its needle protected by a plastic cap.

"What is that thing?" Gabriel asked.

Without removing the syringe from its holder, she examined it more closely. Inside the thick cylinder, a very pale blue liquid sparkled in the sunlight.

Some kind of medicine? A drug? Twenty milliliters of an unknown substance.

Frustrated, she zipped the travel bag shut again. If she were in Paris, she'd be able to run an analysis on the substance, but here, that was impossible.

"If you wanted to know what that stuff does, you'd have to be brave enough to inject yourself with it," said Gabriel.

"Stupid enough to inject yourself with it, you mean," Alice corrected him.

Grabbing his jacket, he used his hand as a visor to protect his eyes from the sun.

"There's a pay phone at the end of the street," he said, pointing. "I'm going to try calling my friend in Tokyo."

"Okay. I'll wait for you in the car."

Alice watched Gabriel walk to the phone. Once again, she had the depressing sensation that her brain was working furiously and getting nowhere, constantly conjuring questions without answers.

Why did she and Gabriel have no memory at all of what had happened to them last night? How had they ended up in Central Park? Whose blood was all over her blouse? Where did she get this gun? Why was a bullet missing from its magazine? Who had written the hotel's phone number on her palm? Who had carved the briefcase code into Gabriel's arm? Why had the briefcase been electrified? What did this syringe contain?

This flood of questions made her reel.

She felt like that other Alice, the one who fell down the rabbit hole into a land where nothing made sense.

She was tempted to call Seymour to ask whether he'd found anything from the security cameras in the parking garage or the list of Parisian airports, but she knew her friend would need more time to carry out his inquiries. In the meantime, it was up to her to keep going. She needed to do what she did best: investigate.

Using only what I have on hand.

A police car appeared at the intersection and drove slowly up the street. Alice lowered her eyes, praying they would not see her. The Crown Vic passed by without stopping. It was a warning, and Alice took it seriously. More than an hour had gone by since they had stolen the Honda. Plenty of time for its owner to have reported the theft and given the cops a description of the woman who stole it. Keeping the car was too big a risk.

Having made her decision, Alice gathered her belongings— the knife from the café, the new cell phone, the packet of ibuprofen, the wet wipes, the travel bag containing the syringe, the scrap of bloodstained fabric—and shoved it all in the army bag. She put the holster she had bought on her belt and slid the Glock inside it, then got out of the car, leaving the keys on the seat.

Use only what you have on hand, Alice.

What would she do if she were in Paris? She would begin with a fingerprint analysis of the syringe. But what could she do *here?* As she walked toward Gabriel, an idea started forming in her head.

"I got a hold of Kenny," Gabriel announced with a big grin. "He's happy to lend us his apartment if we need it. It's in Astoria, in Queens. Not exactly close by, I know, but it's better than nothing."

"Come on, Keyne, let's go! We've wasted enough time.

And I hope you like walking, because we're leaving the car here."

"And where are we going?"

She smiled. "A place you ought to enjoy, given what an overgrown kid you are."

"Is that all you're going to tell me?"

"It's almost Christmas, Gabriel. I'm going to buy you some toys."

10

FINGERPRINTS

ALICE AND GABRIEL weaved between the tourists in the courtyard of the General Motors Building at the corner of Fifth Avenue and Fifty-Ninth Street.

At FAO Schwarz, two doormen dressed as toy soldiers greeted visitors to this old New York institution with wide, welcoming smiles.

The iconic Manhattan toy store was already crowded. The first floor was like a circus tent, almost entirely devoted to life-size stuffed animals: a roaring lion, a tiger jumping through a flaming hoop, an elephant carrying three monkeys dressed as bellboys. Farther off, there was a space outfitted like a hospital nursery, with employees dressed as nurses holding chubby-cheeked dolls so realistic that they could easily be mistaken for real babies.

"Are you ever going to tell me what the hell we're doing here?" Gabriel asked.

Ignoring the question, Alice took the escalator. As she rushed across the second floor, the pianist dreamily followed her, watching the kids around him with a certain amusement. Some were jumping on the keys of a giant piano mat on the floor, while others begged their parents to take a picture of them next to six-foot-tall Star Wars characters made out of Lego. Another group of kids was watching a Muppet-style puppet show.

Still in Alice's wake, Gabriel checked out the aisles, allowing himself a brief nostalgic return to childhood: plastic dinosaurs, five-thousand-piece Ravensburger jigsaw puzzles, Playmobil figures, Matchbox cars, electric trains, labyrinthine tracks.

Kid heaven.

In the costumes section, he put on a Groucho Marx mustache and an Indiana Jones hat, then joined Alice in the Science and Education area. With intense concentration, the cop was carefully examining the boxes on display: microscopes, telescopes, chemistry sets, plastic skeletons, and so on.

"Hey, if you happen to find a whip..."

She looked up at him and frowned at his getup. "Are you ever going to stop clowning around, Keyne?"

"What can I do to help?"

"Never mind," she said dismissively.

Annoyed, he moved away. He returned a few minutes later.

"I bet this is what you're looking for," he said, showing her a cardboard box with the logo of a well-known TV show.

She glanced up at the toy set he was holding—CSI: Junior Investigator Kit, $29.99—then grabbed the box from him so she could study its contents more closely: a roll of yellow crime scene tape, a magnifying glass, a detective's badge, Scotch tape, glue, fingerprint powder, evidence bags, a magnetic fingerprint brush.

"Actually, that's exactly what we need," she admitted.

Alice went to the back of a long line on the second floor to pay for her purchase. It was only when she took the escalator down to the first floor that she saw Gabriel again. The pianist had swapped his Indiana Jones fedora for a magician's top hat. Wearing a black cape, he was performing tricks for a crowd of spectators whose average age was five and a half. Alice watched him for a few seconds, baffled and fascinated in equal measure by this strange man. Dexterously and with evident pleasure, Gabriel was pulling all kinds of stuffed animals from his hat: a rabbit, a toucan, a kitten, a hedgehog, a tiger cub.

Her smile soon faded, however. The presence of children was still difficult for Alice to bear, reminding her brutally of the fact that she would never give her son his bottle, never drive him to school or soccer practice or judo lessons, never teach him to defend himself and face the world.

She blinked several times to rid herself of the tears that

had formed in her eyes and then took a few steps toward Gabriel.

"Stop messing around, Keyne!" she ordered, pulling him by the arm. "The police are looking for us, remember?"

With a sweeping gesture, the magician removed his cape and sent his top hat flying onto the shelf where it belonged.

"Mandrake the Magician bids you farewell!" he called out, bowing at the laughter and applause of the children.

On Madison Avenue behind St. Patrick's Cathedral, the Pergolese Café was one of the oldest diners in Manhattan. With its Formica tables and green leatherette benches, it was like something from the 1960s. It didn't look like much from the outside, but it was famous for its crunchy salads, tasty burgers, eggs Benedict, and pastrami in truffle oil.

Paolo Mancuso himself, the elderly owner of the establishment, brought over the dishes ordered by the young woman with the French accent and her companion: two lobster rolls, two cartons of homemade fries, and two bottles of Budweiser.

No sooner had his food been served than Gabriel dived into it, stuffing a handful of fries into his mouth—crisp and salted to perfection.

Sitting across from him, Alice took only a few bites of her sandwich before clearing a space on the table. She placed her satchel there, unfastened the two straps, and pulled out the travel bag they had found inside the briefcase. Using a paper napkin, she carefully removed the syringe from the pouch's leather lining, then got down to work.

After tearing the plastic wrapping from the CSI kit, she chose a vial of powder, a magnetic brush, and an evidence bag.

"Um, you do realize they're just toys, right?" the pianist said.

"They're good enough."

Alice cleaned her hands with a wet wipe and examined the quality of each item. The black powder, composed of carbon and thin iron filings, would work perfectly. She dipped the end of the brush into the little vial containing the powder and painted the outside of the syringe. The powder stuck to the oils left by the skin that had touched the smooth plastic, gradually revealing several clear fingerprints. Alice tapped the syringe with her nail to get rid of the excess powder, then scrutinized each print, all of them clearly recent. One of them in particular stood out: the almost whole print of an index or middle finger.

"Cut me a piece of Scotch tape," she said.

Gabriel picked up the roll. "Like this?"

"A bit longer. And be careful not to touch the sticky side!"

She took the rectangle of tape from him and used it to cover the fingerprint, smoothing it flat to avoid air bubbles. Then she removed the tape, turned over the coaster that her drink had been sitting on, and applied the tape to the blank cardboard. She pressed down on it firmly with her thumb to transfer the pattern to the coaster.

When she removed the tape, a clear black fingerprint

was visible on the coaster's white surface. Alice squinted, examining the intertwining of grooves. Lines and ridges formed an unusual pattern: an arched print broken by a tiny cross-shaped scar.

She showed the print to Gabriel and then, satisfied, slid the coaster into an evidence bag.

"Okay, that's very nice," he admitted, "but what good does it do us? Wouldn't we have to scan it into a police database to find out whose it is?"

Alice nibbled a few fries while she mused out loud: "Your friend's apartment in Queens..."

"Yeah?"

"I imagine he'll have a computer with an Internet connection."

"He may well have Wi-Fi, but if he has a computer, it's probably a laptop—and that will be in Tokyo. So I wouldn't get your hopes up."

Alice's face crumpled with disappointment. "How should we get there? Taxi, subway..."

Gabriel looked up. On the wall above their table, amid a hodgepodge of photographs of celebrities posing with the café owner, he saw an old city map pinned to a corkboard. "We're not far from Grand Central," he said, pointing to the map.

Grand Central...Alice remembered that extraordinary train station, which Seymour had shown her during one of their trips to New York. Her colleague had taken her to eat oysters and shrimp at the Oyster Bar, a fantastic seafood restaurant situated in a large vaulted room underground. Re-calling that visit, she suddenly had an idea. She looked at the map. Gabriel was right—Grand Central Station was only a few blocks from where they sat.

"Let's go!" she said, sliding out of her seat.

"What, already? Don't you want dessert? You should see their cheesecake!"

"You're getting on my nerves, Keyne."

They went into the station through the entrance at the corner of Park Avenue and Forty-Second Street, finding themselves in the vast main hall with its rows of ticket windows and machines.

In the center, above the circular information kiosk, was the famous four-faced clock in brass and opal glass, used by lovers as a meeting place for more than a hundred years.

They weren't here as tourists, of course, but Alice couldn't help admiring the station. *It's nothing like the Gare du Nord or Saint-Lazare, that's for sure,* she thought, looking around. An autumnal light, soft and peaceful, poured through the large side window, painting the lobby in shades of gold and ocher.

On the immense vaulted ceiling, 125 feet high, thousands of painted stars gave the impression that you were looking up into a clear night sky. It was from here that Cary Grant fled to Chicago in *North by Northwest,* here that Robert De Niro met Meryl Streep in *Falling in Love.*

"Follow me," she said, loud enough to be heard above the roar of voices around them.

She fought her way through the crowd, with Gabriel following, then climbed the steps that led to the eastern balcony of the main concourse. From here, they had a commanding view of the entire hall, which seemed even more monumental.

It was in this majestic, almost open-air setting that a major firm had installed one of its stores. Alice weaved between the pale-wood tables displaying the brand's flagship products: cell phones, MP3 players, computers, tablets. Although secured with anti-theft devices, much of this equipment was freely available to use. The store's visitors—most of them tourists—came here to check their e-mail, go online, or listen to music on state-of-the-art headphones.

They had to act fast; there were police and security guards everywhere. Alice managed to avoid being collared by any of the army of employees wearing blue T-shirts who patrolled the space, and approached one of the display tables.

She handed her satchel to Gabriel. "Grab the coaster," she told him.

While he did this, she touched a key on the keyboard of a MacBook Pro that looked similar to the one she had at home in France. With a click, she activated a program that used the computer's built-in camera, grabbed the coaster from Gabriel, held it up to the screen, and took several photographs of the fingerprint. Using the computer's retouching software, she manipulated the contrast and brightness levels until she had the clearest image possible. Then she connected to her e-mail in-box.

"Can you go buy our subway tickets?" she asked Gabriel.

Waiting until he had disappeared toward the ticket machines, she began writing an e-mail to Seymour, her fingertips flying over the keyboard.

To: Seymour Lombart
Subject: Help
From: Alice Schafer

Seymour,

I need your help more than ever. I'll try to call you sometime in the next hour, but before then you really have to speed up your investigation.

1. Have you gotten access to the security cameras in the parking garage and the airports?
2. Have you found my car? Traced my cell phone? Checked the latest activity in my bank account?
3. What have you found out about Gabriel Keyne?
4. I'm attaching a photograph of a fingerprint. Could you get it analyzed ASAP?

I'm counting on you.
   All best,
   Alice

11

LITTLE EGYPT

Astoria, Queens
Noon

THE SQUARE OUTSIDE the station was a blaze of fall sunlight. Alice and Gabriel left this bright esplanade and
disappeared into the crowd of customers at the market that
had been set up under the elevated railway. The two fugitives
had caught a train from Grand Central to Lexington Avenue,
then taken the local line to Astoria Boulevard. The trip took
only about twenty minutes, but the difference in their surroundings was incredible. Small brick buildings had replaced
the steel-and-glass skyscrapers, while the hectic energy of
Manhattan had given way to an almost village-like calm.

The air was thick with the exquisite odors of olive oil,
crushed garlic, and fresh mint. The stalls were filled with

grilled squid and octopus, moussaka and souvlaki, baklava, grape leaves, and spanakopita. These appetizing specialties left no room for doubt—this part of Astoria was New York's Greek neighborhood.

"Do you know the address, at least?" Alice asked, seeing Gabriel hesitate over which direction to take.

"I've only been here once or twice," he said defensively. "All I remember is that the apartment's windows overlooked Steinway Street."

"Perfect street name for a musician." Alice smiled.

They asked the way from an old man who was selling skewers of beef and bay leaves grilled in a firepit.

Following his directions, they walked down a long street edged with trees and semidetached houses reminiscent of certain areas of London. They turned onto a lively, cosmopolitan shopping street packed with Greek caterers, vegetarian delis, kebab stalls, Japanese restaurants, and Korean groceries—a genuine melting pot of gastronomy concentrated within a few blocks.

As they walked farther down Steinway Street, the borders shifted again. This time they were on the other side of the Mediterranean—in North Africa, to be precise.

"For a few years now, this place has been known as Little Egypt or Little Morocco," Gabriel explained.

In fact, with a little imagination, Alice could easily have believed she'd been miraculously transported to a souk in Cairo or Marrakesh. Delicious scents of honey and tajine floated through the air, and in this part of Queens, there were more hookah bars than Greek taverns. They walked past a golden-painted mosque, a halal butcher, a religious bookshop. In the conversations they overheard, Arabic and English mingled almost naturally.

"I think this is it," Gabriel said, arriving at a brownstone with a pale façade and sash windows that rose above a barbershop.

There was no intercom and no elevator. They walked quickly upstairs and stopped on the fourth-floor landing to pick up the keys from Madame Chaouch, the building's owner. Kenny had phoned her to let her know they were coming.

"Pretty nice here, huh?" Gabriel said as they entered the loft.

Kenny's bachelor pad was a vast and mostly open-plan duplex, with exposed metal girders. Alice looked around at the brick walls, high ceiling, polished concrete flooring, then stood still in front of the large bay window with its view of the street.

She looked out for a good minute before tossing her satchel onto a large, solid-oak table surrounded by two mismatched armchairs and a brushed-metal bench.

"Ugh, I'm wiped out." She groaned, collapsing into one of the chairs.

"Hey, you know what? I'm going to run you a bath!"

"What? No, don't bother. We have better things to do than—"

But Gabriel, ignoring her protests, had already disappeared upstairs.

Alice sighed and for a long moment remained motionless, curled up in the cushions. Her tiredness was suddenly resurfacing. It took her several minutes to recover from the aftereffects of the mental stress and physical strain she had been under since that hallucinatory awakening in the middle of the park. When she felt better, she stood up and rummaged around in the kitchen cabinets in search of a teapot. She put some water on to boil and, as she waited, looked unthinkingly through the books on the shelves (Harry Crews, Hunter S. Thompson, Trevanian...), the magazines on the coffee table, the abstract and minimalist paintings on the walls.

Light-filled and spacious, the apartment was suffused with a thousand shades of gray and beige, a reasonable compromise between the industrial style and the Scandinavian all-wood look. The ascetic and stripped-down décor, the soft lighting... all this came together to create a protective, cocoon-like atmosphere.

She looked around for a computer, a router, or a landline phone.

Nothing.

In a small dish, she saw a car key attached to a key ring decorated with a galloping silver horse. *A Mustang?* she wondered, picking up the keys.

Back in the kitchen, she found some genmaicha, a Japanese green tea mixed with roasted brown rice. She prepared a cup. The beverage was original—the fresh notes of the green tea contrasting with the rice's aroma of hazelnut and cereal—but undrinkable. She poured it out into the sink, then opened the glass door of a wine cabinet next to the fridge. Apparently their host was a wine buff. Apart from a few Californian pinot noirs, his collection consisted entirely of French *grands crus*. Thanks to her father, Alice knew quite a bit about wine. She spotted a Château Margaux 2000, a Cheval Blanc 2006, a Montrose 2005…she was about to open the Saint-Estèphe, when she changed her mind and opted for a burgundy instead, a Romanée-Conti La Tâche 1999—an extremely expensive vintage she had never tasted. She rejected every rational reason not to drink this wine, then opened the bottle and poured herself a large glass. A good garnet color, a powerful nose with notes of roses, red berries, and chocolate.

This is what I need—not a cup of tea!

She drank a mouthful of the burgundy, appreciating every nuance of red fruit and spice. The wine caressed her palate and warmed her chest. She drank the whole glass and then poured herself another right away.

"If Madame would care to come upstairs, her bath is ready," Gabriel declared from the mezzanine above.

"Shall I pour you a glass?"

"What! You opened one of his bottles?" he said, alarmed, running down the spiral staircase. He looked at the bottle and exploded with rage. "Are you insane? Do you know how much this wine costs?"

"Oh, chill out, Keyne."

"You have a strange way of thanking my friend for his hospitality!" he insisted.

"All right, that's enough. I'll pay him back for his stupid wine!"

"With what? Your cop's wages?"

"Yes! Actually, while we're on the subject, do you know if your friend has a car?"

"Kenny has an old beater, yeah. I think he won it in a poker game."

"Any idea where he keeps it?"

"Nope." Suddenly inspired, Gabriel crossed the living room and stared through one of the back windows, which overlooked a gravel courtyard. There were a dozen or so cars parked around a central concrete island. He squinted to make out the different models. "It might be that one," he said, nodding to a white 1960s-era Mustang Shelby with blue racing stripes.

"Why don't you go down and check?" she said, throwing him the keys.

He balked at this. "Why don't you stop giving me orders? I'm not one of your minions!"

"Hurry up, Keyne. We *really* need a car."

"And you, go take your bath, girlfriend. You *really* need to relax!"

"I am not your girlfriend," she shouted, but Keyne didn't hear her. He had already left the room, slamming the door behind him.

Upstairs, in the master bedroom, Alice sat on the bed and opened her canvas satchel. She took out the new cell phone and removed it from its plastic packet. It came with a charger, a hands-free device, and a user's manual. She also found a plastic card containing the phone's serial number.

She plugged in the phone. An icon appeared on the screen showing a credit of ten minutes. She pressed Call and was put through to a recorded message asking her to enter the serial number.

She did this, and the robotic voice asked her to type in the area code of the zone where she planned to use the phone. Almost instantaneously, she was sent a text assigning her a phone number. Once her phone had been activated, she entered the number of the prepaid card, which immediately gave her 120 minutes of communication.

She called Seymour's cell phone, but it went straight to voice mail.

"Call me back at this number as soon as you can, Seymour. I really need your help. Please be quick."

Alice then went into the bathroom, which was separated from the bedroom by a glass-brick wall. It was decorated in a retro style, very 1950s: black-and-white-checkerboard tile floor, cast-iron bathtub with brass feet, antique sink, vintage ceramic faucets, painted wooden cabinet with moldings.

Keyne had done what he'd said he would—beneath a thick cloud of foam, a steaming bath scented with lavender awaited her.

What a strange guy.

Alice undressed in front of a large, adjustable mirror with

a wrought-iron frame, then slipped into the water. The heat increased her blood flow and woke all the pores in her skin. Her muscles relaxed, and the shooting pains in her joints diminished. She took deep breaths. Alice had the pleasant sensation of being swept away by a burning-hot beneficent wave, and for a few seconds she abandoned herself completely to the bath's voluptuous languor.

Then she held her breath and plunged her head underwater.

With the alcohol in her bloodstream and the temperature of the water, she felt herself floating midway between somnolence and numbness. Contradictory thoughts flashed through her mind. Her memory loss made her impatient. Once again, Alice tried to reconstruct the previous evening, but still she ended up in that same black hole, without access to her memories. For the early part of the evening, the pieces of the puzzle slotted into place easily enough: the bars, the cocktails, her friends, the parking garage on Avenue Franklin-Roosevelt. Then walking to the car. The bluish-green artificial lighting. She feels groggy, staggers as she walks. She distinctly sees herself open the door of the little Audi and sit down behind the wheel . . . and there's someone sitting next to her! She remembers now. A face emerges from the darkness, taking her by surprise. A man's face. She attempts to make out his features, but they vanish under a milky fog.

Suddenly, the flood of memories sweeps her further back in time, like a river rushing to its source in the heart of pain.

I remember...

Two years ago

I remember.

Or rather, I imagine.

November 21, 2011.

A rainy day, late afternoon, in my husband's office. An appointment with a patient is interrupted by a phone call:

"Dr. Paul Malaury? This is the surgery department in the Hôtel-Dieu hospital. Your wife has just been brought here. She's in critical condition..."

In a panic, Paul grabs his coat, stammers a few words of explanation to his secretary, and runs out of his office. He sits behind the wheel of his old Alfa Romeo Giulietta, parked, as always, straddling a little bit of sidewalk in front of Paris's public-housing agency. The rain has reduced his daily parking ticket to a pulp. He starts the engine, drives around the square, and turns onto Rue du Bac.

Night has already fallen, after a grim, wet fall day—the kind of day that makes you loathe Paris, this cancerous, polluted, overcrowded hell engulfed in misery and madness. Traffic is crawling on Boulevard Saint-Germain. Paul uses his sleeve to wipe condensation from the inside of his windshield. Then he uses the same sleeve to wipe the tears from his cheeks.

Alice, the baby ... please don't let this be true!

He has been euphoric ever since he discovered he was going to be a father. Already he is looking forward to it all: baby bottles, walks with the stroller in the Jardin du Luxembourg, sandcastles on the beach, the first day of school, soccer fields on Sunday mornings ... a series of moments now dissolving in his mind.

He forces away these morbid thoughts and tries to remain calm, but the emotion is too powerful and his body is shaken by sobs. His pain becomes mixed with anger. He bawls like a kid. Stuck at a traffic light, he smashes his fist against the steering wheel. He can still hear the nurse's words describing the horror: "I'm not going to lie to you, Doctor: It's very serious. She was attacked with a knife. She has several wounds in her abdomen . . ."

The light turns green. He speeds away and jerks his wheel to the side to take the bus lane. He wonders how this could have happened. How could his wife—with whom he ate lunch that very day in a little bar on Rue Guisarde—have been stabbed in a squalid apartment in west Paris when she was supposed to be spending the afternoon with her midwife, preparing for the birth?

Images flash through his head again: Alice lying in a pool of blood, the ambulance arriving, the paramedic making the first report: "Patient unstable, systolic pressure dropping, weak pulse, heart rate one hundred. We're going to intubate her."

Paul flashes his headlights, passes two taxis, and is about to turn left, when he sees that Boulevard Saint-Michel is cordoned off by cops because of a protest march. He clenches his jaw. *Fuck! I don't believe this!*

He lowers his window to talk to the police officers, hoping they will let him through, but he comes up against the brick wall of their inflexibility and drives away angrily, yelling insults at them.

He turns back onto Boulevard Saint-Germain without signaling and a bus driver honks his horn.

He has to calm down. Focus all his energy on saving his wife. He has to find a doctor capable of performing miracles. He wonders if he knows any of the doctors at Hôtel-Dieu.

Pralavorio, maybe? No, he works at Bichat. Jourdin? He's at Cochin, but he knows everyone. He's the one I should call. He reaches for his phone, which he left on top of his coat on the passenger seat, but he can't find it.

The old Alfa Romeo drives along narrow Rue des Bernardins and joins the Pont de l'Archevêché, the "lovers' bridge," its guardrails covered with thousands of padlocks shining in the night.

Paul switches on the dome light, looks around, and finally spots his cell phone on the floor. Keeping one hand on the steering wheel, he leans down to pick it up. When he sits back up, he is dazzled by a headlight and realizes, to his shock, that a motorcycle is coming right at him on this one-way bridge. It's too late to brake. Paul jerks the wheel right to avoid the collision. The Alfa Romeo skids onto the sidewalk, takes off, and collides with a streetlamp before ripping open the bridge's metal barrier.

Paul is dead before his car falls into the Seine.

I remember
    that on one day,
    November 21, 2011,
    out of pride, out of vanity, out of sheer blindness,
    I killed my baby.
    And I killed my husband.

12

FREE JAZZ

MUFFLED BY THE bathwater, the ringing of the telephone takes a while to reach Alice's brain. Startled, she snaps out of her reverie. She grabs a towel, wraps herself in it, and reaches for her cell phone.

"Schafer," she says.

"Alice? It's me."

"Seymour! Finally!"

"Are you okay?"

"Yeah, but I need information. Did you find anything?"

"I got your fingerprint. Nice work. I think it's usable. I put Savignon on the case. He's sending it to the lab now, and we should have the results in half an hour."

"Okay. What else? The security cameras in the parking garage?"

"I went over to Franklin-Roosevelt and looked at their tapes, but you can't see much. Your car entered the garage at eight twelve p.m. and came out again at twelve seventeen a.m."

"Could you see me on the video?"

"No, not really..."

Goddamn it! "Was I alone when I came out? Was I driving?"

"It's not clear. The camera picked up your license plate, but the inside of the car is too dark to see."

"Shit, I don't believe this! Have you tried manipulating the images?"

"Yeah, but it didn't help. Their hardware is crap. And I'll warn you now: I haven't found anything from the airports. Without a warrant, it's impossible to access their databases or their stored video. This would be a whole lot easier if we informed Taillandier about it."

"Absolutely not. Did you talk to my friends?"

"Yeah, all three. Sounds like you had a lot to drink, Alice. They were worried about you. Malika and Karine offered to go with you, but you refused."

"Please tell me you have something else, Seymour."

"Yep, I saved the best for last. Are you alone?"

"Yes, why?"

"It's about your friend Gabriel Keyne. Castelli did some checking on him. There is no trace, anywhere, of a jazz pianist with that name."

"Listen, he's not Ray Charles or Michel Legrand. He's strictly small-time—"

"Come on, you know Castelli. He's the best researcher in the division. If there had been anything to find, he would have found it. But there's nothing. Nada! There are dozens of Gabriel Keynes, but none of them are musicians or in any way connected with jazz. And I haven't even told you the best bit yet."

Seymour let his phrase hang, as if waiting for a drumroll.

Spit it out, for God's sake!

"You told me he claimed to have played at the Brown Sugar Club in Dublin last night?"

"That's what he told me."

"Well, it's not true. Castelli called the owner of the club—they had a salsa-and-mambo night yesterday. The only guys onstage were members of a big Cuban orchestra who arrived that morning from Havana."

Alice was stunned by this revelation. She was having trouble getting her head around it. Strangely, she caught herself thinking up excuses to defend Gabriel: Maybe he was using a stage name? Maybe he was part of a group? Maybe…

"I don't know who this guy really is," Seymour said. "I'm still digging. But until we discover his real identity, you should watch your back."

She hung up and remained motionless for a few seconds. No, her theories were bullshit. The truth was, she'd been suckered. She had let her guard down, and Keyne had lied to her from the moment they first met.

CENTRAL PARK   149

But why?

She quickly dressed and shoved all her belongings into the bag. She could feel the fear spreading through her veins. Heart pounding, she walked downstairs, gun held out in front of her. "Keyne?" she shouted as she moved into the living room. Staying close to the walls, she stole furtively into the kitchen, her hand gripped tightly around the butt of the pistol. Nothing. The loft was empty.

In the middle of the table, next to the wine bottle, she found a note scrawled on the back of an envelope.

Alice,

I found the car, but the tank is nearly empty. I'm going out to fill it. I'll meet you in the hookah bar across the street.

Gabriel

PS: I hope you like Moroccan pastries.

13

HOOKAH BAR

ALICE WENT HURTLING down the stairs and out onto the street. She had put her gun back in its holster and was carrying her satchel over one shoulder. The cold wind carried the scent of apricots, spices, and powdered sugar. She saw the Mustang parked out in front of the hookah bar; it had a cream-colored body, shiny chrome bumpers, blue racing stripes—a sleeping tiger ready to roar.

On her guard, she crossed the road and pushed open the door of the Nefertiti Bar.

The interior was an eclectic blend of Arabic and Western influences; scattered haphazardly throughout the room were low tables, overstuffed armchairs, and gold-embroidered cushions, but there were also shelves overflowing with books, an upright piano, an old bar made of zinc and polished oak, and even a dartboard straight from an English pub.

It had a pleasant, relaxed, early-afternoon atmosphere, full of autumn sunlight. Hipster college students with laptops cohabited harmoniously with the neighborhood's elderly Egyptians and North Africans, who tranquilly pulled on their hookahs. The sweet fumes mingled with the scent of mint tea, creating an all-enveloping olfactory cocoon.

Sitting at a table, Gabriel had already started playing chess with a long-haired geek dressed in an improbable fluorescent-yellow spandex turtleneck and a blue down vest.

"Keyne, we have to talk."

The young chess player looked up and complained in a squeaky voice, "Ma'am, you can see we're in the middle of a—"

"Beat it, kid!" she barked, sweeping the chess pieces from the board.

Before he could react, she grabbed the student by his vest and lifted him off his chair. He looked scared. Quickly, he picked up the chess pieces and scurried off without another word.

"So, your bath doesn't seem to have calmed you down any," Gabriel remarked. "Maybe a delicious Moroccan pastry will do the trick. Apparently their honey-and-nut doughnuts are delicious. Unless you want rice pudding instead? Or a cup of tea?"

She calmly sat down opposite him, determined to confront him with his lies. "You know what would *really* make me happy, Keyne?"

Smiling, he shrugged. "Tell me. If it's something I can do..."

"Well, it ought to be, with you being a pianist. You see that piano at the bar?"

He turned around and she noticed a look of apprehension flicker across his face.

"I would love it if you could play something for me," Alice said. "I mean, it's not every day that I get to have tea with a professional jazz pianist!"

"I don't think that's a good idea. The other customers might not like it."

"Oh, come on, don't be ridiculous. They'd be thrilled! Everyone loves listening to a good song while they smoke their water pipes."

Again Gabriel hedged. "It probably hasn't been tuned..."

"Who cares? Come on, Keyne, play a few standards: 'Autumn Leaves,' 'Blue Monk,' 'April in Paris'... or better still, play 'Alice in Wonderland' and dedicate it to me! You can't refuse me that."

Gabriel writhed in his chair, obviously uncomfortable. "Listen, I think—"

"Well, *I* think if you're a jazz pianist, then I'm a nun!"

He rubbed his eyes and gave a long sigh of resignation. Sounding almost relieved, he stopped trying to deny it. "Okay, I admit it, I lied to you. But only about that."

"And I'm supposed to believe that, Keyne? Or is Keyne even your real name?"

"Everything else is true, Alice! My name is Gabriel Keyne, I was in Dublin last night, and I woke up this morning handcuffed to you without any clue about how I'd gotten there."

"So why lie about your job?"

He sighed again, aware that the next few minutes were not going to be easy. "Because I'm the same as you, Alice."

She frowned. "The same as me?"

"Yeah. I'm a cop too."

A heavy silence fell between them.

"You're what?" Alice demanded after a few seconds.

"An FBI special agent assigned to the Boston bureau."

"Stop bullshitting me!" she exploded.

"I'm not, I swear. I really was in Dublin last night at a club in Temple Bar, across the street from my hotel. I went there to relax and have a few drinks after work."

"And what the hell were you doing in Ireland?"

"I'd gone there to meet one of my counterparts from the Garda Síochána."

"Why?"

"We're cooperating on an investigation."

"What investigation?"

Gabriel took a sip of tea, as if to slow down the flood of questions and win himself some time. "We're investigating a series of crimes," he said finally.

"A serial killer?" she asked, trying to back him into a corner.

"Maybe," he admitted, looking away.

Alice's phone vibrated in her jacket pocket. She looked at the screen—it was Seymour. She hesitated, unwilling to interrupt Keyne's wave of revelations.

"You should answer that," he advised her.

"What's it to you?"

"It's your cop friend, isn't it? Aren't you curious to find out who the fingerprints on the syringe belong to?"

She gave in. "Hello?"

"It's me, Alice," Seymour said, sounding distraught.

"Did you analyze the fingerprint?"

"Where did you get it, Alice?"

"From a syringe. I'll explain later. Did you get a match or not?"

"Yes, we have a result, but...shit..."

"What?"

"According to the files, this fingerprint belongs to ..."

"To who? Tell me!"

"To Erik Vaughn," he replied tonelessly.

"Erik Vaughn." The news hit Alice like a sucker punch.

"Yes, the man who tried to kill you, and—"

"I know who Erik Vaughn is, for fuck's sake!"

She closed her eyes. For a moment, she felt shaky, but a restoring force prevented her from collapsing. "That's impossible, Seymour," she said calmly.

There was a sigh on the other end of the line. "I know

it's difficult to believe, but we checked and rechecked the results. There are more than thirty points of correspondence. We have to tell Taillandier now, Alice."

"Just give me a few more hours. Please."

"I can't. Anything involving Vaughn is highly sensitive. You already got us in trouble once with this case."

"How thoughtful of you to remind me."

She glanced up at the old Pepsi-Cola clock on the wall behind the bar—1:15 p.m. "What time is it in Paris, seven fifteen? Just give me till midnight."

Silence.

"Please, Seymour!"

"This is a really bad idea."

"And keep digging with the fingerprint. I'm sure it's not Vaughn."

Another sigh. "And *I'm* sure Vaughn is in New York, Alice. I think he's looking for you and he's going to try to kill you."

14

TWO PEOPLE

Tɪɴʏ ᴍᴜʟᴛɪᴄᴏʟᴏʀᴇᴅ ᴘᴀʀᴛɪᴄʟᴇꜱ danced in the light.
Rays of sunlight filtered through the half-open lou-
vered wooden shutters. The hookah bar hummed with
conversation. Strong aromas of orange, date, and hazelnut
floated through the spacious room, where a scattered clien-
tele pulled nonchalantly at hookahs or nibbled pastries.

Alice and Gabriel faced each other in silence. A young
man approached their table to serve Gabriel more mint tea.
He poured it Moroccan-style, lifting the teapot very high
above the glasses so a head of foam formed on the surface
of the tea.

Both elbows resting on the table, Gabriel sat with his

chin on his hands. His face had grown harder. It was time for explanations. "So, let me guess: The fingerprint on the syringe belongs to Erik Vaughn?"

"How do you know his name?"

"He's the one I was tracking in Ireland."

Alice stared into his eyes. "Why in Ireland?"

"Long story. Ten days ago, the Boston FBI office was alerted by Maine State Police about an unusual murder committed in Cumberland County. I was sent to the crime scene with my partner, Special Agent Thomas Krieg."

"Who was the victim?" Alice asked.

"Elizabeth Hardy, age thirty-one, a nurse working at Sebago Hospital. Found murdered at her home. Strangled—"

"With a pair of tights," Alice guessed.

Keyne nodded.

Alice's heart began to race, but she tried to channel her emotions. It might be the same MO as Vaughn's, but that didn't necessarily mean it was the same criminal.

"After the murder," Keyne went on, "we checked the ViCAP database—without luck. I shouldn't tell you this, but we have hackers capable of getting into the databases of European police computers: the ViCLAS in Germany, the SALVAC in France."

"I hope you're joking!"

"Don't look so outraged—we do what we have to do. Anyway, that's how I found out about the series of murders and attacks committed by Erik Vaughn in Paris from November 2010 to November 2011."

"And you made the connection?"

"I arranged a meeting with your boss, the director of the Criminal Division."

"Mathilde Taillandier?"

"I was supposed to meet her next week in Paris, but first I went to Ireland. I checked the international database and found another murder that had been committed eight months earlier in Dublin."

"Same victim profile, same signature?"

"Mary McCarthy, age twenty-four, a student in her junior year at Trinity College. Found strangled with a pair of tights in her room on campus."

"And you think it's Vaughn?"

"That's obvious, isn't it?"

"No."

"They lost track of Vaughn in Paris after you were attacked. Since then, he's been like a ghost. The French police have made no progress at all on the case."

"So?"

"Let me tell you what I think. Vaughn is a chameleon killer, capable of changing his identity whenever he feels threatened. I think he left Paris a long time ago, stopped over in Ireland for a while, and is now in the U.S."

"All that just because you have two murders with apparently similar MOs?"

"They're not similar—they're exactly the same."

"Oh, come on. Vaughn isn't the first killer to strangle his victims with a pair of tights!"

"Don't play dumb, Schafer. Vaughn killed each of those women with the *previous* victim's hose. That's what makes the signature his, as you already know."

"And your first victim in Maine, what was she strangled with?"

"A pair of pink-and-white tights. The same tights the Irish student was wearing the day she died!"

"You're jumping the gun. Your killer in Ireland or in the States is just a copycat. An accomplice. A straw man. Some sort of admirer who reproduces the crimes in minute detail."

"You think so? Copycat killers are all over the movies and TV shows, but in fifteen years as a cop, I've never come across one. They don't exist in reality."

"Of course they do! The New York Zodiac killer, the Hance case—"

He lifted his hand up to interrupt her. "Those cases are thirty years old. They're in all the criminology manuals."

Alice would not let it drop.

"I thought the FBI was more thorough than this. Do you always charge blindly at every red flag people wave at you?"

Gabriel lost his temper. "Listen, I was going to spare you, Alice, but if you want irrefutable proof, I have it."

"Oh yeah?"

"You know what kind of tights the young Irish girl was strangled with?"

"Go on."

"A pair of lace pregnancy tights, with a blue-green pattern. The pair you were wearing two years ago when Vaughn almost killed you."

A silence. This revelation sent a chill down her spine. The police had never revealed that detail to the press. How could any copycat have known about those tights?

She massaged her temples. "Okay, let's say it's true. What's your theory?"

"I think Vaughn wanted to take us on. That's why he brought us together. And the fact that we found one of his prints certainly supports that theory. You, first of all, the French cop who knew him best after tracking him so relentlessly. You, whose unborn child he killed. You, with all your anger and your hatred for him. And then me: the FBI agent in charge of the investigation that identified him in the States. Two of us against him, determined to catch him but each with our own flaws and demons—two people who have suddenly gone from being the hunter to the hunted."

Alice considered this possibility with a mixture of dread and excitement. There was something terrifying about the idea.

"Whether Vaughn is behind these killings or not, he must have a protégé or an accomplice," she said. "Last night, you were in Dublin and I was in Paris. He had to get us both on a plane somehow, and the guy can't be everywhere."

"Agreed."

Alice held her head in her hands. The case had taken an

unexpected twist that, for the past few hours, had stirred up trauma and pain she had been wrestling with for years.

"One thing bothers me, Keyne. Why did you wait all this time to tell me who you are?"

"Because I had to find out more about you, about your involvement in this case and your motivations. Most important, I had to gather enough information to make it impossible for the Bureau to take me off the case. And, just between you and me, I hate being humiliated. And last night someone definitely got the jump on me."

"But why pretend to be a jazz pianist?"

"It just popped into my head. I've always liked jazz, and Kenny, my best friend, really is a saxophone player."

"So what do you suggest we do now?"

"First we go to the hematology lab on the Upper East Side to drop off a sample of the blood from your blouse. The Bureau works with that lab often. They're incredibly expensive, but they have the best equipment and staff. They should be able to get us a genetic profile within two hours."

"Good idea. And then what?"

"We drive to Boston, get our stories straight, go to the field office, and tell them everything we know. And we pray that they don't take me off the investigation."

Watching Gabriel, she noticed that his appearance had changed since his real identity was revealed. The jovial jazz pianist had given way to a serious cop. His look was darker, his features harder, his expression much more worried. It was like meeting him for the first time.

"All right, I'll go with you," she agreed. "But on one condition: I want to be part of the investigation."

"That's not up to me."

"Officially or unofficially, we work as a team: you give me your information and I give you mine. Otherwise, we go our separate ways now—and you can kiss the blood sample goodbye. Take it or leave it."

Gabriel removed a cigarette from the pack he'd found in the Honda. He lit it and took a few nervous drags, giving himself time to think.

Alice watched him from the corner of her eye. She recognized him now as one of her own kind: a monomaniacal cop prepared to do anything to stay on the case. The kind of cop who stayed up nights trying to get into the heads of criminals in order to understand their motives. The kind of cop who considered catching murderers an almost sacred duty.

He took out the keys to the Mustang and dropped them on the table. "All right, it's a deal," he said, stubbing out his cigarette in an ashtray. "Let's go."

15

PREPARE FOR WAR

T HE HEMATOLOGY LABORATORY occupied the top floor of an ultramodern building with a crystalline façade located on Fifth Avenue between Mount Sinai Hospital and the Museum of the City of New York.

It didn't take Gabriel and Alice long to reach the border of the Upper East Side and Spanish Harlem. Luckily, it was midafternoon, so there were plenty of parking spaces. They found a spot on one of the streets surrounding the immense medical complex.

"Wait for me in the car, okay?" Gabriel said.

"Are you kidding? No way—I'm coming with you."

"All right." Gabriel sighed. "But let me do the talking. I'm leading this investigation. Understood?"

"Got it, Chief," she mocked, opening her door.

Gabriel got out of the car too. "And let's not waste any time, okay?" he said.

Alice nodded and followed him into the lobby and then the elevator. At this time of day, the lab reception area was practically empty. Behind the desk, an employee was eating a salad from a plastic container.

Gabriel introduced himself and asked to see Eliane Pelletier, the lab's deputy director.

"She's French?" said Alice, surprised.

"No, she's from Quebec. And I'd better warn you, she's kind of strange," he said, raising an eyebrow.

"Meaning?"

"I'll let you figure it out for yourself."

Eliane Pelletier appeared almost immediately at the end of the corridor.

"Gabe, my boy," she called to him from down the hall. "Have you brought your fiancée to see me?"

She was a small, sturdy woman with short gray hair. She wore square-framed glasses and a white lab coat open over a baggy black tunic. Her face, round and soft, was like a Russian doll's.

"I'm so happy you finally settled down!" she teased, giving him a hug.

He took care not to prolong the joke.

"Eliane, this is Captain Schafer, from the Paris Criminal Division."

"Bonjour, ma jolie," she said, embracing Alice. "A Frenchie, eh?"

They followed her into her office.

"We don't have much time, Eliane. Can you do a DNA test based on this blood sample? Our labs are overwhelmed."

Alice took the evidence bag with the scrap of blouse in it from her satchel and handed it to the scientist.

"I'll give it to one of my biologists," she promised, taking the bag. "What are you looking for, exactly?"

"A usable genetic profile. How quickly can you do it?"

"Is six hours okay?" she asked, adjusting her glasses.

"Are you serious?"

"Well, I could reduce the DNA extraction and amplification time by using miniature probes, but it's more expensive."

"Just do it as fast as you can. As soon as you have the results, send them to Agent Thomas Krieg, along with your invoice. I'd like to call him so he knows to expect it. Can I use your phone?"

"Make yourself at home, Gabe. I'll get right to work."

And she walked out, leaving them alone in the office.

"What's your cell phone number?" he asked. "If you don't mind, I'll give it to Thomas so he can get hold of us easily."

Alice nodded and wrote her new number on a Post-It that was lying on the desk.

While Gabriel called his colleague, she went out into the hallway. She switched on her phone and called her father's number, but it went straight to his terse voice-mail greeting: "Alain Schafer. Not here right now. Leave a message," growled a grumpy voice.

"Papa, it's Alice. Call me when you can. It's urgent. Very urgent."

She hung up. After a few seconds of reflection, she decided to call Seymour.

"It's me again."

"Thank God. I was getting worried. Have you spoken to Keyne?"

"Yes, he claims to be an FBI agent based in Boston."

"Seriously? This guy is taking you for a ride, Alice!"

"You can try checking it, but I think he's telling the truth this time. He's investigating a murder similar to the Erik Vaughn killings."

"I'll call Sharman, that guy in Washington who we helped on the Petreus case."

"Thanks, Seymour. Are you still at work? I've got another favor to ask."

He couldn't hold back a sigh. "Alice, favors for you is all I've done today!"

"I want you to take your car and—"

"Now? I can't. My shift doesn't end till eleven."

She ignored his objections. "Take the highway to Metz, then continue on to Sarreguemines."

"Alice, that's over two hundred miles!"

She went on as if he hadn't said anything. "There's an old, abandoned sugar factory between Sarreguemines and Sarrebourg. I don't know exactly where it is, but ask Castelli to find it for you—there can't be that many sugar factories in the area."

"I said no, Alice!"

"Take a flashlight with you, a large pair of pliers, and some glow sticks. Call me when you get there. I want you to check something."

"Alice, we're talking about an eight-hour round trip!"

"I wouldn't ask you if it wasn't important. Please, if you're my friend, do this!" she begged. "Damn it, you're the only person I can trust right now!"

Sensing her distress, Seymour yielded. "At least tell me what I'm supposed to be looking for." He sighed.

"A corpse, I hope."

The road.

Speed.

The landscape rushing past.

The roar of the V-8 engine.

On the car radio, the timeless voice of Otis Redding.

A huge tachometer in the center of the antique dashboard.

And the amber and honey highlights in Alice's hair.

They had left Manhattan and driven for almost two hours, crossing through most of Connecticut on I-95, then getting on I-91, which took them north. Traffic was moving easily, the sky cloudless, the road edged with pine trees and occasional ginkgos, elms, maples, and oaks. They had hardly exchanged a word on the trip, both of them lost in their thoughts, alone in their suffering.

The Shelby GT drove like a dream. Behind the wheel, Gabriel imagined himself for a moment as a young man in the sixties, proud of his Mustang, driving his girlfriend to see the latest Steve McQueen movie while listening to Roy Orbison or the Doors and worrying about being drafted, maybe sent to Vietnam.

He turned toward Alice. Her face hard and closed, she had sunk into her own thoughts, fingers tensed around her cell phone, waiting for a call. With her army jacket, her pale face, high cheekbones, and hair tied in a ponytail, she was beautiful in a wild, almost warlike way. But that was hardly surprising; Alice Schafer was at war. Behind the toughness of her features, though, it was possible to glimpse, now and then, the shadow of another woman, softer and more peaceful.

He wondered what she had been like *before*. Before the tragedy. Smiling, calm, happy? Could he have fallen in love with such a woman if he'd met her on the streets of Paris? Would he have approached her? Would she have looked at him? He played the scene over in his head, enjoying these mental ramblings.

On the car radio, Otis Redding was replaced by the Clash, then U2, then Eminem, and the spell was broken. Goodbye to the 1960s and these romantic digressions. Back to reality.

He glanced again at Alice, catching her eye as she rearranged her ponytail.

"Keep your eyes on the road, Keyne."

"I'd like you to explain something to me."

He left the phrase hanging. She held his gaze.

"How can you be so sure that the fingerprints on the syringe aren't Vaughn's?"

She shrugged, visibly irritated. "It's an assumption, not a certainty."

"Don't bullshit me. In spite of all the evidence, you haven't believed for a moment that Erik Vaughn is in the U.S. I've interrogated enough suspects to know when someone is lying to me."

She defended herself half-heartedly: "What gives you the right to—"

"Let me remind you that I am the only cop with the authority to investigate this case!" he interrupted, raising his voice. "I've been aboveboard with you. I gave you all my information, even though I didn't have to."

She sighed.

He went on: "You said you wanted us to work as a team and you asked me to plead your case with my bosses so they'll let you join the investigation. Fine, I agree, even if I'm risking my own credibility. But if we're partners, we have to tell each other everything. Okay?"

She nodded. This was the type of speech she liked.

"So I'm asking you again, Alice: How can you be certain that the prints on the syringe are not Vaughn's?"

She massaged her temples and took a deep breath, then confessed.

"Because Vaughn is dead, Keyne. He's been dead a long time."

I remember...

Less than two years ago

I remember.

December 5, 2011.

The pale brightness of a hospital room.

A low winter sun, its light barely leaking between the blinds.

The foul smell of antiseptics and microwaved meals.

Wanting to die.

Two weeks have passed since I was attacked by Erik Vaughn, two weeks since Paul's death. I am lying on my back in bed, staring into space. There's an antibiotic drip attached to my forearm. Despite all the painkillers I'm being given, the slightest movement cuts into my abdomen. Despite all the antidepressants and antianxiety drugs I'm taking, the slightest thought rips open my heart.

By the time the paramedics got me to the hospital, I had lost a lot of blood. They did an ultrasound that confirmed that the baby was dead. The knife blade had perforated the wall of my uterus, severed an artery, and damaged my small intestine.

I had never needed Paul by my side more than I did at that moment. I needed to feel his presence, to mourn our baby together, united in our pain, and to ask his forgiveness. *Forgive me, forgive me . . .*

Just before they took me into the operating room, they told me he was dead. Just before they opened up my abdomen to remove my murdered baby. The last ties holding me to life were broken. I screamed with rage and despair, hitting out at the doctors who tried to calm me, before I sank under the waves of anesthesia.

Later, when the operation was over, some bastard of a doctor told me that I had been "lucky in a way." My pregnancy meant that the fetus occupied so much space that my organs were pushed toward the back. So my baby took the full brunt of the knife wounds that otherwise would probably have killed me. My baby saved my life.

This idea is unbearable to me.

My internal wounds were sutured and part of my intestine removed. They told me that they had managed to save my uterus, meaning I could get pregnant again in the future.

As if, after all this, I might ever have another love, another pregnancy, another baby.

My mother came on the train to visit me but stayed only twenty minutes. My brother left a message on my voice mail. My sister just sent me a text. Thankfully, Seymour drops by twice a day and does all he can to console and encourage me. The other guys from the division come too, but in their silences I can sense their disappointment, their anger—not only did I double-cross them, but I screwed up one of the department's biggest investigations in years.

I see it in their eyes as they stand at the foot of this bed: the bitterness, the reproach. I know what they're all thinking— that it's my fault Erik Vaughn is still at large. However horrible the things that happened to me, I have no one to blame but myself.

The pills I am given leave me in a haze of half-consciousness. Anesthetizing my brain, numbing my heart—this is the only way the doctors have found to keep me from slitting my wrists or jumping out the window.

Despite my wooziness, I hear the shrill creak of the door as it opens to reveal the heavy figure of my father. I turn to watch as he moves slowly toward my bed. Alain Schafer in all his splendor: salt-and-pepper mane, drawn features, three-day beard. He's dressed in the same cop "uniform" he always wears—leather coat with a fur lining, turtleneck sweater, worn jeans, square-toed boots. On his wrist is an old steel Rolex Daytona just like the one Belmondo wore in *Fear Over the City*—a gift from my mother the year before I was born.

"How are you doing, champ?" he asks, dragging over a chair to sit next to me.

Champ. His old childhood nickname for me. He hasn't called me that in twenty-five years. A memory emerges of him taking me to tennis tournaments on the weekends when I was a kid. It's true that we won plenty of trophies together— me on the court and him in the stands. He always knew what to say and when to say it. Always knew how to encourage me with his eyes. The love of victory, at any price.

My father comes to see me every day. Most often in the evenings; he stays with me until I fall asleep. He's the only one who understands me, who doesn't judge me. The only one who defends me, because in all likelihood he would have acted the same way. An adrenaline junkie, he too would have risked everything; he too would have gone alone, gun raised, head down.

"I went to see your mother at the hotel," he says now, opening a leather case. "She gave me something I've been asking her about for years."

He hands me a photo album bound in faded cloth. I struggle to sit up, switch on the lamp above my bed, and turn the pages separated by glassine paper.

The album is from 1975, the year I was born. Pictures are stuck to the thick cardboard pages with captions written in faded ballpoint below each one.

The first photos are from the spring of that year. I see my mother, six months pregnant. I'd forgotten how much I look like her. Forgotten, too, how much my parents loved each other back then. As I flip through the album, a whole era comes to life through these yellowed photographs. I see the little studio apartment they shared on Rue Delambre in Montparnasse. The psychedelic orange wallpaper in the living area; the egg-shaped chair; the cube shelves filled with vinyl albums by Dylan, Hendrix, and Brassens; a Bakelite telephone; a poster of the Saint-Etienne soccer club at the height of its glory.

In every single picture, my parents are smiling and obviously thrilled at the prospect of becoming parents. They kept everything related to the big event, including the blood-test result that had announced my mother's pregnancy, the first ultrasound, ideas for names scrawled in a spiral-bound notebook: Emma or Alice for a girl, Julien or Alexandre for a boy.

I turn the page and my throat constricts with emotion. The maternity ward on the day of my birth. A newborn baby screaming in her father's arms. Beneath this picture, I recognize my mother's handwriting: *July 12, 1975: Our little Alice is here! And she's just as sensible as her mom and dad!*

Stuck to the opposite page is my hospital ID bracelet and another photograph taken a few hours later. This time, "little Alice" is sleeping peacefully in her crib, watched over by her parents, who have dark bags under their gleaming, euphoric eyes. And, again, my mother's handwriting: *We are starting a new life, full of new feelings. We are now parents.*

Bitter tears roll down my cheeks at the description of these feelings, which I will never experience.

"Why the hell are you showing me this?" I say, pushing the album away.

Then I notice that my father is wet-eyed too.

"After your mother gave birth to you, I was the one who gave you your first bath and your first bottle," he tells me. "Never in my life have I felt as moved as I was then. That day, when I took you in my arms, I made you a promise."

His voice is cracking with emotion and he pauses for a few seconds.

"What promise?" I ask.

"I promised you that, as long as you lived, I would never let anyone hurt you. That whatever happened, whatever the consequences, I would always protect you."

I swallow. "But you should never make promises like that, because it's impossible to keep them."

He sighs and rubs his eyes to wipe away the tears he can't hold back. Then he takes a manila folder from his briefcase.

"I did what I could. I did what I had to do," he says, handing me the folder.

Before opening it, I look at him questioningly.

That's when he tells me: "I found him, Alice."

"Found who?"

"Erik Vaughn."

I am speechless. Dumbfounded. My brain cannot process what I have just heard. I ask him to repeat it.

"I found Erik Vaughn. He will never hurt you again."

I am paralyzed by an icy wave. For a few seconds, we stare at each other in silence.

"That's impossible!" I say finally. "Half the cops in France have been searching for him since he went on the run. How the hell did you manage to find him on your own?"

"Doesn't matter. All that matters is I did it."

I become irritated. "But you were fired. You're not a cop anymore. You don't have a team or—"

"I still have my contacts," he says, his eyes never leaving mine. "Guys who owe me favors. People who know people who know people. You know how it works."

"Actually, I don't."

"I have snitches who are taxi drivers. One of them had Erik Vaughn in his cab near Porte de Saint-Cloud on the evening you were attacked. He left his phone when he realized he'd been identified."

I feel as if my heart is about to explode. My father continues.

"The taxi took him to Seine-Saint-Denis, in Aulnay-sous-Bois, to a crappy hotel near Place du Général-Leclerc."

He takes the folder from me and pulls a few photographs from it, the kind of pictures cops take when they are on a stakeout.

"While everyone thought he'd gone overseas, this piece of shit was hiding less than twenty minutes from Paris. He stayed there for five days under an assumed name using a fake ID. He didn't go out much, but he needed a fake passport. On the fifth day, around eleven p.m., he came outside. He was alone. He stayed close to the walls, head down. That was when I got him."

"Just like that, in the street?"

"That place is deserted at night. I hit him twice with a crowbar on his head and neck. He was already dead when I loaded him in the trunk of my Range Rover."

I try to swallow, but my throat is too tight. I grip the metal security bar at the edge of my bed. "What did you do with the body?"

"I drove most of the night toward Lorraine. I'd spotted the perfect place to dump this monster, an abandoned sugar factory between Sarrebourg and Sarreguemines."

He hands me other pictures. The place looks like something from a horror movie: a series of derelict buildings hidden behind chain-link fences out in the middle of nowhere. Boarded-up windows. Redbrick chimneys that look like they're about to collapse. Huge metal crates half buried in the ground. Busted conveyor belts. Carts on rails overgrown with weeds. Rusted old backhoes.

He points to one of the pictures. "Behind the storage area, there are three stone wells, built side by side, that lead down to an underground tank. Vaughn's corpse is rotting in the middle one. No one will ever find him there." He shows me the last photo—the edge of a well covered by a heavy metal grate.

"This vengeance is ours," my father says, hugging me. "The case will fade away now, partly because there won't be any more murders. And anyway, Vaughn has family in Ireland and the States, so everyone will think he's gone overseas or that he's committed suicide."

I hold his gaze, unblinking. I am paralyzed, unable to say a single word, filled with violent and contradictory feelings.

After the first wave of relief comes a sort of blind rage. I ball my fists, digging my nails into the flesh of my hands. My whole body contracts. Tears rush to my eyes and I feel my cheeks go hot.

Why did my father deprive me of this vengeance? Of *my* vengeance?

After the death of my husband and my baby, finding and killing Erik Vaughn was the only reason I had to stay alive.

Now I have nothing at all.

Part Three

BLOOD AND FURY

16

TRACKING THE KILLER

THE MILES RUSHED past.

Lost in his thoughts, chain-smoking, Gabriel drove with his eyes fixed on the road.

A road sign announced NEXT EXIT HARTFORD, then immediately afterward, there was another: BOSTON 105 MILES. At this speed, they would be at the FBI office in less than two hours.

Leaning her forehead against the window, Alice tried to put her thoughts in some kind of order. In light of recent revelations, she categorized her information, rearranging evidence and facts in imaginary folders in her brain.

One thing bothered her—what Seymour had said about the security camera footage. *The camera picked up your license plate, but the inside of the car is too dark to see.*

If only she could see those images *herself*...

Always this need to control everything.

To check every detail.

But how could she? Call Seymour back? Pointless. *I went over to Franklin-Roosevelt and looked at their tapes, but you can't see much,* he'd said. Seymour had watched the video, but he didn't have it with him. That was logical. Without a warrant, he wouldn't have been able to seize the tapes. He had gone to the parking garage and had to negotiate with the security guy just to watch them.

In her head, she went through her contacts list. Then she picked up her phone and typed in the number for Captain Maréchal, the regional transportation police chief.

"Hi, Franck, it's Schafer."

"Alice? Where are you? My phone says you're calling from an international number."

"I'm in New York."

"For work?"

"Long story. I'll tell you later."

"Okay, I get it. Working your own personal investigation, as usual. You'll never change!"

"Actually, that's true. And it's also why I'm calling you."

"Alice, it's after ten at night! I'm at home. What do you want?"

"Security-camera footage. The Vinci parking garage on

Avenue Franklin-Roosevelt. I'm trying to find out everything I can about a silver Audi TT—"

"Well, let me stop you there. It's a private garage!"

After a silence, he spoke again: "What do you want me
to do?"

"Do what you do best. You know people at Vinci—
negotiate with them, threaten them, persuade them. Do you
have a pen and paper?"

"I'm not—"

"Remember how I arrested your kid when I was working
for the drug squad? You were pretty happy that he didn't go
to jail, weren't you? Want me to remind you how much shit
he had on him?"

"God, Schafer, that was nearly ten years ago! I'm not going
to owe you for the rest of my life, am I?"

"Of course you are. That's the rule. So, are you ready to
write down the license number?"

Maréchal sighed with resignation.

Alice gave him the information, then said, "As soon as you
have the images, send them to my personal e-mail address,
okay? And be quick; I need them tonight."

Alice hung up, satisfied, and then, in response to
Gabriel's raised eyebrows, summarized the conversation.
The FBI agent wanted another cigarette, but his pack was
empty.

"Still no word from your father?"

Alice shook her head.

"He holds the key to this mystery, though," Gabriel

insisted. "If he was telling you the truth—if he really did kill
Vaughn—then we're after the wrong guy."

"You think I don't know that?"

Gabriel crumpled the empty cigarette pack and threw it
into the ashtray. "I don't see why he would lie to you
about it."

Alice shrugged. "Maybe he wanted to help me move on
after the attack."

He frowned doubtfully. "To the point of inventing that
whole story?"

"You obviously don't know my father."

"Well, no."

She watched the roadside safety barriers as they zoomed
past, a blur of steel and concrete.

"He has his flaws and his virtues," she explained. "He
knows me, so he must have realized I would want to get
revenge by killing Vaughn with my own hands. It's possible
he was trying to stop me from doing something stupid."

"Still, don't you think you should try to call him again?"

"There's no point. If he'd gotten my message, he would
have called me."

"Come on, try one more time, and then I'll stop bugging
you about it." He smiled.

With a sigh, Alice pressed speakerphone and dialed the
number again.

"Alain Schafer. Not here right now. Leave a message."

"It's strange he's not calling you back, isn't it?"

"My father is not the kind of guy who checks his messages

every five minutes. And since he retired, he's become crazy about spelunking. He's probably with his old cop buddies in a cave somewhere."

"So we're shit out of luck," Gabriel muttered.

Alice had barely hung up, though, before her phone rang. She answered it in French: *"Papa, c'est toi?"*

"I'm afraid not. This is Thomas Krieg. Gabriel gave me your number. May I..."

She pressed speakerphone again and handed the phone to Keyne. He took it, looking surprised.

"Hey, Gabe, it's Thomas Krieg. Eliane Pelletier sent me the results of the DNA test you ran on the blood from that blouse. I put it into the CODIS database, and guess what— we have a winner!"

Alice and Gabriel exchanged a look. Both felt their hearts accelerate.

Alice pointed out a road sign to Gabriel.

"Thomas, we're driving, but there's a rest area coming up in a mile. Let me pull off there and I'll call you back," he said.

Grille 91 was in a long, rectangular, and fairly old-fashioned building, roomy and high-ceilinged like many 1970s constructions. It may not have overlooked the Pacific (in fact, it overlooked the parking lot of a rest area on I-91), but its geometric lines and big glass windows were more reminiscent of Californian houses than the gable-roofed Capes of New England.

Emblazoned with the slogan MILES AWAY FROM ORDINARY, the wall clock, decked out in the bright colors of a famous Mexican beer, indicated that it was nearly five p.m. Slanting sunlight poured into the almost empty dining room. Behind the counter, a waitress daydreamed while listening to Stan Getz play saxophone.

Alice and Gabriel sat at a table as far back in the room as possible. Gabriel placed the cell phone in the center of the table and put the call on speaker, and the two of them listened attentively to Thomas Krieg's deep, resonant voice as he told them a strange story.

"The blood on the blouse belongs to a Caleb Dunn, age forty-one, who has a record for minor offenses—he was arrested eight years ago in California for drug-dealing and resisting arrest. He spent six months in prison in Salinas Valley, then he settled down—moved to the East Coast, where he found a job. No further problems until now."

Alice took notes on a paper napkin. Gabriel asked: "What's his job?"

"Security guard in a retirement home in Concord, New Hampshire."

"Retirement homes are hiring ex-cons now?" Gabriel asked, amazed.

"Everyone deserves a second chance, don't you think?"

Alice fiddled with the cap of the ballpoint pen she had borrowed from the waitress.

"Do you have his home address?"

"Yes," Krieg replied. "A place in Lincoln, in the middle

of the White Mountains. What do you want us to do, Gabe?"

"Nothing much right now. Just keep digging at your end. We'll talk again later. We should be in Boston in two hours."

"You need to fill me in. The boss thinks you're still in Ireland."

"Don't tell him anything yet. I'll explain it all when I get there. Actually... do you have a photo of Dunn?"

"I'll text it to you."

"That's not going to work. This phone is prehistoric." Gabriel glanced at the menu, which included the restaurant's address and phone numbers. "Can you fax it?"

"Seriously? Do people still use those things?"

"Apparently. I'm at Grille 91, just off the interstate. Not far from Hartford. I'll give you the number. Send me the picture and include the phone number and address of the retirement home and Dunn's home address."

Gabriel read out the fax number and then hung up. He and Alice looked at each other in silence. Their investigation was going nowhere. Too many leads. Too many questions. Not enough to connect all these apparently unrelated elements. Gabriel broke the silence.

"Fuck! None of this makes any sense! What was that security guard's blood doing on your blouse?"

"You think I shot him?"

"We can't rule it out. You told me yourself that there was a bullet missing from the Glock's magazine."

Alice scowled at him. "And what would my motive be, exactly? I've never even heard of that guy!"

He raised his hands in a calming gesture. "Okay, you're right. I have no idea."

He cracked his knuckles, then announced he was going to buy cigarettes from the gas station. "Do you want anything?"

She shook her head and watched him walk away.

Again, Alice felt a burning sensation in the pit of her stomach that rose up to the base of her throat. She stood and walked over to the counter to warn the waitress that a fax would be arriving for them.

"Are you feeling okay, ma'am?"

"Yes, it's just heartburn. I'll be fine."

"Oh, my mom gets that! I could make you a papaya smoothie? It works real well!"

The waitress was a little blond Barbie doll with a slight lisp. In her cheerleader outfit, she looked as if she'd just stepped out of the movie *Grease* or an episode of *Glee*.

"Okay, that sounds good—thank you." Alice sat on a bar stool. "You don't happen to have a map of the area, do you?"

"We might. I'll go look in the office."

"Thanks."

Less than two minutes later, Barbie returned with a map of New England. Alice unfolded it on the counter. It was a good old-fashioned AAA map from before the age of GPS, smartphones, and the Internet, before this crazy time when people had become slaves to technology.

"Do you mind if I write on it?"

"It's yours. On the house. And here's your smoothie."

Alice thanked her with a smile. She liked this girl—kind, easygoing, sweet. How old was she? Eighteen? Nineteen at most. Alice was thirty-eight. The sentence formed inside her mind, irrefutable: *I'm old enough to be her mother.* An observation she made more and more often these days when encountering young people. She found herself in a no-man's-land—feeling twenty years old in her head but being almost twice that age in her body.

Damn the passing of time. Master of those who have no master, as the Arab proverb says.

She pushed away these thoughts and concentrated on the map. She had always needed to visualize things in order to orient herself. With the ballpoint pen, she circled various places. First New York, which they had left two hours earlier, then Boston, where they were heading. They were currently close to Hartford, Connecticut, midway between the two big cities. Another ink circle—Krieg had told them that Dunn worked in a retirement home in Concord, New Hampshire. That was much farther north, at least 150 miles away. Krieg had also stated that Dunn lived in Lincoln. It took Alice almost a minute to locate it on the map. It was a little village stuck in the middle of a mountain range.

"Do you know this place?" she asked her new friend.

"Yeah, there's a ski resort near there, Loon Mountain. I've been there with my boyfriend."

"What's it like?"

"Kind of boring. And it's not exactly next door."

The cop nodded. It was so hot in the restaurant that she took off her sweater and sat there in a T-shirt.

Gabriel returned, cigarette pack in hand, and sat on the stool next to Alice's.

"Can I get you a drink, sir?"

"Do you have any espresso?"

"Sorry, we don't."

"Maybe a Perrier?"

"We don't have that either."

Alice became annoyed. "Stop being so picky, Keyne!"

"Okay, just give me a regular coffee."

While the waitress poured the coffee, Gabriel looked her up and down, lingering shamelessly on the fleshiest part of her anatomy.

"Have a good look, why don't you?" Alice whispered.

He rolled his eyes.

"You're such a typical *guy*." She sighed.

"I never claimed otherwise," he said, taking a cigarette from his pack and tucking it behind his ear.

Alice had her reply in mind, but she never got a chance to deliver it.

"I think your fax just came through," Barbie trilled. She slipped into the office for a few seconds and then returned to the counter, holding two printed pages that she had stapled together.

Gabriel and Alice examined Caleb Dunn's mug shot.

"Well, it's better than nothing, I guess," Alice said, disappointed.

The photograph was a grainy black-and-white image that did not reveal much. Dunn looked like Joe Average: dark-haired, medium height, no distinguishing features, ordinary in every respect.

"Just barely," Gabriel agreed. "It could be anyone."

Overcoming his disappointment, he turned the page and saw that Thomas Krieg had written the address of Dunn's house and the address and phone number of the retirement home.

"Doesn't that strike you as weird?" he asked. "A retirement home employing an ex-con?"

Alice didn't reply. She was still staring at the mug shot, attempting to figure out the mysterious Dunn.

Gabriel took a sip of his coffee and made a grimace of disgust. "Can I borrow your phone? I need to check something."

He called the retirement home where Dunn worked. He identified himself to the receptionist—"Special Agent Keyne, FBI"—and asked to speak to the manager. As had become their habit, he pressed speakerphone so Alice could listen in on the conversation.

"Julius Mason. How can I help you?"

Gabriel said it was a routine inquiry and asked for information about Dunn.

"I hope nothing has happened to Caleb," Mason said, sounding worried.

"Did he turn up today?"

The manager almost choked. "What do you mean? Caleb Dunn hasn't worked for us in almost two years!"

"Really? Sorry, I wasn't aware of that."

Gabriel struggled to sound unfazed. Alice couldn't help smiling. So, even the FBI couldn't manage to keep its files updated. The slowness of bureaucracy was not solely a French phenomenon.

Embarrassed, Gabriel hardened his voice and began interrogating the manager.

"Did you know that Dunn had a criminal record when you hired him?"

"Criminal record? Come on, all he did was sell a few ounces of pot and yell at the cop who arrested him. So what? He hardly merited a prison sentence."

"That's one way of looking at it."

"That's right—*my* way."

Alice smiled again. This guy was not easy to interrogate.

"When Dunn worked for you, did he ever behave in a strange or inappropriate way? Anything strike you as unusual?"

"Not at all. Caleb was always very professional, very helpful. Our staff and our residents all spoke very highly of him."

"So why is he no longer working for you?"

Mason sighed. "The board of directors wanted to reduce costs. To save a few dollars, we now use an external security firm. It costs less, but it's much more impersonal."

"Do you know if he found other employment?"

"Of course, and very quickly. I recommended him myself to a hospital in Maine that needed a reliable security guard."

"Do you know the name of that hospital?"

"So you can update your damned files and continue harassing honest citizens?"

"Mr. Mason, please."

"Sebago Hospital. In Cumberland County."

Gabriel and Alice exchanged an astounded look. The same tension electrified their bodies. Sebago Hospital was where Elizabeth Hardy had worked—the nurse found murdered at her home ten days earlier.

Cops from their heads to their toes.

Cops to their bones.

Cops to the very cores of their beings.

They didn't have to discuss it for long to come to their conclusion. Why waste time in Boston? They would work as partners and strike out on their own, driving north to Lincoln to question Caleb Dunn themselves.

"I must have missed this guy in my investigation," Gabriel admitted. "Elizabeth Hardy was killed in her house near Augusta. She had deactivated the alarm system, which led us to think she knew her attacker. I interrogated lots of people who knew her: friends, work colleagues. I even went to Sebago Hospital, but this guy's name never came up. He wasn't a close friend of hers, I'm sure of that."

"How long will it take us to get there?"

He examined the map, tracing the journey to Lincoln

with his finger. "I would say three and a half hours. Less if we don't stick to the speed limit."

"That long, really?"

"As far as Haverhill, we can stay on the interstate, but after that we'll have to go into the mountains. This is not a bad car, but it's pretty old. The oil level worries me, and I happened to notice that the spare tire is flat. We should really stop at a garage before we go any farther."

Barbie, who had been hanging on their every word, exclaimed, "My cousin has a garage! I can call him for you!"

Gabriel raised an eyebrow. "Where is he?"

"In Greenfield, Massachusetts," she said, pointing out the little town on the map.

He looked at where her finger lay. It was less than an hour away. "You think he'll know how to take care of an old Mustang?"

"Why don't you just call him and find out?" Alice suggested.

The cop nodded and Barbie went to get her phone.

Alice shot her a wink but felt another burning in her throat, stronger than before, as if acid were eating away at the lining of her stomach.

When she got the telltale metallic taste in her mouth, she leaped off her stool and ran to the bathroom.

My kingdom for a Nexium!

Retching, Alice leaned over the toilet bowl. Her throat was on fire. She tried rubbing her stomach, but it didn't help to calm the burning. Why was the pain so intense? Stress? The excitement of the investigation? Fatigue?

She continued to massage her belly for over a minute, then stood up and washed her hands. She did not look in the mirror; she had no desire to see herself reflected, with the rings under her eyes and the drawn features. She splashed cold water on her face and stood there for a moment. Why had she woken up this morning with her blouse stained with Caleb Dunn's blood? And who was he? A disciple of Vaughn's, using the same MO to murder that nurse?

Or Vaughn himself?

No—she refused to imagine this possibility. Her father had no shortage of flaws, but she didn't want to believe that he would lie to her to such an extent. It was too messed up. Too dangerous. The best cops in France had been relentlessly tracking Vaughn for the past two years, without success.

That in itself is proof that the serial killer is dead, she told herself.

As Seymour would soon assure her, Vaughn's corpse was moldering at the bottom of a well in a scary-looking abandoned factory in a godforsaken hole in eastern France.

Water had trickled down to her chest. She grabbed two paper towels and wiped her neck and the tops of her breasts. Embarrassed, she lowered her eyes.

And that was when she saw it.

A foreign body implanted under her skin, about two inches below her collarbone. Alice pressed down hard on the flesh to make the object stand out.

It was the size and shape of a large SIM card: a rectangle half an inch square. She could see its edges quite clearly when she pulled at her skin.

Her pulse sped up and beat loudly in her temples.

Oh, fuck, who could have done this?

Instinctively, she looked for traces of a recent operation. Standing in front of the mirror, she took off her T-shirt and examined her chest, throat, armpits.

No sign of any recent incision. Not even the tiniest wound was visible.

Sweat ran down her forehead. A hundred questions swarmed in her brain, but two emerged most urgently from the confusion:

How long had she had this thing under her skin?

And what did it do?

17

THE DEVIL'S TRICKS

THE MUSTANG LEFT the interstate, entered a traffic circle, and took the first exit.

Greenfield, on the border of Massachusetts and New Hampshire, was a small town that seemed frozen in time. The town hall, the post office, the courthouse, and the large white church with its pointed steeple were all clustered within a mile along Main Street. Also on this stretch of road were the public library, a bunch of restaurants, little stores, and an old movie theater, its sign blazing with dozens of electric bulbs. Over each building hung the Stars and Stripes, flying proudly in the wind, colored by the late afternoon sunlight.

"Let me out here," Alice said, adjusting the strap of her holster.

"Here? But Barbie said her cousin's garage is at the other end of town."

"I need to do something, Keyne."

He sighed. "I thought we'd stopped being secretive."

"I don't want to just sit there twiddling my thumbs while they repair the car! I'm going to a café with Wi-Fi. There's something I need to check."

"What?" he said, suspicious.

"I want to look at some old newspaper articles about Vaughn. I'll explain later."

The car stopped at a red light. Gabriel took out his pack of cigarettes. "There won't be a café in this hole."

"I'll find one, Keyne."

He thought for a few seconds. "Okay, I'll drop you off here, but leave your gun in the car."

Alice was not thrilled with this idea, but she didn't have time to go into endless discussions about it. The light turned green. She opened the glove compartment and put the holstered Glock inside it.

"I'll see you at the garage," she said, opening the door.

She crossed the road and walked up the sidewalk to the town hall. In front of the building, she saw a town map displayed under a wooden canopy. She looked at it and found what she needed: the address of a medical center on Second Street.

The advantage of small towns like this was that everything

was bunched close together. Alice had to walk only a couple hundred yards to reach a brand-new building with a resolutely modern façade: a vertical metallic-blue wave that stood out like a sore thumb amid the town's old-fashioned architecture.

The sliding doors opened and she entered the lobby of the medical building. She went to the front desk and told the receptionist she wanted a chest X-ray. She was asked for a photo ID and her insurance card. As she had neither of these, she spoke the first lie that came to mind: she said she was a French tourist with lung problems and she wanted to see a doctor and get an X-ray. The receptionist looked skeptical.

"It's quite important," Alice insisted. "I would like to see the physician so I can explain my problem. I would pay all the costs, of course."

"Let me find out," the receptionist said, picking up the phone.

She spoke to someone for about two minutes, then hung up and told Alice, "Dr. Mitchell in the urgent-care clinic will see you. Could you show me some ID, please?"

"Oh, I'm sorry, I left my purse in the car. But my husband is on his way here and—"

"All right, you can go up. The clinic is on the fifth floor." She pressed a button that opened a Plexiglas security barrier, allowing Alice access to the elevator.

Fifth floor. Another reception desk. A waiting room decorated in soft, bright colors with white walls, PVC flooring, cushioned wooden benches and chairs. An old lady, sagging under the weight of her years, was turning the pages of a celebrity magazine. Opposite her, a burly young man with his leg in a cast and a swollen black eye was playing on his iPad and taking up almost the entire couch.

Alice sat next to him and started a conversation. "Car accident?"

"Football," he replied, looking up from the screen. "I got taken down by the guys from Albany this weekend."

Handsome face, cocky Ultrabrite smile, shining eyes. The girls must go nuts over him, Alice thought. And some boys, for that matter.

"Is there a Wi-Fi connection here?"

"Uh-huh."

Alice didn't beat around the bush. "How would you like to earn a quick fifty bucks?"

He raised an eyebrow. "I'm listening."

She took a fifty-dollar bill from her pocket. "Lend me your iPad for five minutes, and this is yours."

"I'll do it for a hundred."

"Go fuck yourself."

"Okay, okay, don't get mad!" he said, handing her his tablet.

Alice opened a web browser and connected to the sites of France's three main newspapers: *Libération, Le Monde,* and *Le Figaro.* Strange as it might seem, Alice had never seen Vaughn's face. He had been wearing a helmet when he attacked her, and whenever she thought of him, that was the image that came to mind: a predator's black helmet, with sharp lines and bright edges; a metallic mirrored visor; a mouth vent and an aerodynamic chin bar, like a terrifying smile.

Later, during therapy, Alice had agreed with the psychiatrist that it was counterproductive to keep twisting the knife in her mental wounds by compulsively reading news articles about the case. But what the shrink didn't know was that by then, Alice was convinced that Vaughn was dead.

That was no longer the case.

She found several photographs of the killer published in the weeks after her attack, a dozen different pictures in which Erik Vaughn appeared more or less distinctly. A man in his mid-thirties, dark-haired, reasonably good-looking without being unusual in any way.

What disturbed her was the difficulty she had in establishing a definitive portrait of Vaughn based on the different images. Alice thought of those chameleonic actors who seemed to metamorphose from one film to the next: Hugh Jackman, Christian Bale, John Cusack...

She took the fax of Caleb Dunn's mug shot from her pocket and compared it to the other photos. Were Vaughn and Dunn the same person? It didn't immediately strike her that way, but it could not be ruled out.

Alice knew that, with modern plastic-surgery techniques, it was possible to modify a human face in an almost infinite variety of ways. Some of her colleagues had recently dealt with criminals who had been physically transformed in the operating room with rhinoplasty, the insertion of barbed threads under the skin to redraw the shape of the face,

otoplasty to correct ear deformations, injections of hyal-
uronic acid to emphasize the cheekbones, dental surgery to
create a whole new smile.

She was handing the iPad back to its owner when she felt
her phone vibrate in her pocket.

Seymour.

The man who could bring her nightmare to an end.

"Are you at the factory yet?" she asked, skipping the usual
niceties.

"Not yet. I've only just left Sarreguemines. The traffic
in Paris was hell, and it took Castelli a while to locate
the place."

"Where is it?"

"It's supposed to be on Kastelsheim Street. I entered the
address into my GPS, but nothing came up. Don't worry,
I'll find it eventually. The problem is this goddamn rain. It's
pouring, so I can only see about ten feet in front of me."

Alice could hear the windshield wipers beating frantically
in the background.

"I'm calling you about something else," Seymour said. "I
had to bring Savignon and Castelli into the loop. I can't ask
them to do extra work without telling them why. They're
spending the night in the office, working every angle they
can find."

"Thank them for me, will you?"

"Savignon just called me about the serial number of the
Glock you gave me this morning."

She swallowed. She had completely forgotten about that lead. "Yeah, the gun I found in my jacket. So?"

"I tried the stolen-weapons list first, but it wasn't on there. But when I mentioned Vaughn to Savignon, he had an idea right away. Two years ago, after Vaughn attacked you, we searched his apartment—and found a weapon."

"And?"

"Savignon checked the paperwork—it was a Glock with the same serial number."

"What? That's impossible. That gun was held as evidence."

"Savignon spent an hour in the evidence room. The gun is nowhere to be seen."

Fuck.

The nightmare was not over.

"Tell me the truth, Alice: Did you take that gun?"

"Seymour! How can you even ask me that?"

"Because we're really in the shit here."

"Well, this isn't the first time we've had problems with the evidence room. Remember a year ago, when we found out that security guard who worked there was selling guns and drugs? Maybe it was him."

"Hmm, I guess."

"And even if I had stolen that gun, how could I have brought it into the States? I'd never have gotten it through security."

She heard her colleague sigh.

"I want to believe you, Alice, but we really need to clear this up."

She sensed there was something he wasn't telling her. "What else do you have?"

"You won't like it. It's about your car."

"You found it?"

"Yep. At the impound lot in Charléty. Savignon checked; the police prefecture officers towed it last night from Île de la Cité."

"From where, exactly?"

Seymour took a deep breath. "Your Audi was found at four in the morning in the middle of the Pont de l'Archevêché. Right where Paul had his accident."

Alice was so shocked that she almost dropped her phone. At that moment, the waiting-room door opened and a white-coated giant poked his head out.

"Ms. Alice Schafer?" he called out.

18

SUCKER PUNCH

D R. OLIVER MITCHELL was a big man with a shaved head and thick M-shaped eyebrows that met above the bridge of his nose. Despite his impressive height and lack of hair, he looked like he was barely out of college; he had a round, chubby face lit up by a childlike smile and he wore sneakers. A Ramones T-shirt was visible under his coat.

"Sorry, I didn't quite understand this thing about your lung problems," he said when he entered the examining room.

Alice decided to be honest. "That was a lie. I just needed to see a doctor."

"Oh, really? Well, that's original…and kind of ballsy. You're French, right?" he guessed, recognizing her accent.

"Yes, I'm captain of the Criminal Division of the Paris police."

His expression brightened. "Seriously? At thirty-six Quai des Orfèvres? Like Jules Maigret?"

Alice's eyes widened. This was unexpected; what were the odds that a punk-rock urgent-care physician in Greenfield, Massachusetts, would be a Simenon fan?

"My wife is doing a PhD in French literature at Harvard," he explained. "Her dissertation is about Paris in the novels of Georges Simenon."

"Ah, well, that explains it."

"We went there last summer. Man, I love Paris. The Quai des Orfèvres, Place Dauphine, duck confit with sautéed potatoes at the Caveau du Palais..."

Pinch me, I've got to be dreaming!

Alice decided to take advantage of the situation. "If your wife would like, I could give you both a tour of the precinct next time you're in France."

"Wow, that's very kind. She—"

"But first, I need your help," she said, taking off her army jacket and her sweater. She pulled down the neck of her T-shirt and pointed to the rectangular implant under her skin.

"What is that?" he asked, frowning.

"That's exactly what I'm trying to find out."

He washed his hands with antibacterial soap and examined the upper part of Alice's chest, pressing on the skin so he could make out the little rectangle. "Does this hurt?"

"Not really."

"It looks like some sort of miniature pacemaker. Do you have heart problems?"

"No. I don't even know who implanted this thing or how long it's been there."

Unfazed, the doctor said, "Let's take a chest X-ray so we can get a better look."

Alice nodded. Mitchell gave her a paper gown and left the room; she removed her T-shirt and bra and put the gown on. Two minutes later he came back and brought her to the X-ray room. An X-ray tech told her where to stand. Alice did as she was told.

"Take a deep breath and hold it," the tech said. "Okay..."

She heard a click.

"Now breathe normally. We're going to get another view."

The process was repeated, then Dr. Mitchell asked Alice to follow him into an adjoining room. Mitchell sat down behind a bank of monitors, pulled up the images on the screens, and made a few adjustments. "Well, that's something I've never seen before!" he exclaimed, pointing at a white rectangle.

"Is it a microchip?" Alice asked.

"I can't imagine what kind it would be," he replied, scratching his head.

"I was thinking an RFID chip," said Alice. "You know, radio-frequency identification—the kind they use on pets. I went to a conference about this last year, for work. Apparently in South America, some rich people get them implanted so they can be found quickly if they're kidnapped."

"The army uses them more and more with soldiers sent into combat." Mitchell nodded, still staring at the X-ray. "The chip stores all their medical information. If something happens to them, the doctors have immediate access to their medical files with a quick scan. That type of procedure is becoming more common, but those chips are much smaller, no bigger than a grain of rice. Yours is pretty big."

"So what could it be?"

The physician frowned in concentration. "I've seen quite a few articles in medical magazines in recent years about researchers developing electronic chips that can deliver regular doses of medicine. It'd be a convenient way to treat certain conditions. It's already used in medication for osteoporosis, for instance, but in that case the chip would be in your abdomen, and it would also be much bigger."

"So?"

"I still think it looks like a pacemaker."

"But I told you, I don't have any heart problems!"

The doctor returned to his monitor and zoomed in on the chip.

"The shape of your implant is nonstandard, but I'm pretty sure it's made of titanium," he said.

Alice moved her face closer to the screen. "All right, assuming it is a pacemaker...I have a colleague with one, and he needs surgery every seven years to have the battery changed."

"Yeah, that sounds about right. Generally, the operation

takes place every six to ten years. And most pacemakers have lithium batteries."

Alice gestured at the image. "How could there be batteries in such a small device?"

Looking pensive, Dr. Mitchell said, "I imagine yours doesn't have a battery."

"Then how would it work?"

"Maybe some kind of self-generating system. A piezo-electric sensor that would transform the movements of your rib cage into electricity. That's one of the methods they're currently working on to reduce the size of pace-makers."

He took a plastic ruler from the console and used it as a pointer. "You see this slightly rounded part that looks like a notch?"

Alice nodded.

"I think it's a connector that links the pacemaker to your heart via a catheter."

"So where's the catheter?"

"Nowhere. That's exactly why it's strange."

"So what is the pacemaker connected to?"

"Nothing," the doctor admitted. "The way it's currently configured, it can't send electrical impulses."

Doubtfully, Alice asked: "Could you remove it?"

"One of my colleagues might be able to, but it would require an operation and more tests."

Alice's brain was working at a hundred miles an hour. "One last thing. I checked, and I don't have any wounds at all on my chest, neck, or armpits. How could it have been implanted without leaving any trace?"

Mitchell bit his lip. "Either you've had it for a long time . . ."

"Impossible. I would have noticed."

"Or it was implanted via another opening."

To the doctor's amazement, Alice unbuckled her belt, removed her ankle boots, and pulled off her pants. She examined her ankles, her legs, knees. At the top of her thigh, she noticed a transparent Band-Aid, and her heart began to pound again. She peeled it off and found a small incision.

"Yeah, my guess is that's where it was introduced," the doctor said, looking closely at the wound. "The implant is so small that they could have placed it using a catheter."

Perplexed, Alice put her clothes back on. This investigation had moved beyond the realm of the baffling, frightening, and surreal and was now becoming completely insane.

"So, to sum up," she said, "I have a pacemaker with no battery and no catheter that is not connected to any of my organs?"

"It makes no sense, I agree," Mitchell said, "but yeah."

"Then what does it do?"

"That's exactly what I'm wondering."

19

IN THE LAND OF
THE LIVING

NIGHT FELL SLOWLY.

The final rays of the setting sun blazed like a fireworks display. The forest was incandescent. In the foreground, the maples, ashes, and birches were a whirlwind of bright flames, the larches all gold and the lindens pure fire. Then the golden-brown glow of the beeches, the black blood of the sumacs and red oaks, the crimson embers of the rowan trees. And, farther off, a high green wall of pines was overhung by the angular, mineral mass of mountains.

In Greenfield, Gabriel had filled the car with gas, added oil, and found a new spare tire. When Alice met him at the garage, she told him the latest news from Seymour about the origin of the Glock and where her Audi had been found. Instinctively, she decided not to tell him about the foreign body she had discovered under her skin. She wanted to know more about it before she shared this unlikely piece of information.

They began driving again, but on I-91 near Brattleboro, a fuel tanker had overturned and gas had spread everywhere, so emergency services had closed that part of the interstate.

Forced off the highway and onto minor roads, Gabriel had to drive more slowly. At first, Alice and Gabriel had cursed their bad luck, but gradually they let themselves be lulled by the peacefulness of the land they were driving through. They listened to a local radio station that played rock standards— "American Pie" by Don McLean, "Me and Bobby McGee" by Janis Joplin, "Heart of Gold" by Neil Young—and they even bought cider and cinnamon doughnuts from a road-side stand.

For nearly an hour, their investigation was put on a back burner.

The landscape was picturesque, punctuated by footpaths, covered bridges, spectacular views, and mountain streams. Mostly full of rolling hills, the area became flatter for several miles and they found themselves on a country road passing through a succession of pretty villages, timeless farms, and wide-open fields where cows grazed.

For a while, Alice was calmed by the purr of the engine. The region reminded her of family vacations in Normandy when she was young. Time seemed to have stopped here.

Whenever they drove through a village, they felt as if they had gone back a hundred years. It was like living in a New England postcard of old barns with pitched roofs and trees with flame-colored leaves.

The spell was abruptly broken when Alice opened the glove compartment to get her gun. When she had first joined the police, she used to make fun of her older colleagues who carried their weapons even when they weren't on duty. But as time passed, she became just like them—she needed the weight of the gun against her ribs in order to feel at ease, to feel like herself.

The pistol was where she had left it, strapped inside its leather holster, but next to it, she found a child's toy, a metal car painted white with blue racing stripes—an exact replica of the Mustang Shelby they were driving at that moment.

"What's this?"

Gabriel glanced at the toy. "Just one of Kenny's little gadgets, I assume."

"It wasn't here earlier."

Gabriel shrugged. "Maybe you didn't look properly."

"I'm sure that the glove compartment was empty when I put my gun in it," Alice barked.

"Does it matter?" Gabriel scowled.

"I thought we were being honest with each other."

He sighed. "Okay. Barbie's cousin gave it to me. Very nice guy, actually. He collects Hot Wheels. He must have at least three hundred of them. Unbelievable, isn't it?"

"You're right. It is unbelievable," she repeated, staring into his eyes.

Exasperated, he raised his voice: "What? Look, the guy was just being nice. He offered me this toy and I took it to be polite. That's all. Do we really have to spend the whole evening discussing it?"

Alice exploded. "Stop treating me like an imbecile! Are you seriously trying to convince me that this guy and you became so friendly that he gave you a car from his collection? And anyway, the price tag is still on the box."

Gabriel gave her a hostile stare before lighting the cigarette that he had tucked behind his ear. He took a few drags. The odor of tobacco filled the car, and Alice lowered her window to get rid of the smoke. She kept staring hard at her partner, scrutinizing his dark eyes, his angry expression, hoping to pierce his secretiveness and guess at some hidden truth.

And suddenly, it came to her: "You have a son," she murmured, as if talking to herself.

He froze. There was silence.

She went on. "You bought the toy for him."

He turned toward her. His black eyes gleamed like oil. Alice realized she had touched a nerve.

"Yes," he admitted, taking a drag on his cigarette, "I have a little boy. I just wanted to get him a gift. Is that okay with you?"

Embarrassed, Alice wasn't sure she wanted to continue this conversation. But she did anyway, asking in a soft voice: "What's his name?"

Gabriel turned up the volume on the radio and shook his head. He had not expected this untimely intrusion into his privacy.

"I think we have more important problems to deal with, Schafer."

His expression grew sad. He blinked several times and finally said: "His name is Theo. He's six."

From his intonation, Alice realized that this was a painful subject.

Moved, she turned down the music and made a peace offering. "It's a nice little car," she said, holding the miniature Shelby. "I bet he'll like it."

Suddenly, Keyne grabbed the toy from her hand and threw it out the window. "It's no use. I never see him anyway."

"Gabriel, no!"

She gripped the steering wheel, forcing him to stop the car. Incensed, he slammed on the brakes, pulled over to the side of the road, and leaped out of the car.

Alice watched him walk away in the rearview mirror. They were on a narrow road that wound down toward a valley. She saw Gabriel sit on a rocky outcropping that jutted into the void like the plank of a ship. He finished his cigarette and immediately lit another one. Alice got out of the car, picked up the toy from where it was lying on the grassy roadside a few yards back, then walked up to Gabriel.

"I'm sorry," she said, joining him on the rock.

"Don't sit there, it's dangerous."

"If it's dangerous for me, it's dangerous for you too." She

leaned forward and saw a lake down below. The ephemeral palette of fall colors was vividly reflected in the water.

"Why don't you see him more often?"

He made a dismissive gesture. "He lives in London with his mother. It's a long story."

She stole a cigarette from him, but the wind made it difficult to light. He handed her his and, just when she was least expecting it, unburdened his heart to her.

"I haven't always worked for the FBI. Before I joined the Bureau, I was a street cop in Chicago." He narrowed his eyes, letting the memories rise to the surface of his mind. "Chicago is where I was born, and it's where I met my wife. The two of us grew up in Ukrainian Village, the neighborhood where a lot of the Eastern European immigrants live. It's a pretty quiet place, northwest of the Loop."

"Were you in the homicide unit?"

"Yeah, on the South Side, which covers some of the city's toughest neighborhoods: Englewood, New City..."

He took a long drag on his cigarette before continuing. "Those areas are all run by gangs. They're places of fear and despair, and as a cop, there's not much you can do. Whole neighborhoods under the control of little thugs with guns who think they're Scarface. They rule through terror."

Memories filled his mind. A past he preferred to keep at a distance but that was now, against his will, submerging him again.

"Don't you ever get the feeling that we—cops, I mean—are working for the dead? If you think about it, they're our real clients. They're the ones we're accountable to. They're the ones who haunt us at night when we fail to find their murderers. My wife often used to complain about that: 'You spend more time with the dead than the living.' I guess she was right, when it comes down to it—"

Alice interrupted Gabriel. "That's not true! We work for their families, for the people who loved them, to allow them to grieve, to give them justice, to make sure that the killers never do it again!"

He frowned doubtfully and continued his story. "Well, one day, I decided to *really* help the living. In Englewood, I was in daily contact with a mediators' association. They were all types of people, a lot of them social workers and local ex-cons, who had joined together to try to do what police, as representatives of the law, couldn't—smooth things out, de-escalate conflicts, reduce tensions. And, most important, save the people who could still be saved."

"The youngest ones?"

"The ones who weren't drug addicts yet. Sometimes, the volunteers would blur the lines of legality. A few times, I helped them 'exfiltrate' young prostitutes from the neighborhood by providing them with fake IDs, some money seized from arrested drug dealers, a train ticket for the West Coast, a place to stay once they got there, the promise of a job..."

Like Paul, Alice thought in spite of herself.

The forest was reflected in Gabriel's eyes, giving his gaze a disturbing intensity. "I was so sure I was doing good, I didn't realize the risks I was taking. I'd decided to ignore all the warnings and threats I received. That was dumb—pimps and drug lords don't just sit back and take it if you rob them of their livelihood."

He kept talking, silences punctuating his words. "In January 2009, my wife's younger sister was supposed to go skiing for the weekend with her friends to celebrate her birthday. She asked to borrow our SUV, and we agreed. I can still see myself, standing on the porch, waving and saying, 'Be careful, Joanne! Take it easy on the black diamonds!' She was wearing a pom-pom hat that evening. Her cheeks were red with cold. She was eighteen. Full of life. She got behind the wheel of the Jeep, turned the key in the ignition. And...the car exploded. Those bastards in Englewood had planted a bomb in my car."

Gabriel took his time lighting another cigarette with the butt of the last one. Then he began speaking again.

"The day after her sister's funeral, my wife left, taking our son with her. She moved to London, where some of her family live. It all happened very fast after that. She filed for divorce and her lawyers got to work smearing my name. They accused me of being violent, being an alcoholic, going to prostitutes. They came up with false witnesses and used text messages taken out of context. I wasn't able to fight back, and she got sole custody of Theo."

He took a final drag on his cigarette and crushed it against the rock.

"I was allowed to see my son only twice a year. So one day, I cracked. I went to visit my wife in England. I tried reasoning with her, but she dug her heels in. Her lawyers did their stuff and they got a restraining order. Now I'm not allowed to see Theo ever again."

A look of resignation passed over his face. Night was falling. The wind had grown stronger and it was getting cold. Touched by his story, Alice put her hand on his forearm. Suddenly, the phone rang, bursting the bubble of their intimacy.

They looked at each other, aware that the half-open door to this secret garden was about to close. She picked up.

"Seymour?" she answered, switching on the speaker.

"I found the sugar factory. I'm here now. Shit, this place is scary. Out in the middle of nowhere. This must be where they shot *Evil Dead,* right?"

"Tell me what you see."

"It's like the antechamber to hell."

"Come on, don't exaggerate."

"And it's pissing down, and I don't have an umbrella."

"I don't give a shit, Seymour! Do you have the flashlight, the pliers, and the glow sticks?"

"Yeah, yeah. It's all in the bag."

Amplified by the speakerphone, the cop's crackly voice echoed through the valley, bouncing against the mountainsides.

"According to Castelli, this place has been abandoned for over thirty years. I'm in the main building now. It's half falling down. Everything's rusted, and there are weeds taller than me."

Alice closed her eyes and methodically re-created the

topography of the factory as her father had described it to her. "Okay. Go out the back and look for a storage area. A building that looks like a silo."

A few seconds passed before Seymour spoke again. "All right, I see a sort of high, narrow tank, covered in ivy. It looks like the Jolly Green Giant's cock!"

Alice ignored this joke. "Walk around the silo until you find three stone wells."

Another silence.

"Yeah, I see them. They're covered."

Alice felt her heart accelerate. "Start with the middle one. Can you remove the cover?"

"Hang on, I'm going to use my earbuds . . . okay, yeah, the cover's off. But there's a metal hatch underneath it."

"Can you lift it?"

"Jesus, this thing weighs a ton! All right, it's open."

Seymour was breathing heavily.

"What do you see inside?"

"Nothing."

She lost her temper: "Point the flashlight down there, for Christ's sake!"

"That's what I'm doing, Alice! I'm telling you, there's nothing down there."

"Try a glow stick."

She heard him mutter at the other end of the line, "How do these damn things work?"

Exasperated, she yelled, "Pick it up, bend it in half, shake it, and throw it down the hole."

A few seconds later, Seymour reported, "The well is empty. It's completely dry."

Fuck, I don't believe this!

"What was I supposed to find?" Seymour asked.

Alice put her head in her hands. "Vaughn's corpse."

"What? Are you crazy?"

"Try the other wells," she ordered.

"The covers are rusted up. I can't move them. No one's opened them in years."

"Use the pliers to get them free!"

"No, Alice, I'm not going to do that. I've had enough of this bullshit. I'm going back to Paris."

Powerless, stranded in the middle of a forest nearly four thousand miles from that old French factory, Alice balled her fists with rage. Seymour was wrong. There *was* a corpse in that factory. She was sure of it.

She was about to hang up, when she heard a groan and a flood of curse words.

"Seymour?" she said, alarmed.

Silence. She exchanged a worried look with Gabriel, who, even if he could not understand every word of the French conversation, was aware of the rising tension.

"Seymour, what's happened?" she shouted into the phone.

There was a long pause, during which they heard a series of metallic creaks. Then Seymour finally said: "Fucking hell. You were right, there's . . . there really is a corpse!"

Alice closed her eyes and began to thank God.

"But it's not in the well!" the cop went on.

Not in the well?

"There's a corpse in the cab of an old backhoe."

White-faced and breathless, Alice asked, "Is it Vaughn?"

"No, it's a young woman. She's been tied up and gagged. Hang on . . . oh, fuck! With a pair of tights! She was strangled with a pair of tights!"

Alice tried to stay calm. "What state is the body in?"

"I can't see much, with the darkness and this goddamn rain, but in my opinion, she's been dead a few days at the most."

Gabriel's face was a mask of confusion and frustration. "Can you tell me what's happening?"

Alice briefly summarized the situation in English. Immediately, the federal agent formed a question.

"Ask him what color the tights are. According to eyewitnesses, on the day she was murdered, Elizabeth Hardy was wearing *pink* tights."

Alice translated this into French for Seymour.

"Impossible to tell," he replied. "It's too dark to see . . . I'm going to have to hang up, Alice. I need to inform the local cops."

"Seymour, wait!" she screamed. "Please tell us the color of the tights!"

"Ugh . . . red, I think. No, more like pink." And he hung up.

Alice and Gabriel looked at each other, petrified.

The nightmare was continuing.

20

INSIDE THE HOUSE

A NEARLY FULL MOON hung heavy in the sky, defying the clouds.

It was icy cold.

The Mustang Shelby's heater blew only lukewarm air. Alice rubbed her hands to warm them up and covered them with the sleeves of her sweater. She had turned on the dome light and was looking at the road map folded out on her lap. Gabriel drove, leaning forward, face somber, his hands tightly gripping the wheel. They had driven about three hours since the phone call with Seymour, still heading north. After such a long trip, they were becoming painfully aware of how uncomfortable the Shelby was: very low seats, prehistoric suspension, faulty heating...

Focused on the road, Gabriel rounded a hairpin bend and accelerated. The road wound between the gorges of the White Mountains. They had not seen another car for miles. The whole area seemed deserted.

All around them was unfettered nature. The forest was dark and menacing. The palette of fall colors had given way to a single shade of black—the black of shadows, the black of the bottom of the ocean.

As the car meandered around the road's curves, they sometimes glimpsed the valley, veiled in fog, or a tiered waterfall, the rock silver beneath the rushing foam.

Her eyes ringed with fatigue and sleeplessness, Alice went over what Seymour had told them: Not only was Vaughn not dead, but he was still killing. Ten days earlier, he had murdered a nurse here in New England, and soon afterward he had returned to France, killed again, and left the body in the old sugar factory.

Vaughn was not acting alone, Alice was sure of that. It wasn't by chance that she and Gabriel had been brought together. Vaughn had engineered this in order to provoke them, to defy them. But this macabre setup could not possibly be the work of one person. Materially, logistically, there was no way a single individual could have orchestrated such a gigantic puzzle.

Alice rubbed her eyes. Her thoughts were growing murky, her brain slowing down.

But one question wouldn't stop torturing her: Why had her father lied to her about Vaughn's death?

She rubbed her shoulders and wiped the condensation

from the windshield. The gloomy landscape was affecting her mood. She felt fear in her gut, and only Gabriel's presence prevented her from yielding to panic.

They drove another ten miles before reaching the opening to a forest path framed by wooden logs.

"That's it!" Alice said, looking up from the map.

The car veered to the left and entered a path through the woods bordered by pine trees. After a hundred yards or so, the passage narrowed, as if the trees were uniting to repel the intruders. They kept going, pine needles scraping against the Mustang's bodywork, branches hitting the windows and doors, the ground becoming ever more unstable. Almost imperceptibly, the conifers were closing in around them.

Suddenly, out of nowhere, a dark mass burst out in front of the car. Alice screamed; Gabriel slammed on the brakes and jerked the steering wheel to the side to avoid the obstacle. The Shelby skidded into the trunk of a pine tree, breaking off the side mirror, smashing one of the windows, and short-circuiting the interior light by which Alice had been reading the map.

Gabriel turned off the engine. Silence. Fear. And then a long bellowing noise.

A moose, Alice thought, watching the silhouette of a large animal with fan-shaped antlers running away.

"Nothing broken?" Gabriel asked.

"No, I'm okay," Alice said. "How about you?"

"I'll survive," he assured her, then started the car again.

They drove five hundred yards and came to a clearing with a cabin at its center.

They parked the Shelby near the building and turned off the headlights. The moonlight was bright enough for them to make out the little house. It was a rectangular wood-paneled construction with a cedar-shingle roof. Two dormer windows seemed to observe them suspiciously. The shutters were open and the darkness inside was absolute.

"There's no one here," Gabriel said.

"Or that's what they want us to think," Alice replied.

She buckled the straps of her satchel and handed it to Gabriel. "Take that," she ordered, then took her gun from the glove compartment, removed the Glock from its holster, checked the magazine, and pressed her finger to the trigger.

"You're not planning on going in there without backup?" Gabriel asked.

"Do you have another solution?"

"We might as well just paint targets on our faces!"

"If Vaughn had wanted to kill us, we'd be dead already."

They went out into the cold and moved toward the house. Steam escaped their mouths, forming silvery clouds that vanished in the night.

They stopped in front of a mailbox with peeling paint: CALEB DUNN.

"At least we don't have the wrong house," said Gabriel, opening the mailbox.

It was empty. Someone must have picked up the mail recently.

They continued until they reached the porch, where they found a newspaper.

"Today's *Concord Monitor*," Gabriel noted after ripping off the protective plastic. He dropped the newspaper onto an old rocking chair.

"So Dunn hasn't been home today," Alice deduced, glancing at the paper.

Gabriel stood in front of the door and seemed to hesitate.

"You know, legally, we have no right to be here. Dunn is not officially a suspect. We don't have a warrant or—"

"So?" Alice asked impatiently.

"So maybe we should get in without breaking down the door."

Alice holstered her gun and knelt in front of the lock. "Hand me my bag." She rummaged inside the satchel and took out a large manila envelope containing the chest X-ray films she'd asked Mitchell to print out for her.

"Where did you get those?" Gabriel asked, seeing the images.

"I'll explain later. What do you want to bet that there's no dead bolt? How many burglars can there be around here?"

Alice slid the rigid plastic sheet between the door and the frame and pushed it in several times. No luck.

"Forget it, Schafer. This isn't a movie. It's locked."

But Alice did not give up. She slid the X-ray in again, this time while shaking the door and giving it little upward kicks; the latch came loose and the door opened.

She shot a triumphant look at Gabriel and unholstered her Glock again. The two moved into the cabin.

First observation: the house was heated. First deduction: the last time he had gone out, Dunn expected to be back pretty soon.

Gabriel turned the light on. The interior was simple, a sort of large, old-fashioned hunter's cabin with a brick floor, wood-paneled walls, and a wood-burning stove. The living room was arranged around a moth-eaten L-shaped couch in front of a huge stone fireplace, above which hung a stuffed deer head. Four rifles stood in the gun rack.

"They're just old pheasant-hunting guns," said Gabriel.

The only concessions to modernity were some Red Sox pennants, an HDTV, a video-game console, a laptop, and a small printer standing on a raw-wood table. They went through the kitchen. Similar plain décor: faded walls, a cast-iron stove, and a collection of old saucepans.

They went upstairs and found three small, austere, practically bare bedrooms off a single corridor.

Back on the first floor, the two detectives opened cabinets and drawers, looked on shelves, lifted cushions and the plaid blanket on the couch. They found nothing of interest besides a few ounces of pot hidden in a fruit bowl. It was hard to believe this house was the lair of a serial killer.

"Strange," said Gabriel. "Not a single personal photograph."

Alice sat in front of the laptop and opened it up. No password prompt. No photo software. The browser history had been cleared, and the e-mail application was not configured. A hollow shell.

Alice stopped to think. She decided that Dunn must send

e-mails by using his service provider's website. She connected to it—it was the only site on his favorites list—but found only monthly bills and spam.

Meanwhile, Gabriel kept searching. In a kitchen cabinet, he found some plastic sheeting and a roll of duct tape that he put aside to patch up the Shelby's broken window. At the back of the house was a large window that looked out onto the forest. He opened it out of curiosity and let in a gust of wind that banged shut the front door. Alice looked up, and her face went pale.

She jumped up from her chair, walked to the front door, and froze. Attached to the door with big rusty nails were three pictures that she always kept in her purse.

One was a photograph of Paul smiling, taken in the Ravello gardens on the Amalfi Coast. Another was a printout of her ultrasound from the fifth month.

Seeing this, Alice closed her eyes. In a second, all the emotions she had felt when she saw her baby that day flashed through her again. You could already see all his features—the delicate shape of his face, the ovals of the eyes, the tiny nostrils, the little hands and sculpted fingers. And you could hear the hypnotic rhythm of his heart. *Ba-boom, ba-boom, ba-boom...*

She opened her eyes and saw the third image: herself on her police ID card. She too was nailed to the door, but the perpetrator of the crime had made sure to tear her in two.

Ba-boom, ba-boom, ba-boom... the sound of her own heart pulsing in her chest mixed with the memory of her son's heartbeat, and suddenly the room spun around her. She was overcome by a wave of heat and a violent desire to vomit. She had just enough time to feel someone holding her before she lost consciousness.

Thunder rumbled, making the windows tremble. A series of lightning flashes strobe-lit the house's interior. Alice had quickly regained consciousness, but she was still as white as a ghost. Gabriel was taking control of the situation.

"Listen, there's no sense in staying here forever. We have to find Caleb Dunn, and there's no reason to assume he's ever coming back."

Alice and Gabriel were sitting facing each other across the wooden table in the living room. Their map was spread out between them. The FBI agent continued, "Either Dunn and Vaughn are one and the same person or Dunn will lead us to Vaughn. Either way, this man knows an important part of the truth."

Alice nodded. She closed her eyes so she could concentrate more easily. The DNA test had indicated that the blood on her blouse belonged to Dunn. So Dunn had been injured recently. Last night or early this morning. And his wound must have been bad enough to prevent him from going home. But where was he now? Hiding out somewhere, probably. Or maybe in the hospital.

As if reading her thoughts, Gabriel said: "What if Dunn is in the same hospital he works at?"

"We could call them to check," Alice suggested, bringing the laptop to life with a touch of its keyboard.

She found the address and phone number for Sebago Hospital, then tried to find the place on the map.

"Here it is," she said, pointing to a lake shaped like a light bulb. "Only eighty miles away."

"Still, it'll take us a good two hours. We have to get out of the mountains first."

"Let's call the hospital and ask if Dunn is there."

He shook his head. "They won't tell us anything over the phone. And they might even warn Dunn."

"So we just go there blindly?"

"Maybe not—I have another idea. Give me your phone."

Gabriel typed in the hospital's number and was answered by the main switchboard. Instead of asking whether they had a patient named Dunn, however, he asked to be put through to the security guard's office.

"Security," said a laid-back voice that seemed at odds with the job description.

"Good evening, I'm a friend of Caleb Dunn's. He told me I could get hold of him at this number. Could I speak to him?"

"Ha, well, that might be kinda tricky, man. From what I hear, ol' Caleb got in the way of a bullet. So he's here, all right, but on the other side of the fence, if you see what I mean."

"Dunn is there? At Sebago Hospital?"

"That's what the boss told me, anyway."

"The boss?"

"Katherine Koller, the hospital assistant director."

"Do you know who shot him?"

"No idea, man. They don't like it when we ask questions here, you know."

Gabriel thanked the security guard and hung up.

"Let's go," said Alice. "We've got him this time!"

She was about to close the laptop, when she suddenly changed her mind. "Just a minute..." She would check her e-mails while she was online. More than five hours had passed since her phone call to Franck Maréchal, the regional transportation police chief. Maybe he'd gotten hold of the images of her car from the security cameras in the Franklin-Roosevelt parking garage.

In all honesty, she didn't have much faith in Maréchal's diligence. But she was proved wrong; there was an e-mail from him in her in-box.

From: Franck Maréchal
To: Alice Schafer
Subject: Vinci/FDR security footage

Hi, Alice,

Here are the images from the security cameras corresponding to the license plate number you gave me. The video file was too big to send by e-mail, but I've attached a few screenshots. I hope it's enough.

Cheers,
Franck

There were four photos attached.

Alice put her face as close to the screen as possible. At 8:12 p.m., two pictures showed the Audi entering the parking garage. The quality of the images was not as bad as Seymour had claimed. Alice could see her own face through the windshield quite clearly, and it was obvious that she was alone. At 12:17 a.m., two other photographs showed the Audi exiting. This time, Alice was not alone—and she was not driving. She looked as if she had collapsed; she was slumped in the passenger seat. A man was behind the wheel. His face wasn't visible in the first picture, but in the second he was looking up.

Alice opened the image on the full screen and used the touchpad to zoom in.

Her blood froze in her veins.

There could be no doubt about it.

The man behind the wheel of the Audi was Seymour.

21

THE VEIL

THE MUSTANG MOVED through darkness.

The storm lashed against the mountain with devastating power. The wind buffeted the car, the rain hammering noisily against its windows and the plastic sheet.

They had reached the summit of the mountain a half hour ago and begun the long descent to the valley. The road, made slippery by the rain, swept vertiginously through endless curves.

Alice held a printout of the image from the parking garage in one hand and stared at Seymour's face, illuminated by the pale light of her phone. She had tried calling her friend several times, but each time it had gone straight to voice mail.

She looked again at the picture, this time at herself sitting next to Seymour in her Audi. She looked drunk, a crumpled figure but not completely unconscious.

How could she have no memory of this incident that had happened only last night? She tried again to unfreeze this part of her memory, but her way was still barred by the same gauzy veil. Through force of will, however, the clockwork of her brain suddenly seemed to come unblocked. Alice's heart raced. Yes, the memories were there! Hidden in the misty maze of her subconscious. The truth was there—she could discern its outline, circle it, but whenever she came close to grasping it, it would wither, scatter, dissolve inside the freezing car.

She felt like Tantalus.

Suddenly, a flash of crimson diluted the night's blackness. Alice turned; the red gas warning light was blinking on the dashboard.

"Shit," breathed Gabriel. "We might not have enough to get to the hospital. This car is a real gas-guzzler!"

"How much farther do you think we can get?"

"Thirty miles, max."

Alice shone her phone light on the road map. "Look, it looks like there's a gas station just here. You think we can make it that far?"

Gabriel squinted at the map. "It'll be tight, but we might be able to. We don't have much choice."

The wind tried to infiltrate the Shelby. The rain kept bucketing down. Eyes glued to the road, Gabriel spoke: "I have to admit, with that Seymour guy, I never felt like he—"

Alice sighed wearily. "You don't know him."

"He just always seemed kinda shifty to me."

"You're talking out of your ass. Let's hear his version before we judge him."

"What difference does it make what his version is?" Gabriel demanded testily. "He's been lying to you from the beginning. Lying to *us!* Fuck, maybe everything he told us today is bullshit!"

Alice thought anxiously about this possibility. Gabriel fumbled in his shirt pocket, found a cigarette, and lit it without taking his eyes off the road. "Same goes for your father!"

"That's enough. Leave my father out of this."

He exhaled a few smoke rings that drifted and dissolved inside the car.

"All I'm saying is that you're surrounded by people who are lying to you and putting you in danger."

Now that they were back in the valley, there were other vehicles on the road. A truck was coming in the other lane now, its high beams on.

"And you keep making excuses for them!" Gabriel went on.

Exasperated, Alice defended herself angrily. "Without Seymour and without my father, I wouldn't even be here. How do you think someone can keep living after a madman has stabbed her, killed her child, and left her for dead in a pool of blood?"

Gabriel tried to argue his point, but Alice talked over him: "I was devastated after Paul died, and they were the *only* ones who supported me! How can you not understand that?"

Gabriel let it drop. He continued smoking his cigarette in silence, his face pensive. Alice sighed and turned toward the window. The rain drummed on the glass. Memories bombarded her mind.

I remember...

December 2011–July 2013

I remember.

I remember being certain that I was going to end it all.

I couldn't imagine any other outcome; as soon as I got home, I would take my service pistol and fire a bullet into my head.

One shot, and at least I wouldn't slip any closer to hell.

I had played this movie over and over again in my mind while I was stranded in that hospital bed—the sound of the magazine clicking into place, the taste of cold metal in my mouth, the barrel pointing up so it would explode my brain.

I used to fix on that image as a way of getting to sleep: My finger on the trigger. My head blown to pieces. Salvation.

And yet, that was not the trajectory my life took.

"You're going to live with us," my father told me when he came to pick me up from the hospital.

I looked at him, wide-eyed. "What do you mean, 'with us'?"

"With me and your friend, that nice young gay fellow."

Without telling me, while I was in the hospital, my father had rented a large house with a garden on Rue du Square-Montsouris—a former painter's studio surrounded by greenery. Like a little bit of countryside in the middle of the fourteenth arrondissement.

Seymour had just broken up with his partner, and my father took advantage of this to persuade him to move into the house with us. I knew that my colleague had a complicated romantic life; for professional reasons, his long-time boyfriend—a dancer and choreographer with the Paris Opera—had left France for the United States, and their relationship had not survived the trial by distance.

And so, for almost two years, the three of us lived together. Our odd arrangement worked surprisingly well. Against all expectations, Seymour and my father put aside their prejudices and became the best of friends, each strangely fascinated by the other. Seymour was impressed by the legendary cop that was Alain Schafer—his flair, his big mouth, his sense of humor, his ability to impose his point of view, and his rebellious streak. As for my father, he realized that he had been too quick to judge my young colleague, who was an unusual character—rich, dandyish, and highly cultured but always ready to use his fists and happy to down glasses of twenty-year-old whiskey.

Most of all, the two men were united by their fierce determination to protect me from myself. During the weeks that followed my return, my father took me on vacation in Italy and Portugal. In early spring, Seymour took time off work to go with me to Los Angeles and San Francisco. These trips, coupled with a cocoon-like family atmosphere, helped me get through that period without falling to pieces.

I went back to work as soon as I could, even though, for the first six months, I remained on desk duty. Seymour had taken my place as the head of the Schafer squad, and I made do with the position of paper-pusher, gathering and organizing all the documents that made up the legal file used in court. For a year, I was "closely monitored" by a psychiatrist who specialized in dealing with post-traumatic stress.

In the Criminal Division, I was in a difficult situation. After the Vaughn fiasco, Taillandier had me in her sights. In other circumstances, the department would simply have fired me, but the media had gotten hold of my story. *Paris Match* devoted a four-page spread to my tragedy, transforming my bad decision-making into a romantic thriller where I had the starring role—I was a Parisian Clarice Starling, risking everything to catch a killer. After that, I was even given the Medal of Honor by the minister of the interior for my acts of courage and dedication. This media benediction and the bonus I received had angered my colleagues, of course, but at least it allowed me to keep doing my job.

Some ordeals you never really get over, but you survive them all the same. Part of me was undone, wounded, destroyed. The past still choked me, but I was lucky enough to have people around me who stopped me from sinking.

Paul was dead. My baby was dead. Love seemed impossible now. But, deep down, I had the confused feeling that the story was not over. That maybe life still had something to give me.

So, little by little, I began to live again. A blurry, impressionistic life, fed on scraps: a walk in the woods on a sunny day, an hour spent running on the beach, something sweet my father said to me, a fit of uncontrollable laughter with Seymour, a glass of Saint-Julien out on the terrace, the first buds of spring, weekly outings with my old college friends, an old edition of Wilkie Collins discovered at a used-book stall...

In September 2012, nearly a year after the attack, I took over as head of the team again. My fascination with police work and my passion for investigation had not gone away, and for a year or so after that, the Schafer squad was on a roll—we quickly solved every case we were assigned. The dream team was back.

The wheel of fortune turns fast. By early the next summer I had regained my credibility in the Criminal Division. I had also regained my self-respect and the respect of my men. It felt like we were all on the same side again.

I had the sharp sense that maybe life still had something to give me.

I never would have guessed that it would take the form of another ordeal.

22

VAUGHN

WIND HOWLED ALL around them. The duct tape had finally given way in the powerful gusts, freeing the plastic sheet over the window and creating a gaping hole at the back of the Shelby. The rain beat down in a rage, flooding the sports car's floor and seats.

"We're almost there!" Alice shouted over the din of the storm. The map that lay on her lap was soaked, disintegrating in her hands.

Slowing down, they carefully crossed an intersection where the traffic lights had stopped working due to the storm, then, just afterward, they sighed with relief as they saw the sign for the Grant General Store and Gas Station shining in the night.

They stopped next to the two gas pumps in front of the store. Gabriel honked the horn several times to let the owners know they were there. Protected by an umbrella and a windbreaker, a toothless old gas attendant ran up to them and leaned down to their window.

"My name's Virgil. How can I help you folks?"

"Fill her up, please."

"Sure. You should get that back window fixed too!"

"Can you give us a hand with it?" Gabriel said. "Maybe if you have a tarp or a piece of canvas?"

"I'll see what I can do," Virgil promised. "In the meantime, why don't you go inside and warm up?"

They got out of the car and ran to the shelter of the store's awning. Rain streaming down their faces, they opened the door and found themselves in a large, noisy, lively room. The place was divided in two. On the right was a traditional general store with creaking wooden floorboards and old-fashioned shelves filled with jams, maple syrup, honey, snacks, candy bars, and so on. A small stand displayed homemade pies and brownies. On the other side was a long diner-style counter. A large woman stood behind it serving food and drinks.

It had a good-natured, family atmosphere, with customers at the counter digging into eggs with bacon, hash browns, or steaks, washed down with pints of home-brewed beer. There were rock-and-roll concert posters from the 1950s on the walls, and the diner seemed such an anachronism that Alice and Gabriel would hardly have been surprised to find out that Chuck Berry, Bill Haley, or Buddy Holly was playing there the next weekend.

Alice and Gabriel sat on two red leather stools at the back corner of the counter. That way, they were able to face each other.

"What can I get for you lovebirds?" the waitress asked, handing them two plastic-covered menus.

They weren't especially hungry, but they realized they couldn't sit there without ordering something.

While they made their choices, she filled two large glasses with water and pushed a metal napkin holder toward them. "Look at you, you're soaked to the bone! You should dry yourselves off before you catch your death."

They thanked her. Gabriel ordered a toasted BLT and Alice a clam chowder. While they waited for their food to arrive, they used the napkins to wipe the water from their faces and necks and to rub their hair dry.

"Enjoy!" the waitress said, bringing them a sandwich cut in triangles and chowder served in a hollowed-out loaf of bread.

On the bar in front of them, two glasses of whiskey appeared as if by magic in her large hands.

"On the house," she said, "to warm you up. This is from ol' Virgil's personal supply."

"Thank you so much!" Keyne said warmly, tasting a mouthful of rye. He bit into his sandwich and waited until the woman was out of earshot before looking at Alice.

"We're about ten miles from the hospital, Schafer, so we should probably discuss our options now."

She sipped her soup. "Go ahead."

"I'm serious, Alice. I know how much pain Vaughn put you through, you and your family."

"Kind of an understatement."

"But let's be clear about one thing: We're not here to punish him. Understood? We go to the hospital, we arrest the guy, and we take him straight to Boston to interrogate him *legally*."

Alice looked away. She too tasted the whiskey. It had notes of apricot, plum, and clove.

"Agreed?" Gabriel insisted.

"You take care of your responsibilities, I'll take care of mine," Alice replied.

Refusing to be deflected, Gabriel raised his voice. "All right, well, my first responsibility is to take that gun off you. Give it to me right now or you're not leaving this bar."

"Go screw yourself!"

"This isn't negotiable, Alice."

She hesitated, but then, realizing Gabriel was not going to compromise, she removed the Glock from its holster and handed it to him under the counter.

"Believe me, it's better this way," he said, sliding it into his belt.

With a shrug, she downed the rest of her whiskey. Just like every time she drank, she seemed to almost physically sense the alcohol flowing through her bloodstream. The first glass always gave her a rare sense of well-being, an adrenaline shot that sharpened her senses. The exhilarating impression of losing control just a little.

Her gaze flitted around the room from one person to another, one object to another, finally landing on Gabriel's glass of whiskey. There, she stared in fascination at the variations of light floating on the surface of the liquid, the shifting gleams of gold, copper, bronze, and amber. The world was spinning around her. Right now, she felt the same sensation that had gripped her earlier in the car—the euphoric certainty that she was closer to the truth than ever before. The conviction that she was finally approaching the critical moment when she would be able to tear away the veil of ignorance.

Her gaze dissolved in the myriad colors of the whiskey. She felt paralyzed, incapable of tearing her eyes away from her partner's glass. And then, suddenly, she got goose bumps on her arms and felt her throat tighten. And she realized that what she was staring at was not the glass of whiskey but the hand that encircled it—Gabriel's hand. To be more precise, at his finger tapping nervously, rhythmically, on the side of the glass. She could see it with amazing clarity, as if she were looking through a magnifying glass. Gabriel's hand— the curved fingers, the little wrinkles on his knuckles, the tiny cross-shaped scar on his right index finger. The type of injury you get in childhood by carelessly closing the sharpened blade of your first jackknife, the trace of which, left by the doctor's stitches, will stay with you all your life.

Without warning, Virgil's hairy face suddenly appeared between them at the corner of the bar.

"I fixed something up for your window, folks. You wanna come take a look and see if it'll do?"

Gabriel stood up. "Stay here, where it's warm," he said to her. "I'll come and get you when I know for sure we're all set to go."

Her cheeks burning, Alice watched Gabriel walk away. She could feel her heart savagely pounding in her chest, her whole being blazing up, out of control. Her head spinning. The sensation of drowning. The need to know.

"You okay, darling? Can I get you anything else?"

Alice picked up her glass of rye and drank it down in one gulp. She wanted to believe that the alcohol would clear her thoughts. Or at least give her courage.

Do or die!

She opened her satchel and took out the fingerprint kit. With a paper napkin, she picked up the glass Gabriel had been drinking from and carried out the same procedure she had performed earlier on the syringe: using the magnetic brush to sweep the black powder over it, finding the print of the index finger, trapping it with sticky tape, and affixing it to the bottom of the drinks coaster, next to the print from the syringe. Her movements were precise, mechanical. Time was passing quickly. There was no room for even the slightest error.

Alice had brought the coaster close to her face and was examining the two fingerprints when the bell above the door jingled.

She turned around and saw Gabriel coming toward her.

"We can go now," he called out over the hubbub of voices.

Sweat prickled her scalp as Gabriel moved closer with an easy, open smile.

"That Virgil guy did a great job. The old car's waterproof again!"

One last roll of the dice...

"Go start the car. I'll settle up here and be there in a minute," she said, hoping he would make a U-turn.

"No need, I—"

From behind the counter, the woman grabbed him by the arm. "Hey, darling, how about one for the road? Virgil makes this gin himself. Tastes like honey and juniper. You can tell me what you think of it."

Clearly surprised and annoyed by this familiarity, Gabriel pulled away. "No, thanks. We have to get going."

Alice used those few seconds to shove the fingerprint kit back in the satchel. Then she took three ten-dollar bills from her pocket and left them on the counter.

"Ready to go?" Gabriel asked when he reached her.

As casually as she could, she followed him to the front door. Outside, the rain was still pouring down.

"Wait for me here under the awning," Gabriel said. "I'll go get the car."

While he ran to the Shelby, Alice turned her back on the parking lot and took the coaster from her bag. In the light from the neon sign above the general store, she compared the two fingerprints. To the naked eye, they looked identical.

Most compelling, they both had the same arch of ridges interrupted by the tiny cross-shaped scar.

In that moment, she understood that Gabriel had lied to her from the beginning.

When she looked up, she sensed the sports car parked behind her. Gabriel leaned over and held the door open for her. She got inside and buckled her seat belt.

"Everything okay? You look kind of pale."

"I'm fine," she replied, suddenly aware that she had given him her Glock and was now unarmed.

He pulled the door shut. Trembling, Alice turned toward the window, lashed relentlessly by rain.

As the car sped off into the night, it took her several seconds to admit the truth to herself: Gabriel and Vaughn were one and the same.

Part Four

COME UNDONE

23

DO OR DIE

THE RAIN FELL heavily and aggressively against the windows.

Thunder rumbled almost incessantly. At regular intervals, lightning flashed through the sooty clouds, illuminating the line of pine trees on the horizon like a giant camera flash.

Sebago Hospital was located at the end of a peninsula bordered by pines that stretched out ten miles into the center of the lake.

Fully focused on his driving, Gabriel was going too fast. The road, strewn with torn-off branches and debris, was treacherous. The wind screamed through the trees, making them bow until they broke, shaking the car as if trying to slow its progress.

Alice stole surreptitious glances at her cell phone. Unsurprisingly, service was spotty, but even so, she did have a signal at times. In some places, the bars showed perfect reception; in other places, there was no service at all.

She tried not to tremble. She needed to buy time. As long as Gabriel didn't suspect that she had guessed his identity, she was safe. There was no way she could try anything on this road without a weapon, but once they were in the hospital, she would be able to act.

What I need is lots of people, activity, security cameras. This time, Vaughn won't get away.

Her hatred was stronger than her fear.

It was unbearable, sitting next to her son's killer like this. To know his body was only inches away. Unbearable, too, to have felt so close to him, told him some of her secrets, been moved by his lies, been deceived in this way.

Alice breathed deeply. She tried to think rationally, to find answers to her questions: What was the point of this wild-goose chase? What was Vaughn's plan? Why hadn't he killed her when he had the chance?

The Shelby rounded a tight bend before coming to a sudden halt. A tall white pine tree just off the road had been hit by lightning. The intensity of the rain must have put the fire out before it could spread, but the tree was still smoking, its trunk split in two. Bits of wood, bark, and

burned branches were scattered across the pavement, blocking the road.

"Damn it!" Gabriel exclaimed.

He put the car into gear and accelerated, determined to
force his way through. A large branch lay in the way. The
Shelby veered to the side, to the edge of the ravine, and its
wheels started skidding in the mud.

"I'm going to try and clear the road," Gabriel said, pulling
over and putting on the emergency brake.

He got out and closed the door, leaving the engine running.

Too good to be true?

She could try to escape as soon as he moved the branch, of
course, but it wasn't the desire to flee that drove her. It was
the need to know. And to go all the way.

Alice glanced at her phone and saw the signal was weak,
just two bars. But who could she call—911? This story was
too long to explain. Her father? Seymour? She no longer
knew if she could trust them. One of her other Criminal
Division colleagues? Yes, that was a good idea. Castelli?
Savignon? She tried to remember their numbers, but nothing
came to mind; she was too used to speed-dialing them from
her own phone.

She closed her eyes to concentrate; the only number she
could come up with was that of Olivier Cruchy, the youngest member of her team. Well, it was better than nothing.
She quickly dialed his number, holding the phone below her
seat. Gabriel kept looking over at the car, but the curtain of
rain was thick enough to protect Alice from his prying eyes.

She turned on the speaker. It rang once. Twice. Three times. And then went straight to voice mail.

Shit.

She left a brief message asking him to call her back at that number and hung up. Another idea came to her. She rummaged in the satchel at her feet and found the knife she had stolen from the café in the Bowery. The blade wasn't as sharp as a steak knife, but the point would still go through flesh. She slid it inside her right sleeve just as Gabriel walked back toward the car.

"All right, it's clear," he said, satisfied. "We can go!"

SEBAGO HOSPITAL
SECURE ZONE
SLOW DOWN

Illuminated by a white light, the wooden sentry box manned by hospital security could be seen from a distance. A luminous halo shone in the night, as if a flying saucer had landed in the middle of New England's cranberry fields. Gabriel drove the Shelby up the ramp to the security post, but when they reached it, they discovered that it was empty.

Gabriel stopped in front of the metal barrier and lowered his window. "Hey! Hello? Anyone there?" he shouted over the noise of the storm.

He turned off the car, got out, and moved toward the shelter. The door was open and banging in the wind. He poked his head in and decided to enter. No security guard.

He looked at the wall of security-camera monitors and then at the electronic dashboard covered with a vast number of buttons and switches. He touched the one that lifted the barrier and got back in the car with Alice.

"No security guard—that's not a good sign," he said, restarting the engine. "I guess he must have gone inside somewhere."

As he accelerated, Gabriel lit another cigarette. His hands were trembling slightly. The Shelby moved along a driveway edged with pine trees and came out on a wide gravel square that served as the hospital's parking lot.

Constructed on the edge of the lake, the hospital building was both unusual and impressive. Under the hammering rain, its lit façade, punctuated with Gothic windows, stood out from the backdrop of black clouds. The ocher-brick manor retained its old character, but on either side of the original building rose two huge modern towers with bluish, transparent façades and geometric multilevel roofs. An audacious glass walkway linked the structures, a hanging hyphen between past and future, the two harmoniously bonded. In front of the main entrance, attached to an aluminum pole, an LCD screen provided real-time information.

Hello, today is Tuesday, October 15, 2013
It's 11:57 p.m.
Visiting hours: 10 a.m.—6 p.m.
Visitor parking: P1–P2
Staff parking: P3

The Shelby slowed down. Alice slid the knife from her sleeve into her hand and gripped it as tightly as she could. *Now or never.*

She could feel her pulse pounding. A wave of adrenaline made her shiver. Her mind was a riot of contradictory feelings—fear, aggression, pain. Yes, pain most of all. She would not be content with merely arresting Vaughn. She was going to kill him. That was the only way she could purge the world of this evil, the only reparation possible to avenge the deaths of Paul and her son. Her throat constricted and tears rolled down her cheeks.

Now or never.

With all her strength, she stabbed Gabriel in the upper chest with the knife, driving the blade in hard. She felt the muscle in his shoulder tear. Caught by surprise, he screamed and let go of the steering wheel. The car veered off the gravel path and collided with a low wall, blowing out one of the tires. It stopped dead. Taking advantage of the confusion, Alice grabbed the Glock from Gabriel's belt.

"Don't move!" she yelled, pointing the gun at him.

She leaped out of the vehicle, checked the magazine, and wrapped her hands around the butt, arms tensed, ready to fire. "Get out of the car!"

Gabriel shifted down in his seat to protect himself but remained inside the Shelby. The rain was falling so hard that Alice couldn't tell what he was doing.

"Get out now!" she repeated. "Hands up!"

Finally the door slowly opened and Gabriel put a foot on the ground. He had removed the knife from his shoulder and blood was trickling over his shirt.

"It's over, Vaughn."

Despite the rain and the darkness, Gabriel's crystal-clear gaze pierced the gloom.

Alice felt an emptiness in the pit of her stomach. In all these years, she'd had only one desire: to kill Vaughn with her own hands.

But there was no way she was going to eliminate him before she'd gotten answers to all her questions.

Just then, she felt her phone vibrate in her jacket pocket. Keeping her eyes trained on Vaughn and the gun aimed at him, she took out her cell phone. Olivier Cruchy's number appeared on the screen.

"Cruchy?" she said.

"You called me, boss?" said a sleepy voice. "Um, you know what time it is, right?"

"I need you, Olivier. Do you know where Seymour is?"

"No idea. I've been on vacation with my in-laws for the last week."

"What are you talking about? I saw you in the office yesterday."

"Boss...you know that's impossible."

"Why?"

"Come on, boss, this is—"

"*Why?*" Alice yelled.

A silence, then a saddened voice: "Because you've been

on medical leave for the past three months. You haven't even set foot in the office for three months..."

This answer chilled her blood. Alice dropped her phone on the wet ground.

What the hell is he talking about?

Through the rain, behind Vaughn, her gaze fell on the hospital's electronic sign.

Hello, today is Tuesday, October 15, 2013
It's 11:59 p.m.

There was a mistake on this sign. Today was Tuesday, but it was the eighth, not the fifteenth. She wiped the rain from her face. Her ears were buzzing. The red flame of a distress flare burst in her mind like a warning. From the beginning, she had been hunting down not only Vaughn but a more insidious and tenacious enemy: herself.

A succession of moments flashed through her mind, like a montage from a movie.

First she saw the young pawnbroker from Chinatown, fiddling with the push button on Paul's watch. "I'm adjusting the time and date," he'd explained.

Then the front page of the newspaper she'd seen by Caleb Dunn's door. That, too, had been dated October 15. As had Franck Maréchal's e-mail. All these details she'd paid no attention to...

But how was it possible?

Suddenly, she understood. The gap in her memory was

not just one night long, as she'd thought. It stretched over at least a week.

Tears of sadness and anger mingled with the rain on Alice's face. She was still pointing the gun at Vaughn, but her whole body was trembling. She swayed, then struggled fiercely against the possibility of collapsing, gripping her gun with all her might.

Again, the iridescent veil appeared in her mind, but this time her arm was long enough for her to seize it. Finally, she could tear it away, allowing the memories to resurface. Fragments began slowly reforming.

Lightning split the darkness. Alice turned away for a fraction of a second. That instant of inattention was fatal. Gabriel rushed at her and shoved her violently onto the hood of the Shelby. Alice pulled the trigger, but the shot missed.

Her enemy pressed down on her with all his weight, immobilizing her with his left hand. Again, lightning flashed in the sky and set the horizon ablaze. Alice looked up and saw the syringe that the man was holding in his right hand. Her vision blurred. A taste of iron in her mouth. She watched, powerless, as the shining needle came down as if in slow motion and stabbed her neck. She could do nothing to stop it.

Gabriel pressed down on the plunger to inject the liquid. The serum burned inside her body like an electric shock. Pain seared through her, abruptly unlocking the gates of her memory. She had the impression that her entire being was on fire and that her heart had been replaced by a grenade with its pin removed.

There was a blinding flash of white light, and she caught a glimpse of something.

It terrified her.

Then she lost consciousness.

I remember...

Three months ago

July 12, 2013

An atmosphere of fear reigns in the capital.

One week earlier, just as people were going home from work, there was a terrorist attack that left Paris dazed and bloodied. A suicide bomber with explosives attached to his belt blew himself up on a bus on Rue Saint-Lazare. The effect was devastating: eight dead, eleven injured.

The same day, a backpack containing a propane cylinder filled with nails was found on line 4 at the Montparnasse-Bienvenue Métro station. Thankfully, the bomb-disposal team managed to defuse it before it could do any damage, but the discovery caused mass panic.

The specter of the 1995 attacks is on everyone's mind.

More and more tourist sites are evacuated every day. "The return of terrorism" is all over the papers and headline news on TV every evening. The SAT, the Criminal Division's anti-terrorism unit, is under pressure and constantly swooping down on enclaves of Islamists, anarchists, and extreme-left activists to check ID papers and make arrests.

In principle, their investigations have nothing to do with me. Not until Antoine de Foucaud, the deputy head of the SAT, asks me to take part in interrogating suspects who have already been in custody for the maximum period allowed and are about to be released. In the 1970s, at the start of his career, Foucaud worked for several years with my father before their paths diverged. He was also one of my instructors at the police academy. He has a high opinion of me and of my abilities as an interrogator—maybe too high.

"We need you on this, Alice."

"What do you want me to do, exactly?"

"We've been trying to make this guy talk for more than three days, but he's not saying a word. I think you can break him."

"Why? Because I'm a woman?"

"No, because you have a talent for it."

I would normally be excited by such an offer. This time, though, to my amazement, I feel no rush of adrenaline, only an immense fatigue and the desire to go home. My head has been screaming with a violent migraine since this morning. Now it's evening—a heavy, oppressive summer evening. The air in Paris is thick with pollution and it has been a mercilessly hot day. With the air-conditioning not working, the Criminal Division's headquarters has been transformed into a furnace. My blouse is sticky with sweat, and I would kill for a cold can of Diet Coke, but the vending machine is out of order.

"Listen, if your guys haven't gotten anything out of him, I don't see what I'll be able to do."

"Please just give it a try," Foucaud begs. "I've seen you do it before."

"I'm just going to waste your time. I don't know anything about the case."

"We'll bring you up to speed on that. Taillandier's already agreed to let you do it. Just get in there and make him give us a name. After that, we'll take over again."

I hesitate, but do I really have a choice in the matter?

We sit in an upper-floor room with two fans blowing warm air at us, and for an hour I am briefed about the suspect by two SAT officers. The man, Brahim Rahmani—aka the "cannon dealer" and the "powder monkey"—has been under close surveillance by the anti-terrorist unit for a long time. He is suspected of having supplied explosives to the group that blew up the Rue Saint-Lazare bus. Small quantities of C-4 and PEP 500 were found in his home during a search, along with plastic charges, cell phones converted into detonators, and a huge arsenal: guns of every caliber, steel rebars, bulletproof vests. After three days in custody, the man has not admitted anything to his interrogators, and the analysis of his hard drive and electronic communications during recent months is not enough to prove his participation, even indirectly, in the terrorist attacks.

It is a fascinating case, but a complicated one. The heat makes it hard for me to concentrate. My two colleagues speak quickly, overloading me with so many details that I struggle to retain them. My memory is usually excellent, but tonight I grab a notebook to write down what they tell me.

When the briefing is over, they take me downstairs to the interrogation room. Foucaud, Taillandier . . . all the big bosses are there, behind a one-way mirror, eager to see me at work. And now I, too, feel eager to enter the arena.

I open the door and walk into the room.

Inside, the heat is stifling, almost unbearable. Handcuffed to a chair, Rahmani is sitting behind a wooden table not much bigger than a school desk. His head is lowered and he is sweating. He barely even notices my presence.

I roll up the sleeves of my blouse and wipe the beads of sweat from my forehead. I have brought a bottle of water as a way of establishing contact. Instead of handing it to the suspect, however, I decide to open it and take a long drink myself.

To begin with, the water makes me feel better. Then, abruptly, I feel dizzy and disoriented. I close my eyes and lean against the wall.

When I open them again, I have no idea where I am. My mind is a blank, a void. And I feel the most awful anxiety, as if I've been teleported to an unknown place.

I feel myself reeling, so I sit down in the chair, facing the man, and ask: "Who are you? What am I doing here?"

One week ago
Tuesday, October 8, 2013

I remember everything…

Paris, six p.m. The end of a beautiful fall day.

The last rays of the setting sun set the capital ablaze, reflecting in the windows of buildings, the surface of the river, the windshields of cars, spreading their golden light through the city's streets. A wave of dazzling light and long shadows.

Near the Parc André-Citroën, I extricate my car from a traffic jam and drive it up the concrete ramp that leads to a glass ship moored on the banks of the Seine. The façade of the Georges-Pompidou European Hospital looks like the prow of a futuristic ocean liner that has made a stopover in the south of the fifteenth arrondissement; it hugs the rounded bend of the street and mirrors the Judas trees and hawthorn hedges planted along either side of the esplanade.

Parking lot. Concrete maze. Sliding doors opening on a large central atrium. Row of elevators. Waiting room.

I have an appointment with Professor Evariste Clouseau, the head of the National Institute of Memory, which occupies the building's entire top floor.

Clouseau is one of France's leading specialists in Alzheimer's disease. I met him three months ago as part of the investigation my team was conducting into the murder of his twin brother, Jean-Baptiste, the head of the cardiovascular unit in the same hospital. The two brothers hated each other so virulently that when Jean-Baptiste learned that he had pancreatic cancer, he decided to commit suicide and make it look as if he had been murdered by his brother. The case was big news. Evariste was even briefly imprisoned before we managed to uncover the truth. After his release, he told Seymour that we had freed him from hell and that he would be eternally grateful to us. These were not empty words; when I called him a week ago to book an appointment, he managed to squeeze me in that very day.

After the fiasco during my interrogation of the suspected terrorist, I quickly recovered my memory. My lapse lasted no more than three minutes, but it happened with everyone watching. Taillandier forced me to take medical leave, then blocked my return, pending a doctor's assessment. So I had to undergo an in-depth medical examination and consult a psychiatrist again. Despite my protests, I was prescribed a long break from work.

This came as a surprise to no one. Taillandier had been openly trying to get rid of me for years. She had failed after the Vaughn case, but this new episode handed her the chance at revenge on a silver platter. I refused to go quietly, however. I contacted the union, hired an employment lawyer, and saw several other doctors, who all testified to my perfect health.

I wasn't really worried. My morale was high, and I wanted to fight, get my job back. Sure, I'd had that sudden, brief memory loss, and—like everyone—I sometimes forgot what I was doing, but I attributed these little episodes to stress, tiredness, overwork, the heat...

And that opinion was shared by all the doctors I went to see. All but one, who mentioned the possibility of a neurological disease and asked me to undergo a brain scan.

Figuring that the best defense is a good offense, I decided to be proactive and consult a recognized authority in the field. So it was that I went to see Clouseau, who ordered a whole battery of tests. Last week, I spent an entire day in this damn hospital, enduring a spinal tap, an MRI, a PET scan, and various blood tests and memory tests. Clouseau asked me to come in today so he could talk to me about the results.

I feel confident. And impatient to start work again. I have even planned an evening out with some university friends—Karine, Malika, and Samia—to celebrate my return to the job. We are going to drink cocktails on the Champs-Élysées and—

"The professor will see you now."

A secretary leads me into an office with a view of the Seine. Behind his desk—an unusual piece of furniture made from the wing of an airplane, as smooth and shiny as a mirror—Evariste Clouseau is typing something on his laptop. At first glance, the neurologist doesn't seem especially impressive: wild hair, pale complexion, tired eyes, badly trimmed beard. He looks like he has stayed up all night playing poker and downing glasses of single-malt whiskey. Under his white coat, he wears a checkered shirt that's buttoned wrong and a burgundy sweater that looks as if it were knitted by a drunken grandmother.

In spite of his unkempt appearance, however, Clouseau inspires confidence, and he is highly regarded in the field—in recent years, he has helped implement new diagnostic criteria for Alzheimer's, and the National Institute of Memory—the organization he runs—is one of the leading establishments in research and patient care. Whenever there are reports about Alzheimer's on television or in the papers, he is the first person journalists call on for an opinion.

"Good evening, Mademoiselle Schafer. Please sit down."

A few minutes later, the sun sets and the room becomes dim. Clouseau takes off his glasses and gives me an owl-like glance before turning on an old brass library lamp. He presses a key on his computer keyboard, which is connected to a flat-screen monitor on the wall. I guess the display shows the results of my tests.

"I'm going to be straight with you, Alice. The analysis of your scans is disturbing."

I say nothing.

He gets to his feet and explains. "These are images of your brain taken during the MRI. To be more precise, they are images of your hippocampus, a part of the brain that plays an essential role in memory and spatial location."

He uses a stylus to mark out an area on the screen.

"This part here shows a slight atrophy. At your age, that isn't normal."

Clouseau allows me time to digest this news before show-ing me another image.

"You had another scan last week, a PET scan. We injected you with a radioactive tracer to determine if there was any reduction in carbohydrate metabolism in certain brain structures."

Seeing that I don't understand a word of this, he tries to articulate the problem in layman's terms. "The PET scan enables us to visualize the activity in different areas of your brain and—"

I cut him off. "Just tell me what it shows."

He sighs. "Well, there are signs of damage in certain areas."

He walks closer to the large screen and points with his stylus at a segment of the image.

"You see these red patches? They represent amyloid plaques that form in the areas between your neurons."

"Amyloid plaques?"

"Also known as senile plaques. Protein deposits responsible for certain neurodegenerative diseases."

These words hammer into my mind, but I don't want to hear them.

Clouseau clicks to a document—a page full of numbers.

"This problematic concentration of amyloid proteins is confirmed by analysis of the cerebrospinal fluid taken during your spinal tap. That, too, showed the presence of pathogenic Tau proteins, which proves that you are suffering from an early-onset form of Alzheimer's dis-ease."

Silence in the office. I am dumbstruck, on the defensive, incapable of thinking clearly.

"But that's impossible. I . . . I'm not even forty!"

"It's very rare, admittedly, but it does happen."

"No. You're wrong." I refuse to accept this diagnosis. I know there is no effective treatment for this disease—no miracle drug, no vaccine.

"I understand your emotion, Alice. For now, I would advise you not to do anything rash. Take your time to think this through. At the moment, there is no reason for you to change the way you live your life—"

"I'm not sick!"

"It's a very difficult thing to accept, Alice, I know that," Clouseau says in a gentle voice. "But you are young and the disease is still in the early stages. There are currently new medicines being tested. Up to now, lacking effective ways of diagnosing the disease, we have always identified its sufferers too late. But that is changing, and—"

I don't want to hear another word. I jump to my feet and leave his office without a backward glance.

Lobby. Row of elevators. Central atrium. Concrete maze. Parking lot. Engine thrum.

I lower all the windows and drive with the wind blowing in my hair, the radio on full blast. Johnny Winter's guitar on "Further On Up the Road."

I feel good. Alive. I am not going to die. I have my whole life ahead of me.

I accelerate, pass other cars, honk my horn. Quai de Grenelle. Quai Branly, Quai d'Orsay...I am not sick. My memory is good. Everyone has always told me that—in school, in college, in the police. I never forget a face and notice every detail; I am capable of memorizing and reciting dozens of pages of evidence from the police file. I remember everything. Everything!

My brain is churning, seething, thinking at top speed. To convince myself of this, I begin saying out loud every fact that flashes through my head:

Six times seven is forty-two / Eight times nine is seventy-two / The capital of Pakistan is Islamabad / The capital of Madagascar is Antananarivo / Stalin died on March 5, 1953 / The Berlin Wall was erected on the night of August 12, 1961.

I remember everything.

The name of my grandmother's perfume was Soir de Paris, and it smelled of bergamot and jasmine / Apollo 11 landed on the moon on July 20, 1969 / The name of Tom Sawyer's girlfriend was Becky Thatcher / I ate lunch at Dessirier today—I had sea bream tartare, Seymour had fish and chips, we both had coffee, and the check came to 79 euros and 83 centimes.

I remember everything.

Although uncredited, the guitar solo on "While My Guitar Gently Weeps" from the Beatles' White Album *is played by Eric Clapton / The correct expression is* toeing the line, *not* towing the line, *and it refers to runners standing in the correct place at the beginning of a race / I filled my car with gas this morning at the BP garage on Boulevard Murat. The 98 unleaded was 1.684 euros per liter; I spent 67 euros / In* North by Northwest, *Alfred Hitchcock makes his cameo appearance after the opening credits; the door of a bus closes in front of him, leaving him on the sidewalk.*

I remember everything.

In Conan Doyle's novels, Sherlock Holmes never says "Elementary, my dear Watson" / The pin code for my debit card is 9728 / The card number is 0573 5233 3754 61 / The security code is 793 / Stanley Kubrick's first film is not Killer's Kiss *but* Fear and Desire */ In 1990, the referee of the match between Benfica and Olympique Marseille who allowed a handballed goal by Vata was named Marcel van Langenhove. That goal made my father cry / Paraguay's currency is the guarani / Botswana's is the pula / My grandfather's motorcycle was a Kawasaki H1 / At twenty years old, my father drove a French blue Renault 8 Gordini.*

I remember everything.

The entry code for my apartment building is 6507B and the code for the elevator is 1321A / My sixth-grade music teacher was named Monsieur Piguet. He made us play the Stones' "She's a Rainbow" on the recorder / I bought my first two CDs in 1991, when I was in my junior year of high school: Du Vent dans les Plaines, *by Noir Désir, and Schubert's* Impromptus *on Deutsche Grammophon, performed by Krystian Zimerman / I scored 16 out of 20 in my philosophy baccalaureate. The subject of the dissertation was "Is passion always an obstacle to self-knowledge?" / In my final year of high school, I was in class C3. On Thursdays, we had three hours of coursework in room 207; I sat in the third row next to Stéphane Muratore, and when school was over he would take me home on his Peugeot ST scooter, which struggled up hills.*

I remember everything.

Belle du Seigneur *is 1,109 pages long in paperback / The music for* The Double Life of Véronique *was composed by Zbigniew Preisner / When I was a college student, my dorm room number was 308 / on Tuesdays in the cafeteria, they used to serve lasagna / In* The Woman Next Door, *the character played by Fanny Ardant is named Mathilde Bauchard / I remember the goose bumps I felt listening to "That's My People"—where NTM sample a Chopin prelude—on my first iPod / I remember where I was on September 11, 2001: In a hotel room, on vacation in*

Madrid, with an older lover. He was a married chief of police who looked like my father. The Twin Towers collapsed while I was in that sleazy atmosphere / I remember that complicated time, those toxic men that I hated. That period before I realized that you had to love yourself a little bit before you could love anyone else.

I cross the Pont des Invalides, take Avenue Franklin-Roosevelt, and drive down the ramp that leads to the underground parking garage. I walk to Motor Village on the Champs-Élysées traffic circle, where I meet the girls.

"Hello, Alice!"

They are sitting at a table on the terrace of the Fiat Caffè, nibbling Italian appetizers. I sit down with them, order a champagne spritzer, and drink it in practically a single gulp. We laugh as we talk about life, love, gossip, clothes, work. We order a round of pink martinis and toast our friendship. Then we move on and try several different places: the Moonlight, the Thirteenth Floor, the Londonderry. I dance, let men approach me, flirt with me, touch me. I am not sick. I'm sexy as hell.

I am not going to die. I am not going to wither. I am not going to come undone. I am not going to wilt like a flower cut too early. I drink—Bacardi mojito, violet champagne, Bombay gin and tonic...I am not going to end up in a home for the mentally ill, yelling insults at nurse's aides and staring into space as I slurp applesauce through a straw.

Everything spins around me. I am happily tipsy. Drunk on freedom. Time speeds by. It's past midnight. I kiss the girls goodbye and walk back to the underground parking garage. Third level belowground. Morgue lighting. Stink of piss. Heels tapping on concrete. Feeling nauseated. Staggering. In a few seconds, my drunkenness is tainted with sadness. I feel pathetic, oppressed. My throat tightens and it all comes rushing to the surface—the image of my brain being assailed by senile plaques, the fear of the great collapse. A weary fluorescent bulb blinks and crackles like a cricket. I take out my car keys, press the button that opens all the doors, and sit crumpled behind the steering wheel. Tears come to my eyes. A sound . . . there is someone in the back seat! I sit up in shock. The shadow of a face emerges from the darkness.

"Seymour! Jesus, you scared the hell out of me."

"Good evening, Alice."

"What the hell are you doing here?"

"I was waiting until you were alone. Clouseau called me. I was worried about you."

"Goddamn it, whatever happened to patient confidentiality?"

"He didn't have to tell me anything. Your father and I have been living in fear of this moment for the past three months."

I turn on the ceiling light so I can see him better. He has tears in his eyes too, but he wipes them away with his sleeve and clears his throat.

"It's your decision, Alice, but I think you need to act

quickly on this. That's what you taught me—never put off until tomorrow what you can do today. Take the bull by the horns and don't let go. That's why you're the best cop I know, because you don't spare yourself, because you are always the first one to enter the fray, because you're always one step ahead."

I sniff. "It's impossible to be one step ahead of Alzheimer's."

In the rearview mirror, I see him open a manila folder. He takes out an airplane ticket and a brochure with a cover showing an impressive building at the edge of a lake. "My mother told me about this place. It's in Maine. Sebago Hospital."

"What was your mother doing there?"

"She has Parkinson's, as you know. Two years ago, she was trembling so much that her life was a nightmare. One day, her doctor suggested a new form of treatment—they put two thin electrodes in her brain connected to a little electric box implanted under her collarbone. Kind of like a pacemaker."

"You told me this already, Seymour, and you yourself admitted that the electrical pulses didn't stop the disease from progressing."

"Maybe not, but they got rid of the worst symptoms, and she feels much better now."

"Alzheimer's and Parkinson's are not the same thing at all."

"I know," he says, handing me the brochure, "but look at this place. They use deep-brain stimulation to fight the symptoms of Alzheimer's. Initial results are encouraging. It wasn't easy, but I got you a place in their study. I've paid for it all, but you have to leave tomorrow. I booked you a plane ticket to Boston."

I shake my head. "Keep your money, Seymour. It doesn't make any difference. I'm going to die, period."

"Sleep on it," he insists. "But first, let me take you home. You're in no state to drive."

Too weary to argue with him, I slide over into the passenger seat and let him drive.

It is 12:17 a.m. when the security camera in the parking garage films us on our way out.

24

CHAPTER ZERO

Tribeca
4:50 a.m.
Three hours before Alice first meets Gabriel

THE TELEPHONE RANG six times in room 308 of the Greenwich Hotel before it was finally picked up.

"Hello," said a thick voice, emerging from deep sleep.

"This is reception, Mr. Keyne. I'm terribly sorry to disturb you, but I have a call for you. A Mr. Thomas Krieg is asking to speak with you."

"In the middle of the night? What the hell time is it, anyway?"

"Nearly five o'clock, sir. He told me it was very urgent."

"Okay, put him through."

Gabriel pushed himself up on the pillow, then sat on the edge of the bed. The room was in darkness, but the light from the radio alarm clock gave a vague impression of the chaos within it. The carpet was strewn with clothes and small, empty bottles. The woman sleeping next to him had not woken up. It took him a few seconds to remember her name: Elena Sabatini, from Florida, whom he had met the previous evening in the hotel lounge. After a few martinis, he had persuaded her to go up to his room and they had gotten to know each other much better while raiding the minibar.

Gabriel rubbed his eyes and sighed. He hated what he had become since his wife left him—a lost soul drifting in a downward spiral, a ghost. *There is nothing more tragic than to find an individual bogged down in the length of life, devoid of breadth.* Martin Luther King Jr.'s quote came to mind immediately. It fit him like a glove.

"Gabriel? Hey, are you there?" yelled the voice at the other end of the line.

Receiver pressed to his ear, Keyne got off his bed and closed the sliding door that separated the bedroom from the little living room next to it. "Hello, Thomas."

"I tried calling you on your landline in Astoria, then on your cell phone, but you weren't answering."

"The battery must be dead. How did you find me?"

"I remembered it was the week of the American Psychiatric Association's annual conference. I called their main office and they told me they'd booked you a room at the Greenwich."

"What do you want?"

"I heard you got a great response yesterday for your speech on the psychiatric aspects of Alzheimer's."

"Spare me the flattery, would you?"

"You're right; I'll get straight to the point. I want your opinion on a patient."

"At five in the morning? Thomas, can I remind you that we're no longer partners?"

"Yeah, and that's too bad. We made a good team, the two of us. We complement each other perfectly, the psychiatrist and the neurologist."

"Yeah, yeah, but it's over. I sold you my share in the practice, remember?"

"The biggest mistake of your life."

Gabriel lost his temper. "We're not going to have this discussion again! You know perfectly well why I did it!"

"Yes—moving to London so you could get joint custody of your son. And what did you get out of it? A restraining order that forced you to come back to the States."

Gabriel felt his eyes tearing up. He rubbed his temples while his friend kept talking.

"Could you take a look at my case file? Please. It's an early-onset Alzheimer's. I think you'll find it fascinating. I'll e-mail it to you now and call you back in twenty minutes."

"You've gotta be kidding! I'm going back to bed. And please don't call me again," he said firmly before hanging up.

The window reflected the image of a tired, unshaven, and depressed-looking man. He found his cell phone—battery dead—on the carpet next to the couch. He plugged it in, walked to the bathroom, and spent ten minutes in the shower to wake himself from his lethargy. Wearing a bathrobe, he went back to the living room. Using the pod machine on top of a chest of drawers, he made himself a double espresso and drank it while watching the Hudson shine in the first glimmers of daylight. After that, he made himself another coffee and turned on his laptop. As promised, Thomas's e-mail was waiting in his in-box.

Christ, that guy never gives up!

The neurologist had sent him his patient's case file. Krieg knew that Gabriel would not be able to resist taking a look at it.

Gabriel opened the PDF and skimmed through the first few pages. The patient's unusual profile caught his attention: Alice Schafer, thirty-eight, a pretty Frenchwoman with regular features and an open face framed by blond hair tied back in a ponytail. He lingered for a few seconds on her photograph, on her eyes in particular. Pale irises, with an expression that was both intense and fragile. There was something mysterious, indecipherable about her. He sighed. This damn disease had always wrecked lives, but now it was hitting people younger than ever before.

Gabriel scrolled down in the file. There were dozens of pages of test results and medical images—MRI, PET scan, spinal tap—culminating in a definitive diagnosis by Professor Evariste Clouseau. Though he had never met him, Gabriel knew all about this French neurologist's reputation. He was one of the best in his field.

The second part of the file began with Alice Schafer's admission form for Sebago Hospital, the clinic specializing in memory problems that he had founded with Thomas and two other partners. It was a cutting-edge research facility for Alzheimer's. The young woman had been admitted six days earlier, on October 9, to undergo treatment through deep-brain stimulation, the clinic's specialty. On the eleventh, a tiny neurostimulator—known to the patients as a "brain pacemaker"—had been implanted under her skin to provide constant electrical impulses to her brain. After that, there were no more notes.

Strange.

Under normal circumstances, the implantation of the three electrodes in her brain would have taken place the next day. Without them, the pacemaker was useless. Gabriel was swallowing his last mouthful of coffee when his cell phone vibrated on the desk.

"Have you read the file?" Thomas asked.

"Reading it now. What do you expect from me, exactly?"

"Any help you can give me. I'm in deep shit, Gabriel. That girl, Alice Schafer, she escaped from the clinic last night."

"Escaped?"

"She's a cop. She knows what she's doing. She left her room without telling anyone. She fooled the nurses and even injured Caleb Dunn, who was trying to stop her."

"Dunn? The security guard?"

"Yeah. The idiot pulled a gun on her. He got into a fight with the girl while he was trying to handcuff her, and she came out on top. Apparently, the gun went off by accident, but she ran away, taking the gun and the handcuffs with her."

"Is he seriously hurt?"

"No, the bullet went into the flesh of his thigh. He's being cared for here, and he says he won't involve the cops on the condition that we pay him a hundred thousand dollars."

"Are you telling me one of your patients has wounded a security guard and is now on the run, carrying a weapon, and you haven't informed the police? That's just irresponsible, Thomas. You could go to jail for this!"

"If we tell the cops, we'll have the law and the press all over us. We could lose our accreditation for something like this. It could put us out of business. I'm not going to give up my life's work just because of that stupid security guard. That's why I need your help, Gabriel. I want you to bring her back to me."

"Why me? And how am I supposed to do it?"

"I've carried out my own investigation. Alice Schafer is in New York, and so are you. She went to Portland by taxi at nine last night. From there, she took a bus to Boston, then a train to Manhattan. She arrived there this morning at five twenty."

"If you know where she is, why don't you come here and get her yourself?"

"I can't leave the hospital in the middle of a crisis. Agatha, my assistant, is on a plane now. She'll be in Manhattan in two hours, but I really want you to take care of this. You have a gift for reasoning with people. You have something special, an empathy, like one of those actors who—"

"Okay, okay, don't start on the flattery again. How can you be sure she's still in New York?"

"Because of the GPS tracker we implant in our patients' shoes. She's in the middle of Central Park, in a wooded area called the Ramble. According to the tracker, she hasn't moved in the past half hour, so she's either dead or asleep, or maybe she dumped her shoes. Please, Gabriel, just go over there and look for her—I'm asking you as a friend. We have to find her before the police do."

Keyne took a few seconds to think about this.

"Gabriel? Are you still there?"

"Tell me more about her. I saw that you implanted the stimulator four days ago."

"Yes," Krieg confirmed. "The latest model, completely miniaturized, hardly any bigger than a SIM card. You should see it, it's impressive."

"So why didn't you move on to the next stage and install the electrodes?"

"Because overnight, she went completely crazy! She was in total denial. Add that to the amnesia and—"

"Amnesia?"

"Schafer is suffering from a sort of anterograde amnesia based on her denial of her condition. Her brain has been blocking everything that's happened to her since her Alzheimer's was diagnosed."

"She's not storing any new memories?"

"Not since a drunken night a week ago, just after Clouseau gave her the diagnosis. Every morning when she wakes up, her memory resets. She doesn't know she has Alzheimer's and she thinks that she was partying on the Champs-Élysées just the night before. She has also forgotten that she's been on medical leave from the police department for the past three months."

Gabriel tried to put things in perspective. "Well, we know that denial and the disappearance of past memories are symptoms of the disease..."

"Yes, but this girl doesn't appear sick at all. She's intellectually agile and quite a character."

Gabriel gave a long sigh of resignation. Krieg knew better than anyone how to pique his curiosity. And this girl's case was clearly very mysterious.

"All right, I'll go see if I can find her."

"Thanks, Gabe! You're a lifesaver!"

"I'm not making any promises, though," Keyne said.

"You'll manage, I'm sure you will. I'll text you her exact location. Call me as soon as you have any news."

Gabriel hung up with the disagreeable sensation of having been duped. Since his return to New York, he had created his own medical business in Astoria, specializing in emergency psychiatric house calls. He sent his secretary a text telling her he'd be out of the office this morning and asking her to get someone to cover for him.

He quickly got dressed in his previous day's clothes— dark jeans, pale blue shirt, dark jacket, putty-colored trench coat, Converse sneakers—then opened the door of the closet where he had left his medical kit. He put a syringe filled with a powerful sedative inside a small leather toiletries case. After all, this woman was armed and potentially dangerous. He put the travel case in his briefcase and left the room.

Downstairs, he asked the doorman to call him a taxi, then realized he had left his remote control for the briefcase in his hotel room. If he went more than fifty yards from the receiver, an alarm and an electrical charge would go off automatically.

His cab was on its way, so he decided not to waste time by going back up to his room; instead, he left the briefcase in the hotel cloakroom.

In return, the employee handed him a claim ticket bearing the number 127.

A watermark of the intertwined letters *G* and *H* formed a discreet logo behind it.

25

JUST BEFORE

Manhattan
7:15 a.m.
Forty-five minutes before Alice first meets Gabriel

NOTES FROM A jazz number crackled inside the cab.

It took Gabriel only a few seconds to recognize the legendary recording: Bill Evans playing "All of You" by Cole Porter at the Village Vanguard in 1961. Although he had no talent as a musician, the psychiatrist loved jazz and often went to bars and concert halls in search of new sounds or—the very opposite—in an attempt to rekindle the emotions he had felt as a college student when he first discovered the music in the clubs of Chicago.

There was roadwork on Harrison, so the taxi took a roundabout route to get on Hudson Street. In the back seat of the cab, Gabriel continued reading Alice Schafer's file on his cell phone screen. The final part of the document, written by a psychologist at the clinic, consisted of a long biographical note supported by articles taken from French newspapers, each with a brief translated summary. All these articles mentioned the serial killer Erik Vaughn, who had terrorized the French capital two years earlier. Gabriel had never heard of the case. It wasn't easy to read on such a small screen and with the taxi lurching from side to side. At first, skimming through the early press reports, Gabriel thought it was an investigation that Alice was working on, and he felt as if he were living inside one of those thrillers that he often devoured on train or plane trips.

Then he came to the four-page article from *Paris Match* that described the tragedy in Alice's life: The young cop had found the killer, but she too had become one of his victims. What he read chilled him—Vaughn had stabbed her in the abdomen, killing the baby inside her womb and leaving her for dead in a pool of blood. And then the bitter coda: her husband dying in a car accident as he drove to the hospital to be with her.

The shock of this made Gabriel feel sick, and for a minute he thought he was going to throw up the two cups of coffee he'd drunk earlier that morning. While the car rushed along Eighth Avenue, he pressed his face to the window for several minutes, keeping himself very still. How could fate have been so cruel to this woman? After she'd endured such tragedy, how could fate strike her down with Alzheimer's at only thirty-eight years old?

The sun was rising now, its first rays piercing the forest of sky-scrapers. The taxi moved up Central Park West and dropped Gabriel at the intersection of Seventy-Second Street, near the park's western entrance.

The psychiatrist handed the driver a bill and closed the door behind him. The air was cool, but the cloudless sky gave him hope that this would turn out to be a beautiful day. He looked around him. Traffic was growing dense. On the sidewalk, pretzel and hot-dog carts were already open for business. Opposite the Dakota, a street vendor was laying out his posters, T-shirts, and gadgets bearing the image of John Lennon.

Gabriel entered the park. The atmosphere was bucolic. He passed the triangle garden of Strawberry Fields and walked down the path that ran alongside the lake until he reached the Cherry Hill Fountain. The sunlight was beautiful, the air fresh and dry, and already the area was bustling with life—joggers, skaters, cyclists, and dog walkers all passing by in a sort of improvised but harmonious ballet.

Gabriel felt his phone vibrate in the pocket of his trench coat. Thomas had sent him a text containing a screenshot of a map showing Alice Schafer's precise location. The young woman was still somewhere on the other side of the bridge that went over the lake.

Gabriel had no trouble orienting himself. The towers of the San Remo were behind him; farther up ahead were the

Bethesda Terrace and Fountain; to his left was Bow Bridge, with its delicate arabesque decorations. He crossed this long, cream-colored bridge and went into the Ramble.

The psychiatrist had never been here, in the wildest part of Central Park. Little by little, the copses and bushes gave way to real woods: elms, oaks, a carpet of moss and dry leaves, boulders. He kept walking, eyes fixed on the screen of his phone so he wouldn't get lost. It was hard to believe that a dense forest could exist so close to such a busy area. The thicker the vegetation grew, the quieter the sounds of the city became, and finally they disappeared altogether. Soon, all he could hear was birdsong and the rustle of leaves.

Gabriel blew on his hands to warm them up and looked at his screen again. He was beginning to think he must have gone the wrong way, when he came to a clearing in the woods.

It was a place removed from time, protected from everything around it by the golden dome formed by the foliage of a giant elm tree. There was something unreal about the light here, as if butterflies with luminous wings were fluttering in the sky. Swept by a gentle breeze, red leaves fluttered through the air. An odor of damp earth and rotting leaves permeated the atmosphere.

In the center of the clearing, a woman was lying on a bench, asleep.

Gabriel carefully approached her. Yes, it was Alice Schafer, curled up in a fetal position, wearing a leather jacket and jeans. A bloodstained blouse was visible below her jacket. Gabriel was alarmed, thinking that she must be injured. After examining the blouse, however, he realized the blood must be that of the hospital security guard, Caleb Dunn. He leaned over until he was almost touching the young woman's hair, listening to her breathe. He stayed in that position for a moment, watching the thousand shades of gold reflected in her ponytail, looking at her fragile face, her pale skin, and her dry pink lips, feeling the warm air that blew out from between them.

He felt unexpectedly stirred by this. A fire lit up his entire being. This woman's fragility, the solitude that seemed to emanate from her body, echoed painfully within him. All it took was a few seconds, a single look, and he felt destiny knocking on the door of his life. Seized by some irrational force, he suddenly knew that he would do everything he could to help Alice Schafer.

Time was short. As gently as possible, he searched through the young woman's jacket pockets and found her wallet, a pair of handcuffs, and Caleb Dunn's gun. He left the pistol where it was but took the wallet and the handcuffs. Inside the wallet was Schafer's police ID card, a photograph of a blond, curly-haired man, and an ultrasound image.

So, what now?

His brain buzzed. The glimmers of a crazy scenario began to form inside his mind. The outline had come to him during the taxi ride as he listened to the jazz pianist on the radio, read the articles about Vaughn, the serial killer, and thought over what Thomas had said about Alice's anterograde amnesia and her denial of the disease: *Every morning when she wakes up, her memory resets. She doesn't know she has Alzheimer's and she thinks that she was partying on the Champs-Élysées just the night before.*

He emptied his own pockets and made an inventory of everything he had with him: his wallet, his cell phone, a shiny ballpoint pen, his Swiss Army knife, the claim ticket for his briefcase.

He had to improvise with that. Time was running out. The pieces of the puzzle came together in his head with stunning speed. Inspired, he put together his plan in only a few seconds.

He checked the number of the Greenwich Hotel on his cell phone, then used his pen to write it on Alice's palm, praying that she wouldn't wake up.

Then he left the clearing for a few minutes. About fifty yards north, he found a little pond crossed by a tiny rustic wooden bridge and surrounded by weeping willows and low bushes. To judge from the number of bird feeders attached to tree branches, this place—calm and silent at this time of day—must be a sort of observation point created by the park's bird-watchers.

Gabriel took off his trench coat and cut a long, thin band from the lining that looked like a pale-colored strip of gauze. He removed his jacket, rolled up the sleeve of his shirt, and, with the blade of his knife, carved six numbers into his fore-arm: 141197, the combination for the lock on his briefcase.

He grimaced with pain as he felt the blade dig into his skin. If a park ranger were to come upon him now, he would struggle to explain what he was doing.

He wrapped up his bleeding arm with the makeshift bandage, then lowered his shirtsleeve, put his jacket back on, and bundled up his and Alice's wallets, his Swiss army knife, his watch, and his pen in his raincoat.

Then he decided to call Thomas.

"Tell me you've found her and she's alive!" his friend pleaded.

"Yeah, she's asleep on a bench in the middle of the woods here."

"Have you tried waking her?"

"Not yet. But I need to do it before someone shows up."

"Have you taken Dunn's gun off her?"

"Not yet."

"What are you waiting for?"

"Listen, I'm going to try to bring her back to the clinic, but I want to do it my way."

"Okay, whatever you think is best," Krieg said.

Frowning, Gabriel scratched the back of his head. "Who do you think she'll try to call when she wakes up?"

"Probably Seymour Lombart. He's her best friend and her colleague. He was the one who recommended our clinic to her and paid for her treatment."

"You have to call that guy. Whatever she says to him, ask him not to mention her disease. Tell him to play for time and follow her instructions as she gives them."

"Are you sure about this? Because—"

"I'm not sure of anything. But if you don't like it, you can always come here and get her yourself."

Krieg simply sighed.

"One other thing. Is Agatha in New York yet?" Gabriel asked.

"She called me two minutes ago. She just landed at JFK."

"Tell her to come to Central Park right away. To the north of the Ramble, she'll find a little pond surrounded by azaleas. There's a wooden bridge and some trees with bird feeders in the branches. I'm going to leave all my things along with Schafer's personal belongings in the biggest of those bird feeders. Ask Agatha to pick them up before anyone else finds them. And tell her to be ready to help me if I call her."

"I'll do that right now," Krieg replied. "When will you call again?"

"Whenever I can. There's no point trying to reach me on my cell phone, because I need to get rid of it."

"All right. Well, good luck."

"One last question: Does Alice Schafer have a boyfriend?"

"Not that I know of."

"What about that Seymour guy?"

"I think he's gay. Why?"

"No reason."

Gabriel hung up and slid the cell phone into the bundle he'd made with his trench coat, then pushed this as deeply as possible into the biggest bird feeder he could find.

Back in the clearing, he saw with relief that Alice had not moved.

There, he dealt with the final details. He took the claim ticket for his briefcase and pushed it into the small pocket of Alice's jeans. Then he leaned over her forearm and, very gently, played with the push button of the man's watch she was wearing, changing the date to exactly one week before. On the face of the Patek, the perpetual calendar now said that today was Tuesday, October 8, instead of October 15.

Last, he slipped one of the handcuff bracelets around Alice's right wrist and fastened the other one to his own left wrist.

Now they were inseparable. Chained together for better or worse.

He threw the key to the handcuffs as far as he could into the undergrowth.

Then he curled up on the bench, closed his eyes, and leaned softly against the young woman.

The weight of his body seemed to pull Alice from the depths of sleep.

It was eight a.m.

The adventure could begin.

26

THE MIRRORS

I OPEN MY EYES.

I recognize the room—white, antiseptic, timeless. Tile floor, immaculate walls, a wardrobe, and a small wooden desk. Wide window blinds filter the slanting light. A décor more in keeping with the comfort of a hotel than the asceticism of a hospital.

I know exactly where I am: Room 6 in Sebago Hospital, near Portland, Maine. And I know why I am here.

I sit up against the pillow. I feel as if I am in a sensory no-man's-land, like a dead star extinguished a long time ago. Little by little, however, I regain full awareness. My body is rested, my mind relieved of a great weight, as if I have just emerged from a long, nightmarish journey that has taken me through the palaces of Night, Dreams, and Sleep, has seen me fight Cerberus and defeat the Furies.

I stand up and walk, barefoot, to the sliding glass door. I open it, and the blast of icy air that blows through the room revives me. The view below me is breathtaking. Surrounded by a steeply sloping pine forest, Sebago Lake is a cobalt mirror that stretches out for miles like an azure jewel. There is a huge rock in the shape of a castle and a wooden dock extending over the water.

"Hello, Ms. Schafer."

Surprised, I turn around. Sitting in a corner of the room, an Asian-American nurse has been watching me silently for several minutes without my noticing.

"I hope you are feeling well. Dr. Keyne is waiting for you near the lake."

"Dr. Keyne?"

"He asked me to tell you he was there as soon as you woke up." She walks to the window and points to a spot in the distance. I squint and see Gabriel, hands inside the open hood of the Shelby. He waves, signals me to join him. Inside the closet, I find the suitcase I brought with me. I put on a pair of jeans, a sweater, a jacket, and shoes, and I exit through the sliding glass door.

I walk toward him, mesmerized by the deep blue surface of the lake.

Everything is clear in my mind now. My memories are

neatly ordered in the filing cabinet of my brain. Clouseau's alarming diagnosis, Seymour's mentioning Sebago Hospital, his efforts to have me admitted here, my flight to the United States, my first days in the clinic, the cerebral stimulator implanted in my chest and the panic attack that followed, my forceful denial of the disease, my escape from the hospital, my fight with the security guard, my running away to New York, falling asleep on that bench in Central Park...

And then the bizarre encounter with that strange guy, Gabriel Keyne, who accompanied me on the winding path of that crazy day. A treasure hunt during which my deepest terrors rose to the surface: The specter of Erik Vaughn, the loss of my baby, the trauma of Paul's death, my doubts about the loyalty of my father and Seymour. And my continuing refusal to accept the state of my health, to the extent that I persuaded myself that I was waking up on the morning of October 8 when it was actually one week later.

"Hello, Alice. I hope you've slept well," Keyne says, closing the hood of the car.

He is wearing cargo pants, a wide leather belt, a ribbed-knit sweater. His beard is thick, his hair a mess, his eyes dark-ringed and shining. The grease marks on his cheeks make him look more like a mechanic than a doctor.

I say nothing. He tries to start a conversation.

"I'm sorry about the syringe I stuck in your neck. But sedating you was the only way to get you to sleep."

He grabs the cigarette tucked behind his ear and lights it with an old Zippo lighter. I now know that this man is not

Vaughn. But who is he? As if reading my thoughts, he holds out a hand shiny with oil and grease.

"Gabriel Keyne, psychiatrist," he says, introducing himself formally.

I refuse to shake his hand. "Jazz pianist, magician, FBI special agent, psychiatrist... you really are a chameleon."

He gives a sort of embarrassed grimace. "I understand why you're mad at me, Alice, and I'm sorry to have deceived you. But this time, I swear I'm telling you the truth."

As often happens, the cop inside me gets the upper hand and I bombard him with questions. I discover that it was his former partner Thomas Krieg, the clinic director, who asked him to find me in New York and bring me here.

"But why did you claim to be a pianist? Why Dublin? Why the handcuffs, the cloakroom ticket, and the numbers on my hand? What the hell was all that about?"

He exhales a long plume of smoke. "It was all part of a script that I wrote at the last minute."

"A script?"

"The staging of a role-play psychiatric game, if you prefer."

Seeing my incredulous expression, Gabriel realizes he needs to tell me more.

"We had to find a way to stop you from denying your condition. To make you confront the ghosts of your past in order to free you from them. This is my job: rebuilding people, trying to help them reorder their minds."

"And you came up with this 'script' just like that?"

"I tried to enter into your logic, your way of thinking. It's the most effective way of establishing contact. I improvised as I went along based on what you told me and the decisions you made."

I shook my head. "No, I don't believe a word of this. It's impossible."

He looks at me. "Why?"

In my head, the events of the previous day are replaying on fast-forward. And then the images freeze as they are succeeded by questions. "The numbers in blood on your arm?"

"I scratched them there myself with a Swiss Army knife."

I have trouble believing what I'm hearing. "The claim ticket from the Greenwich Hotel?"

"That's where I spent the previous night, after a conference."

"The electrified briefcase?"

"Mine. The alarm and the electric shock are set off automatically as soon as the briefcase is taken more than fifty yards from the remote control."

"The GPS in my shoe?"

"All the patients in the clinic have a GPS in one of their shoes. It's common practice for hospitals dealing with patients suffering from memory problems."

"But you had one too..." I play the scene over in my head, me standing in front of the thrift store as Gabriel throws his sneaker into a trash can.

"No, I *told* you I'd found one. You didn't see it. You believed me without checking."

He walks around the car, opens the trunk, and takes out a

jack and a tire iron to change the Shelby's blown tire. I still can't believe how easily he tricked me.

"But...what about the whole thing with Vaughn?"

"I wanted a way to get us out of New York," he explains, squatting down to remove the hubcap. "I'd read in your case file about what Vaughn did to you. I knew I could get you to do anything if I dangled him in front of you."

I feel the anger rising within me. I am capable of beating the shit out of him, but first I want to make sure I understand.

"The fingerprints on the syringe...they were yours, of course? Vaughn is dead."

"Yes. If your father says he killed him, there's no reason not to believe him. I'll keep your secret. I'm not normally in favor of vigilantism, but in this case, who could blame him?"

"And Seymour?"

"Krieg called him and asked him to cooperate with us. Later on, I called him myself to ask him to give you false clues and direct you toward the hospital."

"When? We were together the whole time."

He looks at me and shakes his head, his lips pursed. "Not all the time, Alice. In Chinatown, I waited for you to leave the pawnbroker's and then asked the guy to let me make a call. And later, by the community garden in Hell's Kitchen, you stayed in the car while you thought I was calling my friend Kenny from a pay phone."

Using the tire iron, he starts unscrewing the wheel nuts while continuing his story.

"In the train station, while I was buying our subway tickets, a very sweet grandmother let me use her cell phone to make a call. In Astoria, while you were taking your bath, I had time to use the phone in the hookah bar. And when we were driving north, I left you with Barbie for a good ten minutes while I was supposedly buying cigarettes."

"And all those times, you were actually talking to Seymour?"

"He was the one who helped me play that FBI special agent role with some degree of credibility. I must admit he was a bigger help than I could have hoped. That thing with the corpse in the sugar factory—where he never set foot, of course—that was his idea."

"The bastard…"

"He loves you very much, you know. Not everyone is lucky enough to have a friend like him."

He sets up the jack and begins levering the car a few inches from the ground. Seeing him grimace with pain, I remember stabbing him the night before. It must have given him quite a deep muscular wound. I'm not in the mood to get softhearted, though.

"What about my father?"

"Ah, he was the one I worried about. I really wasn't sure that the great Alain Schafer would agree to play along. Thankfully, Seymour was able to steal his phone."

I take all these blows like a boxer caught in the corner of the ring. But I want to know. To know everything.

"The apartment in Astoria? Your friend Kenny Forrest?"

"Kenny doesn't exist. I invented that story of the jazz pianist because I love jazz. As for the apartment, it's mine. And by the way, you owe me a bottle of La Tâche 1999. I was keeping that for a special occasion."

As usual, he thinks that humor will undercut my anger. Or he is provoking me, trying to make me fly off the handle.

"You know where you can stick your bottle! So what about Madame Chaouch, the building owner? How come she didn't recognize you?"

"I called her from the station and asked her not to give me away."

Having unscrewed the nuts, he removes the blown tire, then finishes his explanation.

"Agatha, Krieg's assistant, went to the apartment a few minutes before we got there to get rid of anything that might have identified me: photographs, files, bills...my shoulder really hurts. Could you pass me the spare tire?"

"Go fuck yourself! What about the log cabin?"

Gabriel takes a step away from me and checks the bandages under his sweater and shirt. The strain of removing the wheel must have made his wound bleed again, but he grits his teeth and grabs the spare tire.

"The cabin belongs to the real Caleb Dunn. And I asked Agatha to pin those three pictures to the door after I found them in your wallet."

"The Shelby is yours too, I imagine?"

"I won it in a poker game when I was living in Chicago," the psychiatrist says, standing up and wiping his hands.

Listening to him is unbearable. I feel belittled, humiliated. In tricking me this way, Gabriel has taken the last thing that remained to me: my certainty that I was still a good cop.

"I have to admit, I got lucky," he says. "You nearly found me out twice. First, when you insisted on going with me to the hematology lab to leave the blood sample."

I'm not sure I understand what he means. I let him continue.

"I do know Eliane; the clinic has worked with her lab for a long time. I didn't have time to warn her, but thankfully she never called me 'Doctor' in front of you." He smiles.

I do not see much humor in this story.

"And the second time?"

"Your colleague Franck Maréchal. We really came close to disaster there. To begin with, I was lucky that he didn't know about your medical leave. And then, when he made his request to the parking garage, he just checked the records for your license plate. If he'd mentioned in his e-mail to you that the images were a week old, I would have been screwed!"

I nod. I am so angry, filled with a rage I cannot channel. A torrent of disgust and indignation takes possession of my body. I bend down, grab the tire iron, stand up, move toward Gabriel, and, with all my strength, smash him in the stomach with it.

27

WHITE SHADOWS

I HIT HIM AGAIN and Gabriel crumples into the dust, winded and bent double.

"I hate you, you bastard!"

He wraps his hands over his abdomen. I continue to pour out my rage.

"All that crap you told me about your son, about the death of your wife's sister...inventing lies like that, it's disgusting!"

He tries to stand up, holding his arms crossed in front of him to fend off another blow.

"Alice, that's all true! I swear, that part is all true. The only part I invented was the bit about being a cop in Chicago—I was actually a volunteer psychiatrist in a charity that helped prostitutes."

I drop the tire iron and let him stand up.

"My wife really did go to London with our son," he explains as he gets his breath back. "I quit my job here at the clinic so I could move closer to her."

In spite of this admission, I can't stop the torrent of anger that is flowing through me. "I bet you had fun with your little masquerade, didn't you? But what good did it do *me?*"

I throw myself at him, punching him in the chest and screaming: "Tell me! What good did it do me?"

He traps my fists in his big hands.

"Calm down now!" he orders in a firm voice. "We did all of that to help you."

A gust of wind. I shiver. It's true; I was so obsessed with the investigation that I almost forgot about my condition.

I can't believe that I'm going to die. This morning, my mind is clear and sharp. The windows of the Shelby reflect a flattering image: a still young and slender woman with a pretty face and hair that is blowing in the wind. And yet I now know all too well the ephemeral and deceptive nature of appearances. I know that the senile plaques are attacking my neurons, slowing down my brain. I know that time is running out.

"You have to agree to undergo the second part of the operation," Gabriel insists.

"What's the point? That thing of yours won't do any good.

It's just something you designed to rip off desperate people. Everyone knows there is nothing that can be done to stop Alzheimer's."

He speaks more gently. "That's true, and yet it's also false. Listen, I don't know what you've heard about this operation. But I do know that this clinic specializes in the electrical stimulation of memory circuits and that the procedure has shown excellent results."

I listen to him. He tries to explain it to me.

"We use very thin electrodes to send a small continuous current into a couple of strategic zones in your brain: the fornix and the entorhinal cortex. This stimulation generates tiny tremors that have an effect on the hippocampus. We don't yet understand all the mechanisms, but the idea behind it is to improve neuron activity."

"But it doesn't cure the disease."

"In many patients, we notice a modest but significant improvement in episodic and spatial memory."

"*Modest*? Wow, great."

"Alice, what I'm trying to tell you is that we don't have enough experience to be certain of the results. It's true, this is not an exact science. In some patients, lost memories return, and the symptoms regress or stabilize; in other patients, nothing happens and they continue, sadly, to be overcome by the disease."

"So you can see why I—"

"What I can see is that nothing is certain. The symptoms can accelerate and lead to death or they can slow down.

In young people where the disease was spotted early, there is a significant probability that we will be able to slow its progression. That is your situation, Alice."

I repeat to myself: "Slow its progression..."

"If we can slow down the disease, we can win you more time," he says. "Researchers are making progress every day. There will be advances in the future, that's certain."

"Sure, in thirty years."

"It could be thirty years or it could be tomorrow. Look what happened with AIDS. In the early eighties, being diagnosed as HIV-positive was equivalent to a death sentence. Then came AZT and combination therapy. Now there are people who've lived with the disease for thirty years."

I lower my head and say wearily, "I don't have the strength. That's why I panicked after the first operation. I wanted to go home to France to see my father one last time and..."

He comes closer to me and looks into my eyes. "And what? Put a bullet in your head?"

I stare back defiantly. "Something like that, yes."

"I thought you were braver than that."

"Who are you to talk to me about bravery?"

He takes another step closer. Our foreheads are almost touching; we're like two boxers before the start of the first round.

"Your unhappiness has blinded you to your good luck. You have a friend who is financing this treatment and who pulled strings to get you a place in this study. Maybe you don't know this, but most people have to go on a long waiting list before they get this treatment."

"Well, there you go—I'll be freeing up a place for someone."

"Fine. You clearly don't deserve it."

Just when I least expect it, I see his eyes shine. In those eyes, I can read anger, sadness, defiance.

"You're young, you're a fighter. You're the most stubborn and determined woman I've ever met. If anyone can beat this disease, it's you. You could be an example for other sufferers, a role model."

"I don't want to be a role model, Keyne! This is one battle I can never win, and you know it. So spare me the bullshit."

"So you're just going to give up?" he demands angrily. "Well, you're right—it's much easier that way. You want to put an end to it all? Go ahead! Your bag's on the back seat and your gun's inside."

And with that, Gabriel strides off toward the hospital.

He is provoking me. He is irritating the hell out of me. I'm so tired. He doesn't realize that he shouldn't lead me out to that place, that I've spent too long walking on the edge of the abyss. I open the door of the Mustang and grab the satchel. I unbuckle the straps. The Glock is there, along with my cell phone, the battery almost dead. Without thinking, I put the phone in my pocket, then check the magazine and shove the pistol into my belt.

The sun is quite high in the sky now.

I look into the distance and blink, dazzled by the silver reflections dancing on the surface of the lake. Without a glance at Gabriel, I walk away from the car and toward the dock.

There is a peacefulness to the landscape that radiates a kind of power, serene and harmonious. Up close, the water looks clear, almost turquoise.

Finally, I turn around. Gabriel is no more than a silhouette in the driveway. Too far away to intervene.

I grip the polymer butt of the Glock and take a deep breath.

I am devastated, exhausted. I feel like I have been falling, falling, falling for years.

I close my eyes. In my head, I see fragments of a storyline whose ending I already know. Deep down, didn't I always believe that it would end this way?

Alone, but free.

The way I have always tried to live my life.

28

WITH ONE HEART

I PLACE THE COLD gun barrel inside my mouth.

So I can stay in control. Not become a woman with no memory, a sick, helpless person locked up in a hospital room.

So I can decide, to the end, the path my existence should take.

While my mind is still lucid.

No one can take that away from me.

My last freedom.

Eyes closed, I see moments of happiness from my life with Paul rush past. Thousands of images that the wind will sweep away, carry up into the atmosphere, opening a way to heaven.

Suddenly I see him, holding his father's hand. The child whose name we hadn't even chosen yet, who will never have a name. The child I will never know but whose face I imagined so many times.

They are there, the two of them, in the welcoming darkness. The two men of my life.

I feel tears rolling down my cheeks. I keep my eyes closed, the gun in my mouth, my finger on the trigger, ready to fire. Ready to join them.

And then the child lets go of Paul's hand and takes a few steps toward me. He is so beautiful... no longer a baby. He's a little boy now. Wearing a checkered shirt, his pant legs rolled up. How old is he? Three, maybe four? I stare at him, fascinated by the purity of his gaze, the innocence of his expression, the promises and the challenges that I read in his eyes.

"Mommy, I'm scared. Come with me, please."

He calls out to me. He holds out his hand.

I'm scared too.

The attraction is powerful. I choke on a sob. And yet I know that this child is not real. That he is only a projection of my mind.

"Come with me, Mommy, please..."

I'm coming...

My finger is poised on the trigger. An abyss opens up inside me. My whole body tenses, as if the yawning gap that has existed inside me since childhood is widening.

This is the story of a sad, solitary girl who never found

her place in the world. A human bomb, about to explode. A pressure cooker simmering for too long with resentment, dissatisfaction, the desire to be elsewhere.

Do it. Squeeze the trigger. The pain and fear will vanish instantly. Do it now. You're brave enough, lucid enough, weak enough . . . it's the right time.

A trembling along my thigh.

The cell phone vibrating in my pocket.

I try to keep them with me, but Paul and the child evaporate. Sadness gives way to anger. I open my eyes, pull the pistol from my mouth, and, in a rage, answer my phone. I hear Gabriel's voice:

"Don't do it, Alice."

I turn around. He is fifty yards away from me, coming closer.

"We've said everything there is to say, Gabriel."

"I don't think we have."

In despair, I scream: "Leave me alone! Are you worried about your career, is that it? A patient blowing her head off on the grounds of your beautiful clinic . . . bad for the image, right?"

"You're no longer my patient, Alice."

I frown. "What do you mean?"

"You know the rules. A doctor is not allowed to be in love with his patient."

"Are you kidding? Is that the best line you can come up with?"

"Why do you think I took all those risks?" he says,

continuing to move toward me. "I felt something for you from the moment I saw you asleep on that bench."

"You're ridiculous."

"I'm serious, Alice."

"We don't even know each other."

"I think we do, actually. Or, rather, we recognized something in each other."

I balk at this. "Come on, you're not in love with me. You're a womanizer. You told me so yourself—a girl in every port. You think I forgot that?"

"That was a lie. Part of my jazz-pianist persona."

"You check out every girl you see!"

"I think you're incredible, Alice. I love your bad temper, your quick wit. I've never felt as right with anyone as I feel with you."

I stare at him, unable to speak. The sincerity I sense in his words petrifies me. He risked his life for me, it's true. I very nearly shot him last night.

He keeps talking. "There are so many things I want to do with you. Talk to you about the books I love, show you the neighborhood where I grew up, make you my special truffle mac and cheese recipe..."

Tears blur my vision again. Gabriel's words wrap me up in their gentleness and I want to abandon myself to this feeling. I remember the first time I saw his face on that bench in Central Park. There was a complicity between us from the first second. I see him again in that toy store, wearing his cape and performing magic tricks to amuse the children.

But I interrupt his flow of words. "This woman you claim to love, Gabriel... you know perfectly well she'll vanish in a few months. She won't recognize you anymore. She'll call you *monsieur* and you'll have to lock her up in a hospital room."

"That's a possibility, not a certainty. And I'm ready to take that risk."

I drop my cell phone as the battery finally dies.

Gabriel is standing in front of me, less than thirty feet away. "If anyone can win this battle, Alice, it's you."

Now he is only inches away. "But winning doesn't depend on me."

"We'll fight it together, Alice. I think we make a good team, don't you?"

"I'm scared! I'm so scared..."

A gust of wind blows dust into the air and makes the golden needles of the larch trees tremble. The cold burns my fingers.

"I know how difficult it will be, but there will be..."

THERE WILL BE . . .

There will be bright mornings and others obscured by clouds.

There will be days of doubt, days of fear, gray and futile hours spent in waiting rooms that smell of hospitals.

There will be moments of lightness, moments of hope and youth when the disease will be forgotten.

As if it had never existed.

And then life will go on.

And you will hold tight to it.

There will be Ella Fitzgerald's voice, Jim Hall's guitar, a melody by Nick Drake.

There will be walks by the sea, the smell of cut grass, the color of a stormy sky.

There will be days spent fishing at low tide.

Scarves tied around necks to protect us from the wind.

Sandcastles that stand up to the salty waves.

And lemon cannoli eaten as we walk down the streets of the North End.

There will be a house on a shady road. Gas lamps with colored halos. A ginger cat purring in your lap. A large dog barking its welcome.

There will be a winter morning when I'll be late for work. I'll rush downstairs, kiss you quickly, grab my keys.

Door, driveway, start the car.

And at the first red light, I'll realize that the key fob is a pacifier.

There will be...

Sweat, blood, a baby's first cry.

A shared look.

A pact for eternity.

Baby bottles every four hours, packets of diapers, rain on the windows, sunlight in your heart.

There will be...

A changing table, a baby bath, endless ear infections, a menagerie of stuffed animals, hummed lullabies.

Smiles, outings to the park, first steps, a tricycle in the driveway.

Before bedtime, there will be stories of princes defeating dragons.

Birthdays and first days of school. Cowboy outfits; drawings of animals stuck to the fridge.

Snowball fights, magic tricks, toast with jam at four in the afternoon.

And time will pass.

There will be other stays in the hospital, other exams, other alarms, other treatments.

Each time, you will go there fearful, your stomach in knots, your heart beating fast, armed only with your desire to keep living.

Each time, you will tell yourself that, no matter what happens now, you would not give up any of those moments torn from the hands of fate.

And no one will ever be able to take them from you.

ACKNOWLEDGMENTS

To Ingrid.

To Edith Leblond, Bernard Fixot, and Catherine de Larouzière.

To Sylvie Angel, Alexandre Labrosse, Jacques Bartoletti, and Pierre Collange.

To Valérie Taillefer, Jean-Paul Campos, Bruno Barbette, Virginie Plantard, Caroline Sers, Stéphanie Le Foll, and Isabelle de Charon.

ABOUT THE AUTHOR

Guillaume Musso is the number one bestselling author in France. He has written seventeen novels, including the thrillers *The Reunion,* which is in development as an international TV series, and *Afterwards...,* which was made into a feature film starring John Malkovich and Evangeline Lilly. He lives in Paris.